AMBER ROYER

D0945622

*Grand Openings
Can Be Murder*

**GOLDEN TIP
PRESS**

GOLDEN TIP PRESS

A Golden Tip Press paperback original 2020

Copyright © Amber Royer 2020

Cover by Jon Bravo

Distributed in the United States by Ingram, Tennessee

ISBN 978-0-9914083-4-4

Ebook ISBN 978-0-9914083-5-1

Printed in the United States of America

To all the craft chocolate makers who have shared their expertise and experience with me.

You are all amazing!

I'm sitting in a tall chair at the kitchen island, scrolling through pictures from my recent trip to Colombia. I'm trying to decide which ones are social-media worthy, when I spot a picture of my late husband, in between a close up shot of a cacao pod and a picture of me smiling from between two chocolate farmers in the Sierra Nevada Mountains.

My breath catches, and I sit there staring at it, re-memorizing the curve of his face, imagining the sound of his laugh, lost inside myself.

The smoke alarm goes off, making me jump. I'd lost all track of time.

Aunt Naomi rushes into the kitchen wearing paint spattered jeans and a tee that says *World's Best Mom*. She turns off the oven, before I've even registered the smoke that is rapidly filling the room. "Felicity! What's with you today?"

I look up from my laptop screen, still feeling a bit hazy, and grab a cookie sheet. After sliding off my shoes, I climb up onto the chair I'd been sitting in, and from there onto the island, a modern addition to this historic home, waving the smoke away from the device until it finally quiets. Why on Earth were Victorian houses built with ceilings that were twelve feet tall? "Sorry. It's just . . . you know."

I pull the phone out of my jeans pocket. I'd set a timer when I'd put the cacao beans in the oven. Unfortunately . . . I'd forgotten to press start, though I usually catch the smell of brownies or the first pop of the beans without it. Flavors in chocolate develop by the second. I'd completely lost my focus. How long had I been staring at that photograph?

"Oh, honey." My aunt opens up the windows and back door before coming over. She holds a hand up to help me down from my precarious perch. Sympathy shines in her warm brown eyes. She's barely forty, only eight years older than me, and we bear a passing resemblance to each other, with lightly freckled cheeks and long dark hair, and pale skin that goes red in the sun but never tans. I'm taller, though, by several inches.

I stifle a cough. I'm prone to asthma, and the last thing I want is Aunt Naomi thinking the smoke in the air will give me an attack. She's already worried enough about me making chocolate, with the heat and dust involved. "There-" I start, but my voice cracks. Getting the words out feels a little like someone is stepping on my chest. Grief hits you hard, and weird, and at unexpected times. I wave my hand at the laptop screen, with the picture still up. "There was a picture of Kevin in with all the Colombia shots. I must have copied it off of my phone by mistake."

"Oh, honey," Aunt Naomi says. I wish she wouldn't call me that. The more often she says it in a conversation, the more she's pitying me. "It's next week, isn't it?"

I nod. Next week, on Monday, is my wedding anniversary. Only – Wednesday will be the first anniversary of my husband's death. And I'm not sure I can handle it. He'd been so vibrant, so young. We'd thought we had all the time in the world. Three years ago, we'd been toying around with ideas for starting our own business together, when Kevin hit his buy-in for retirement benefits. Even early retirement had seemed so far away. At least another decade. And then Kevin had had his accident, out on a boat he'd helped design. And then hours later he'd just been gone.

But I don't want to talk about that again with my aunt. Instead, I fake a smile. "Monday's the grand opening party." Which she well knows. She's been social-media-ing about it like crazy, and helping me put up fliers all over the Island, and as far inland as Friendswood and even Houston. "Greetings and Felicitations will be up and running."

The name had been Kevin's idea, something he'd come up with in those last hours between his accident and his death. It was a play on his favorite book as a child. The line from Charlotte's Web had actually been, "Greetings and Salutations." But everything in his life had been about us as a couple. And knowing how brief his life was going to be, he'd wanted me to read about Charlotte again.

"Then let's leave that mess," Naomi gestures with her chin over at the oven. "And go shopping."

"You're the one that asked me to work here today." I move over to the oven and cautiously open the door. The cacao beans inside are beyond burned. More smoke billows out.

"I didn't want you spending all day alone. Again. When those assistants of yours aren't available-" Aunt Naomi scrunches up her nose. "What smells like old chicory coffee?"

"Chocolate gone horribly wrong." I say it like it's the punch line to a joke. It falls flat.

Aunt Naomi forces a smile. "You remember game nights at your Mawmaw's house when the coffee smelled like this by the end of the evening? I know she'd love to see you more at the condo."

"I go when I can." Though truthfully, I've pulled away from my family. They look so . . . sad by the time I leave.

I sigh and turn back to focus on the cacao. At least it's not a huge batch of beans. For that, I would have used the commercial roaster at my tiny chocolate factory. This was just a roasting test using samples I'd brought back from a sourcing trip. When I first got interested in chocolate, I didn't realize I would be networking with farmers in South America and Africa, visiting their small cacao farms to forge relationships and supporting their work so that mine can be successful.

I'm a bean-to-bar chocolate maker. What I produce has to be far superior to what my customers could get from larger companies' blended-origin chocolate, both flavor-wise and from a production standards point of view. If people can't taste the difference, they'll go back to buying cheap chocolate.

I have to choose the beans I purchase wisely, because when you make single-origin chocolate bars, the beans' unique flavor profiles can leave you delighted – or struggling to make up for bland chocolate with inclusions and added flavors. I've tasted chocolate where you would swear someone had added raisins and walnuts, but there was nothing in it but ground cacao and sugar. I've also tasted chocolates with notes of citrus and leather. Some of the most interesting chocolates, at least to me, have flavors that echo pepper, cinnamon, and coffee.

The specific soil and growing conditions found in an individual cacao plantation can make a vast difference. As can the use of different kinds of native wood in the fermentation boxes, and the fermentation, and drying time, and processes . . . and so many other factors specific to a particular farm. I want my chocolate to reflect the places I've visited, the experiences I've had, the sheer amount of life I've managed to soak up. I well know how fleeting life is. Perhaps it is fitting that my mementos should be just as fleeting, edible and delicious, bringing joy to others in a way a photo slideshow never could.

I've made half a dozen bars so far. My newest creation will be a wine-noted, caramelly Sierra Nevada bar, built from my most recent trip. "I don't need to go shopping. I bought decorations and paper goods on-line. Emma and Carmen are setting everything up on Sunday night. Carmen's even making mini-cupcakes from the Chiapas chocolate."

Though I hadn't visited the farm for that one, just split a purchase with another chocolate maker through a broker. But with bean-to-bar, the processes that happen after a chocolate maker receives the beans are just as important, so while we started with the same beans, we will create distinct chocolates. There's a lot of trial and error involved, especially when roasting the beans, as time and temperature affect the flavor notes. And even the grinding and conching processes vary, impacting both flavor and texture inside my factory.

"Then we should go get you a new dress. You never know if some handsome man might come to your opening. In my book, after a year, it's perfectly alright if you want to start dating again." Mischief sparkles in my aunt's eyes. I get the idea that she already has someone in mind for me, and if somebody who is just my type happens to wander into my store on Monday, it won't be by accident.

I close the oven door, leaving the ruined mess inside. I make steady eye contact with Aunt Naomi. "I had love. Real love. The kind where you finish each other's sentences and talk in movie and book quotes because you've shared that much. Where you can be dying, and care more about the pain of the person you're leaving behind. Do you honestly think I'm going to find that again?"

She shrugs, the gleam in her eyes subdued, replaced by determination. "Honey, I honestly do. Someone who loved you like that wouldn't have wanted you to be alone forever."

There's a sudden repeated metallic clicking noise coming from the other side of the room. My lop-eared rabbit, who spends a lot of his daytime hours in the hollow behind the sofa, has hopped in to get a drink from the water bottle inside his cage. I point over to his little gray and white face. "I'm not alone. I have Knightley. And you. And a ton of friends all over the globe, and the rest of our family, what, an hour away."

Mom and Dad had moved to the mainland after the last hurricane.

Aunt Naomi rolls her eyes. "You know what I mean."

It's easy for her to be optimistic. She and her husband have been together since high school, and they have a son who just went away to college. My uncle is a field supervisor for a string of offshore rigs. He's gone for weeks at a time, but when he's here, Aunt Naomi and Uncle Greg give each other looks like newlyweds.

"If I get the dress, and open myself up to the possibility of someday, will you promise not to set me up?" I'm already heading for my purse. "I mean, you remember what happened with Emma."

Aunt Naomi blinks at me. "Your assistant?"

My aunt is not a big reader. I have always been a huge Jane Austen fan, and Emma my favorite Austen heroine . . . though Kevin would have argued for Elinor from *Sense and Sensibility*. He did always have a practical side. But I was lucky enough to find an engineer who reads, so who was I to quibble?

Austen's Emma was a matchmaker and a busybody, but she got herself out of all the problems she caused. And I do have to admit, when I'd been considering assistants, Emma's name alone had bumped her up a few points in my list. And the fact that until recently, Emma had worked at the local indie bookstore had helped even more, since I plan to sell a selection of books I collect on my travels in Felicitations. The one shelf from the trips to Columbia and Ecuador though, seems a little pitiful.

Aunt Naomi grabs her car keys, not even bothering to change out of her paint-spattered clothes. "I promise. No matchmaking."

I absolutely don't believe her.

We get into the car and onto the road. You can smell the salt in the air, and feel the humidity, even though we're in the Historic District, which is pretty close to the center of the East end of the island. We're not close enough to see the Gulf or the Bay, not by blocks and blocks, but Galveston is a long, skinny barrier island, so it's not a long drive from any point on it to the water. The houses flash by. On this street, the tri-color Victorian "painted ladies" are next door to fixer-uppers in desperate need of restoration which are next door to mansions with enough historic value to be surrounded by wrought-iron fences and tropical gardens and open for public tours. It's inconsistent, and a little overwhelming, but there's a grandeur to the neighborhood that's comfortable.

I'm still trying to think of a way to get a sincere promise to leave my lack of a love life alone when Aunt Naomi suddenly turns off the main road, down a tiny, cramped side street.

"Whah!" I try to grab onto something in the car to steady myself. "What's with *you* today?"

"Estate sale." She points at a cardboard sign, a bit battered from today's earlier rain shower. Which might have deterred some of the regular garage salers. There may actually be some good stuff left.

"Cool!"

Aunt Naomi parks haphazardly in a tiny, sandy front yard. The walkway leading up to the house is framed with waist-high palm trees. You don't see palms in most parts of Texas, but they're everywhere on Galveston, along with oleander forming a lush hedge on the property across the street. There is clematis growing up this home's porch posts and hibiscus growing in pots on the porch.

The house itself isn't in great condition, but it's got classic lines. I don't know if my aunt will have finished fixing up the place we're currently living in in time to flip it by the time this place comes on the market, but once we're inside, I catch her examining the window frames, looking for signs of termite damage.

Leaving her to it, I make a beeline for the bookcase I can see through the open door into one of the rooms.

A girl in her twenties is sitting at a table in the main room. She sees where I'm heading and calls out to me, "The furniture in there's all sold, but I'll take five hundred dollars for all the books."

I nod. Some of the books have been haphazardly tossed into boxes, some are still on the heavy oak shelves, but there's enough here to make a decent-looking book section for my shop. Unless they're all encyclopedia sets and cookbooks from the 1970's. Which that first bookcase appears stacked full of. Fighting disappointment, I start digging through one box, picking up each of the books. They're at least fiction. Old editions of the classics, lots of yellowed hardback mystery novels, not bad. The next box has a few covers that are falling apart. I pick up a book with an unassuming brown cover. I tilt it to the side and read the title. *Sense and Sensibility, Volume I.*

My heart squeezes. After what I'd been thinking about Kevin and Austen heroines, how could I have found *this* book? I flip it open carefully.

Sense and Sensibility, a Novel in Three Volumes, by A Lady, 1811. My heart squeezes again, for an entirely different reason. Austen had originally published the book anonymously, paying for it herself. I'm not sure, but 1811 sounds about right for the first printing. I look down into the box, and there's an identical brown cover. I pick it up. *Volume II.* And under that, *Volume III.*

It doesn't matter what the rest of the books are. This alone has to be worth more than five hundred bucks.

I place the three volumes carefully back in the box and go out to talk to the girl running the garage sale, whose too-white makeup, dark eyeliner and "big" hair all seems a bit dated but might just be an old trend coming back around again. She can't be one of those pros who organize and price estate sales, or these books would have been proudly on display. She's probably this house's owner's granddaughter or something. My heart's hammering guiltily as I approach her and ask, "Are you sure they're five hundred dollars?"

She rolls her eyes. "Alright. It's already three in the afternoon. I'll take three hundred and fifty." She gives me a look, like she knows my kind, picking up bargains by being the last at a sale.

Which somehow makes me feel less guilty as I hand over the three hundred and fifty bucks, and take my box to the car, after making arrangements to come back for the rest in my truck. I lost track of Naomi inside the house, and thought I'd find her in the car waiting for me, but she isn't out here. She drives an old car, the kind that still has manual door locks, and I realize that I've forgotten again to lock my door. I put my box in the back seat, and sit in the front, with the door open. Galveston can be humid and sticky on the best of days. Sitting in an enclosed car on a day like today with the engine off would be torture.

A seagull lands near my open door. It looks in at me, as though daring me *not* to give it something to eat. I stare right back. If I make a move that looks like I even might have something to offer, I'll have a cloud of gulls on my hands. I don't know what kind of radar gulls have that lets them do that.

But you know what? I'm having a better day, with my unexpected find. I might as well share the feeling. Aunt Naomi usually has a packet of peanuts or two in her glove box for emergency snacking. I grab one, rip it open and throw nuts to the gull and its rapidly appearing friends.

After a while, Naomi comes out of the house. As she slides back behind the wheel, she tosses a Ziplock holding a set of cabinet knobs onto the back seat. Who other than my aunt carries a screwdriver in their purse, for just such a find?

Aunt Naomi tilts her head to the side studying me. "What makes you suddenly look like the cat who ate the canary?"

At least she hadn't ended the question with *honey*.

"I got a steal on some old books." I don't bother elaborating. She wouldn't understand.

Aunt Naomi laughs. "If that's got you that excited, we really do need to get you that new dress."

Chapter Two
Friday

The next morning, I have an appointment with my GP, so I make my way across the island to Dr. Ricci's office. I'm still thinking about my cool book find while I'm sitting in the waiting room. It is always weird being on this side of the exam area door. When Kevin and I had lived in Seattle, I'd finished school and become a physical therapist. The two of us had met when he'd come to Galveston to study marine engineering at the same A&M where I was doing part of my early coursework. I don't tell that to a lot of people. The reaction you get when you tell someone you quit a thriving practice to follow your dream of making chocolate gets to be a bit soul-crushing. If I have to deal with one more pitying look coupled with a Willie Wonka reference I'm going to slap someone.

But honestly, dealing with the pain of watching someone I loved dying left me empty every time I had to walk in the door of the hospital that housed my office. And I just couldn't face working with one person after another who was also in pain. I wanted to do something that would make people happy. And seriously, watching someone try craft chocolate for the first time. That's happy.

And if people don't know I was something else first, if they assume I was always a chocolate maker – well, they usually think it is cool and fun and adventurous.

The nurse finally calls me back, and Dr. Ricci puts a stethoscope on my back. His manner annoys me – he's always in so much of a hurry to get from one patient to the next, he doesn't really engage in conversation. He's in his fifties sporting salt and pepper hair, obviously Italian, with a craggy nose, his swarthy skin even darker from a golfer's tan.

I try to talk to him anyway, about his day, about the practice. He does seem willing to talk about my lungs. He's impressed that the treatment that I'd started in Seattle and picked up here is working so well.

He takes out a pen from his pocket and scribbles a refill for my prescription onto an old-fashioned paper pad. I cringe. Who does that anymore? It is so much simpler to call the prescriptions in for the patient. And then you have a typed paper trail. Maybe I should change doctors, but he's supposed to be the best GP on the island.

Dr. Ricci tears the prescription off the pad and hands it to me. "You're doing a lot better. Another month, and you won't even need this anymore."

I nod. I'd learned about this experimental treatment, ironically, at the hospital, where they hadn't been able to offer any hope for Kevin. It had completely eliminated asthmatic symptoms in over 60 percent of patients. The drugs involved, though, require I severely limit my caffeine intake. One more month. I sigh happily. "You don't know how much I've missed my second cup of coffee."

Dr. Ricci laughs. "I think everybody on this island knows how much you love coffee. And chocolate."

After the examination, I reach into my purse and give Dr. Ricci a postcard with details about the grand opening party. As I'm leaving the clinic, I text Miles. He's one of Naomi's son's friends, who still seems to think of Naomi as a second mom, even with Wyatt away at college. Aunt Naomi sometimes pays Miles to help out with work when she's flipping a house. Today, he's supposed to help me haul books.

Hey! I text. *What do you want for lunch? Will pick it up on the way to the estate house.*

He texts back: *Aw, thanks, Mrs. Koerber! Maybe a shrimp po boy?*

I know just the place, The Asian Cajun, a fusion joint that serves both po boys and banh mi right on the seawall. You can also get tacos and soul food side dishes, alongside your Cajun-staple boudin balls and alligator tail, and all of it's good – and super cheap. The major culinary traditions of the area together at one spot, it's like a sampler of Galveston itself.

It doesn't take me long to get there. I know what Emma and Carmen like from here, so I order them lunch too.

Miles meets me at the house from the estate sale. Together, we get the books packed up and loaded into my catering truck – which so far I've only used for transporting supplies -- and Miles follows me back to the shop in his Mini Cooper.

I walk towards my shop, balancing the box of books on my hip. Miles is carrying two boxes at once.

The Strand is a tourist draw, playing up its 19th Century history by highlighting the architecture. This makes for a fun juxtaposition of old against new, the vintage streetfront opening into modern, elegant shops that makes this such a great location. The narrow alley behind the strip of buildings is paved with red brick. The backs of the buildings look antiquated – mostly worn brick, covered in places with stucco, with mismatched windows, some arched, some covered with ugly shutters, some more modern. This is counterpointed by banks of electricity meters and bright green trash cans. It's an unfinished version of the front of the buildings, which have been updated and restored.

I hold my breath as I pass the trash. But once I arrive at Felicitations, I inhale deeply as I open the back door, which leads directly into the small kitchen we use for making coffee, dirty horchata, truffles, and the occasional baked good starring one of my chocolates. It's all shiny silver countertops and industrial burners and bakers' racks stacked with baking pans. The smell of chocolate is even more intense than usual. Carmen is pulling out cupcakes, and the earthy, nutty tones of my Chiapas chocolate waft from the oven door. The familiar notes are mixed with sweetness and cinnamon. It smells delicious. Carmen is baking and freezing all the mini cupcakes days early, so that she will have time to take care of more urgent details on the day of the party.

She nods at me. "Perfect timing. Taste one of these."

She breaks one open, and I pop a piece of it into my mouth. They're good, warm, and soft from the oven. Carmen's going to put more cinnamon into the frosting, in the form of cinnamon whiskey, lightened with an herbal hit of lemongrass which she's infusing into the butter she's using to make the buttercream. She's talented, and easy to work with, even if she's got a few gaps in her employment record after her scholarships to El Centro. But she seems to have gotten herself together now that she's turned thirty. Second-generation Mexican American, she's thin but athletic, from surfing and competing in half marathons and helping out at beach cleanup events.

I have a feeling Carmen won't be my assistant for long – someone is going to snatch her away to run a larger kitchen, or she'll open her own shop. I would hate to lose her, but I'm not one to hold someone back.

I put down my box with the rare books where it will be out of the way of the food. Miles goes back for another box of books, while I hand Carmen a banh mi.

I take a plastic container holding a salad out of the bag, and look around for my other assistant, who is supposed to be here today too. "Where's Emma?"

Carmen points with the oven mitt she's holding in her hand. "In the office, updating the spreadsheets. Which she always takes forever to do." Carmen sounds resentful. She jams the mitt on. She has her long, dark hair up in a ponytail and is wearing a vintage polka-dot apron over jeans and a black tee.

I'm confused. "Oh?"

Inside, I'm thinking *what spreadsheets*? What is Emma even doing in the office? I never gave her permission to go in there.

I go into the processing area, where the big melanger is steadily grinding away at the batch of chocolate I'd put in there last night, and on through the bean room, towards the office, which is off the hallway on the far side. That hall, which also has our restrooms, leads back into the main part of the shop.

The office door is ajar. I push it open. Inside, my desk faces the wall. The top of Emma's blonde hair is visible over the headrest of my ergonomic office chair. Which had been a waste of money – I wind up doing all my real work with my laptop. This space is basically a catch-all for junk and chocolate-themed decorations that didn't fit in the shop.

Emma's hand moves on the mouse, and I edge around to get a look at the screen. My breath catches. Oh. My. God. Emma has the LLC's financial software open, and she's transferring money out of the account, as accounts payable to a company called Galaxy Chocolate Supplies.

"What are you doing?" I demand. Though it's obvious. She's stealing money from the shop. Out of my start-up funds. Which is actually the money from Kevin's life insurance policy, which he'd told me in those few hours after his accident that wanted me to use to follow this dream.

Emma jumps, and then whirls around in the chair to face me.

Startled, I flinch backwards and bump into the filing cabinet, knocking the traditional metate – a Mexican stone grinder, for hand grinding chocolate – I had perched there to the floor. Where the bread-box-sized stone cracks in half. Loudly.

"I'm sorry," Emma says, though her large blue eyes are focused on the metate, like that's the larger crime than stealing from the shop.

Emma broke up with her boyfriend about a month ago, and she's been even more conscious of her appearance than usual, wearing tasteful makeup that centers on deep red lipstick even just to work in the kitchen. With her long hair styled around her face, and flawless foundation that implies her cheeks have never seen the sun, she looks like a supermodel.

"Get out of my chair," I say softly. I'm trying to keep myself under control, even though my heart is hammering angrily, and heat is building at the back of my nose.

Emma leaps up. She is barely five feet tall, all of twenty-three years old. And she is trembling visibly. Which mutes my anger. She's terrified. Of me. Emma bites at her lip before she says, "I know I shouldn't have."

"Then why did you?"

Tears start leaking from Emma's eyes. "If I don't get the money – then it will all be over."

I can't tell if she's playing me with those overdramatic tears – or if she's honestly afraid of someone. I step around Emma and sit in the office chair. I do a quick search in the accounts payable records for Galaxy Chocolate Supplies. There are seven total entries. Each for $2,000 dollars.

"Emma," I insist, turning around to look at her. "Tell me what's going on."

She shakes her head. "You wouldn't understand."

"Try me." I try to sound reasonable. "It's better than explaining it to the police."

All the color drains from Emma's already pale complexion. I'd been trying to tell her I *wasn't* going to call the police, but she'd taken it as a threat. And she looks even more terrified of facing the cops than she had of telling me why she's in trouble. "Please. I'll pay the money back. All of it. It might take a while."

"Darn straight, you will." I hold out my hand. "But I'm going to need back the key to the shop."

Emma takes the key out of her pocket, turning it over in her hand. "You're firing me? That's fair."

I hesitate. Something's going on here that's deeper than simple office theft. Maybe if I let Emma keep her job, I can get her to open up to me, and I can get her the help she obviously needs. Maybe helping someone else will ground me after my loss. After all, that's what Kevin meant the money for, anyway. I force a smile. "It will be hard for you to pay me back if you don't have a job. And I don't have time to train anyone else before the grand opening. But I don't want you in this building when no one else is here. And I have to tell Carmen that neither of you are allowed in the office, so she's probably going to figure out what's going on."

There's a sound from out in the hall -- Carmen clearing her throat. She shrugs. "I heard a crash. And then I heard a lot of stuff."

Emma's face goes beet red.

Carmen and Emma have had some kind of grudge between them basically since I'd hired them, and this isn't going to make the two of them working together any easier. Maybe it would have been more professional to fire Emma. Or to report her theft to the police. But I've made my decision, and now, the three of us will have to make this work.

I slip Emma's building key into my own pocket. "Let's get the books organized this afternoon. And then after that, I want you to help Carmen with the cupcakes, and whatever else she's making for the party."

"It's not like I don't know how to bake," Emma says. "Right Carmen?"

Now Carmen blushes, the color less dramatic on her Latina features. She gives Emma an acid look. I have no idea what the subtext is to their exchange. And I'm certain I don't want to know. They'll hash it out, being stuck working together for hours in the kitchen. Or they'll kill each other.

There isn't time to waste feeling betrayed. We have a lot to get done this weekend. Seriously, grand openings can be murder. I've put so much of myself into this venture. It has to succeed.

I go out into the front of the shop. There's a coffee station with prepped carafes near the sunny windows, and a ficus tree in the opposite corner. In the section for books, one case is reserved for rare items, and it is fronted with delicate wrought iron bars. Naomi, who keeps her eye on the local real estate market, had let me know the day this place came up for lease. I still can't believe I scored a space this large on the Strand. It is Galveston's main shopping district, with a number of buildings that survived the Great Hurricane of 1900, which means there are horse drawn carriages and amphibious tour buses bringing people on history tours right past my front door. The strand is also walking distance from the cruise ship terminal, which has made for a number of busy days since my soft opening.

The area open to the customers is all warm brick and gray paint, with half a dozen café tables and one little sofa. Miles is sitting at the table closest to the bookcases, eating his lunch. He makes eye contact with Emma as she walks out behind me. I don't think the two have ever met before.

Emma gives Miles an appraising look, then smiles appreciatively, and walks over to stand close to him. He's got light-toned black skin, with close cropped hair and a trendy five-o'clock-shadow beard. Miles was running back on the high school football team last year. This year, he's on scholarship at the same University I attended on this island. I can see why Emma might be drawn to him, but the last thing he needs right now is someone like Emma derailing his life.

I tell Miles, "Finish that up, and then you can put up the signs outside. I'll hold the ladder. We can leave the girls to unpack things here."

"I'll go get it from next door," Miles says. Since I don't actually have my own ladder.

I doubt I'm imagining the disappointed pout Emma gives Mile's back as he balls up the sandwich wrapper and walks away. I want to help Emma, but she's not making this easy. I can't help but think she might be looking to date a guy who looks like he has money.

I go outside to help Miles. I try not to stare through the window at Emma, though I can't help but picture her stealing my rare volumes and making a run for it.

By the time I get back inside, Emma has shelved the books – except for the three volumes of *Sense and Sensibility*, which are still in the box, which has moved exponentially closer to the back door. I still want to trust Emma. Maybe she just wants to ask me what to do with the books. Maybe she isn't thinking of taking them with her when she leaves today. Feeling just the slightest bit paranoid, and a whole lot judgmental as we leave the shop, I put the Jane Austen volumes in the locked case myself – and then take the key with me.

Chapter Three
Monday

By the time we open on Monday, Carmen and Emma seem to have settled their differences. Or at least agreed not to talk about them. It is a busy day, thank goodness. I'd been terrified that it was going to be just the three of us celebrating the grand opening day alone.

People keep remarking on how clever the packaging is for my bars. The cream-colored wrappers double as all-seasons greeting cards, and the images all feature grayscale versions of Knightley, being his adorable bunny self. I'm even using an imprint of him in profile for the molds.

Aunt Naomi comes in three different times, with different groups of friends, each time acting like it's her first time in. She's had three dirty horchatas – each with an extra shot of espresso, to highlight how willing Carmen is about customizing drinks. My aunt has to be practically levitating from the sugar and caffeine. As she's leaving – again -- she turns back and waves. "See you at six!"

"As long as you don't have any more coffee," I chide. "The caffeine will kill you."

"Just think about everything I'll get done today." She winks, then disappears out the door.

I sigh. I used to be like that. The amount of coffee I consumed would be about equal to the stress of the day. Good thing the coffee roaster we partner with makes a decaf that's almost as good as the real thing.

Aunt Naomi pops her head back into the shop. "And don't forget to change. You never know who you might meet today."

Oh no. My aunt is still trying to fix me up. Here I am trying to un-matchmake the two young people – Emma has asked me for Miles's number three times, and I'm running out of tactful ways to say no – and Naomi's obviously sending someone in here to "accidentally" meet me.

I take a deep breath. Whoever this guy is, I need to treat him like any other customer, no matter what he thinks of my appearance. I was already planning on fixing myself up a bit for the party. It's not like I'm *not* going to change into a fancier outfit, just to spite my aunt. I'm hoping the press will be here – I sent out enough releases.

Almost as soon as Aunt Naomi is gone, Kaylee Goff, who owns the Island's indie bookstore, comes in and takes a look around the shop. She's in her forties, and wears her dark curly hair in a short bob. She's had a spray tan that's left her a tinge orange -- that clashes with her pink tee, which has the word WINE on it in glitter and rhinestones. She heads over to the book section, then she turns back and comes over to me. Word must have gotten around about the First Edition Jane Austen. I'm excited Kaylee left Island Breeze Books and headed over here herself to check it out.

Only she's not cooing with jealousy over my find – her lips are drawn into a hard, thin line, and her brown eyes are dark with anger. "You're selling books in here?"

"Just vintage and rare ones, and things I've picked up on my travels," I say softly. "I want customers to be able to have a cup of coffee and browse for a while. Craft chocolate is such a quick thing to look at-"

Kaylee interrupts. "Galveston already *has* a bookshop. And a historic candy shop. Do you imagine that that many people care about the difference between bean-to-bar chocolate and plain old bon bons to switch loyalties?"

I'm gobsmacked at the aggressiveness of her question, and indignation sparks through my chest. I force a smile. "I think it says something that you know the difference. I'd like to offer you some samples, so you can see what I do here." I pick up a dish that is filled with broken shards of chocolate.

"Some other time," Kaylee says, her Southern politeness kicking in, even though she's obviously still angry. "I see someone else here who needs a piece of my mind."

She turns away from the counter.

"Wait," I say. "We're both businessowners here. I don't want to start out on the wrong foot."

Kaylee turns back, arches one perfectly plucked eyebrow at me. "Then maybe you shouldn't have poached an Island Breeze Books employee."

I groan inside as I remember Emma's previous place of employment from her job application. I hadn't thought about it being such a small island when I'd hired her. "I'm sorry. I didn't realize you needed her. Should I talk to Emma about going back to work for you?"

Although, honestly. Emma had applied with me. I hadn't sought her out.

Kaylee laughs. "Now I didn't say that. You just bought yourself a whole heap of trouble with that one. It is only a just punishment if you keep her."

I glance over at Emma. Had she been stealing from Kaylee too? I don't want to accuse her if she hadn't. So I ask, "What kind of trouble? Was she coming in late? Or napping in the stacks? Or . . . taking things?"

Kaylee's eyes narrow. "Absolutely not. I never would have tolerated any of that." She starts to say more, then that Southern fake-smile comes back onto her face. "I guess you'll just have to see for yourself."

Kaylee makes a beeline over towards Emma. I can't make out what they're saying, but Kaylee pokes Emma in the arm to emphasize her point. Is she that angry over Emma leaving to work for me? Or is it something more personal? I try to ignore what is going on the other side of the shop. Dr. Ricci comes in. I turn to welcome him, grateful for the distraction. After all, I'd invited him to my party before I'd left my office appointment, practically begged him to come.

"Bathroom?" he asks tersely.

I point the way down the hall. So many of my customers have visited the restrooms today – one of us probably needs to go restock the paper goods.

I'll send Emma when she's done talking to her former boss. In the meantime, I make sure that all the chocolate bars have been restocked, along with my new line of bean-to-truffles. I've based them on traditional Cajun-Creole desserts, highlighting my heritage, just as Carmen's highlighting hers in the baked goods and the coffee bar. Bananas Foster. Crème brulee. Pineapple and coconut cake. Whiskey-sauced bread pudding. Candied sweet potatoes. Pecan pralines. The essence of each of them, combined with complimentary chocolate from around the world. This is the me I want to show to everyone – the half Cajun, half Italian world traveler who still embraces home.

I just hope I get good reviews.

I walk through the kitchen, into the chocolate processing area. That's where I have the peanut butter grinder I use to break down the beans before they go into one of the two melangers, as well as a tempering machine which regulates heat so that the chocolate can gain the right crystalline structure and snap to make bars. On the other side of the space, there's a large cooling cabinet for the bars, along with two speed racks for storing trays of molded bars as I work.

Felicitations used to be an oversized café, and some of the walls in the chocolate-making area are still blue and gold, with murals of sunflowers I haven't quite had the heart to paint over. The murals extend onto one wall of the bean room, a separate area where we store small amounts of cacao beans, and have our sorting, roasting, and winnowing equipment. There's a plain white wall dividing the two spaces to keep the heat from roasting and the dust from winnowing – removing the outer shell of the cacao beans – from affecting the finished product. There's a long counter attached to each side of the new wall with cabinets above and below for storage.

Before the remodel, there used to be bathrooms where the processing room is now, sharing plumbing with the kitchen. We used that to our advantage, adding a small sink in both the processing space and the bean room.

I check the melanger, to make sure the chocolate in it is done refining and ready to move into the tempering machine. We already have eleven people signed up for the tour I'm leading tonight. We're capping it at fifteen, so that each participant will be able to temper and decorate their own bar. The molds are neatly stacked on the long counter. The airbrushing equipment is in working order. And the sugar sprinkles – my concession to Emma's point that some people need decorations that are easy to apply – are lined up by color.

I text a few more people a reminder to come to the party. Then I go into the office and get my dressy blouse and black pants from where I've hung them on the wall-mounted coat rack. I take off my wedding band, since I will be working with food, and slip it into the desk drawer where I stick the bag with the extra cash in case we run out of change. I lock the drawer. I never pull that drawer all the way out. Some of Kevin's things are in the back and if I see them today I'll collapse. I grab my makeup bag and head for the ladies' room to change.

I follow the tutorial I'd found for applying flattering on-camera makeup. It's been a long time since I had on eyeliner quite this thick, or lipstick quite this deep a red. I hope Aunt Naomi's mystery guy doesn't get the wrong idea.

I reach for my phone. I don't have it.

"Take some pictures, will you?" I tell Emma. "I left my phone in the office, and we want to plaster all these happy faces all over our accounts."

It's gotten crowded in here. Aunt Naomi's back, with her entire women entrepreneur's group. My friend Autumn is sitting at one of the tables, a coffee in her hand, her afro pulled back from her face with a thick cream band. I've known Autumn since her family moved to Galveston when we were both in the eighth grade. We both did UIL Poetry that year, and on the bus, Autumn had told me that she wished she had the courage to read her own poetry instead of the Langston Hughes piece she'd memorized, even if it got her disqualified. I talked her out of it, because seriously, rules. But she let me see her poetry notebook. I'm the first person she told she wanted to be a writer.

She's one of the few people I've kept up with since high school. Social media makes that so much easier these days, sharing pictures of important events and distant girls' nights. But since I've been back in town, we've been meeting up once a week for lunch. And you just can't get that through Instagram.

Several of my other friends come through the door, wave, and head for Autumn's table.

There's four people sitting at the table with the *Tour Group* sign on it, including Emma's ex-boyfriend, Paul. He looks completely out of place with the others. He's wearing a green long-sleeved tee that does nothing to hide his neck tattoo. And he has a notch shaved out of his left eyebrow, which is doubly-unflattering given his white-guy sandy-blond hair. He's staring at Emma in a way I find a bit unsettling. When he catches me looking, he stares down at his hands. I can't decide if he's being stalker-ish, or if he's waiting until the event ends to talk to her.

I don't want Emma to wind up with Miles – but I don't think she deserves to wind up with this guy either. Which I know isn't really my business. But still.

There's a crew here from a TV station in Houston. They want to do a brief interview. I agree, and it goes really well. The hardest question the reporter asks is why I would choose to make chocolate somewhere with such variable heat and high humidity.

"Galveston is my home," I tell the camera. "And if you've ever spent any time here, you know that we are determined people, who keep overcoming whatever the Gulf winds and weather throw at us. This is a climate-controlled

building, and I have a generator with backup coolers and
dehumidifiers in case of power outages,"

As the news crew is packing up, Dr. Ricci approaches me.
"That will look excellent on the evening news." Then he gestures
to the few rare books. "Of course you have the key to this case."

I pat my pocket. "Right here. I-"

"Excuse me," Carmen interrupts. "But I have a customer
wanting to make a corporate order. He asked to speak to the
owner."

"Sorry," I tell Dr. Ricci. "I'll be right back."

I head towards the counter, walking more and more
slowly as I take in the guy who's leaning against it. He's at least
six-foot four, with a firm jaw and thick lips and slightly untidy
dark hair framing lightly tanned cheeks and intensely green eyes.
He's wearing a flight jacket and tight jeans.

I cut a glance over at Naomi, who from all appearances
isn't even noticing this guy. But my aunt must have been paying
tons of attention to *me* over the years, especially when we've
gone to see rom-coms together. Because the guy she's picked out
for me is exactly my type. Kevin had had green eyes. It was one
of the first things that had attracted me to him. Which makes me
angry. It's almost like Aunt Naomi thinks she can line up
someone to replace the husband I lost. One green-eyed hottie for
another.

I slide through the gap, back behind the counter and try to
put a professional look on my face.

"Logan Hanlon. Ridley Puddle Jumpers flight service."
Which explains the pilot's jacket. His accent's not Texas. It's
subtle, but the soft, rounded vowels make me guess somewhere
up north. He holds out a hand for me to shake.

When our palms touch, instant attraction zings through
me – which almost as instantly turns to hot shame that turns my
chest to lead: I haven't been interested in anyone since Kevin, and
sure, Logan's built and has kind eyes, but that doesn't mean I
should trust him to bring me out of my grief. My heart aches. I

should never have planned this grand opening on my wedding anniversary.

I pull my hand away. "Felicity Koerber. But I suspect you know that."

"Well, yeah." He blinks. His eyelashes are super thick. "Your shop has been in the news. That's how I heard you do custom wrappers."

I match eye contact with him, trying to stare him down and get him to admit the truth. But he doesn't seem prepared to budge from his just-a-customer story. I blink first. But I can't help it. I have to say something. "Look, I'm not interested. It's nothing personal. I'm just not ready for romance right now. I don't want to go out with you. I don't want to go out with anyone – at all."

He blinks again – which sets my heart aflutter. He does honestly look confused. And somewhat amused. Oh God. The crinkle at the corner of his green eyes is enough to fuel my daydreams. "Okay. Not what I expected you to say. But at least you didn't make the obligatory Wolverine joke."

I'm so focused on Kevin and why I'm upset that it takes me a second to remember that the character Wolverine's real name is Logan. He must get that all the time. I take a second to really look at Logan, during which I try to calm myself down. "Nah, Wolverine has facial hair."

He laughs. "That's not a good look for me. Trust me."

"Well, the flight jacket is certainly working for you." I find myself smiling. Look where staring at his eyes has got me. Bantering. Which fills me with guilt again. I feel myself blushing. I look down at the counter, at all the perfect chocolate bars with the Greetings and Felicitations wrappers. I should be remembering Kevin today, not complimenting some stranger.

Logan unzips the jacket, and as he pulls a brochure out of his pocket, I see a gun holstered against his hip.

My eyes go wide, and I suck in a breath that isn't quite a gasp. Nobody would pick out a guy for me who is a ranger or a cop – or a criminal. I don't do dangerous. I like logical and methodical, like my marine engineer late husband. I also appreciate a touch of the romantic and the literary, which Kevin had in spades. We'd both gotten interested in craft chocolate when Kevin had signed us up for a couple's chocolate making class as a spontaneous date night.

That gun means Logan is so not my type.

I glance over at Aunt Naomi. She isn't paying attention to what's going on over here. My heart starts thudding. I think I've made a terrible mistake. I nod towards the gun. "Something tells me you're not the guy my aunt has been trying to set me up with."

He shakes his head and places the brochure on the counter. It's got all the information for his charter flight business. "As flattering as that is, I just came in here looking for chocolate."

I give him quotes for custom wrappers, and let him taste samples of each of my single-origin chocolates. Once he's made his choices and sent me a file of his logo – which includes an endangered Ridley's kemp sea turtle – the flaming embarrassment in my cheeks has settled down. I glance towards the gun again. Why would a guy who flies tourists across the Gulf need to be armed?

Logan pulls his jacket forward, so that the weapon is out of sight. "Old habits, you know?"

I find myself nodding, even though I have no idea what he means. "I guess that makes us all safer here today." Lame. I sounded lame.

He smiles. "Don't worry. If you sister does try to get me to ask you out, I'll be sure to tell her you're not looking."

"My aunt," I say, even more lamely.

But Logan is out of earshot before I can say anything else. He holds the door for some other guy who is coming in.

The new guy smiles shyly at me. Aunt Naomi turns to me and gives me a discreet thumbs up. The guy's not bad looking, but his button-down plaid shirt reminds me of something some of Kevin's less socially adept colleagues might wear. He approaches the counter. "I'd like to sample some chocolate."

"Sure. What do you like?"

He shrugs. "I'm not a huge chocolate fan, to be honest. But one of the girls in my spin class says I should try single-origin chocolates, and that yours are the best. She promised it would change my life."

"I'll just bet." I give Aunt Naomi an acid glance.

But this guy is so shy, and so sincere, that when he finally comes around to asking me out, I don't have the heart to crush him. I find myself saying, "Yes," to be polite, even though it means I'll have to crush him later. Because honestly, after meeting Logan, this guy is quite a letdown. Not that I have any business still thinking about the rugged pilot. Who, as I have said, is not my type. Even if I hadn't made a complete idiot of myself in front of him.

But this guy's name is Sid. I can't believe I've agreed to go out with a guy named Sid. Who is a chemistry professor, but didn't get my joke about H2Go.

As he's walking out of my shop, I reach for my phone to put the details into my calendar, but my phone's still in the office.

I turn to find Emma, to ask her to take over at the counter, since I'm about to have to start my tour and Carmen is still taking to Dr. Ricci. Only -- I can't find her.

I search the crowd. Finally, I peek into the hall and spot Emma coming out of my office.

She holds out both of her hands. "I know what you're thinking. But I just wanted to get Miles's number, and you were always too busy to give it to me. I didn't touch the computer."

She looks slightly out of breath, possibly a little ill. I suck in a breath and let it out through gritted teeth. "We will talk about this when the party is over."

"You left the office door open," she says defensively.

"No, I didn't," I insist. I *know* I didn't. Either Emma's lying again, or someone else went into my office. It's not very hard to guess which.

I still want to help Emma. But where is the point between giving people a second chance or two – and letting them walk all over you? I need to think about whether I can let her keep this job. It hinges on whether or not she's willing to talk tonight, whether I can figure out what has her so nervous.

I realize I never did show Dr. Ricci the books he wanted to look at. But my tour is supposed to be starting now, and there's a couple of members of the local press standing there with the fifteen tour-goers, cameras in hand. They're filming Emma giving me an introduction. Emma is holding a tray full of samples of drinking chocolate made with my Belize chocolate.

I move towards Carmen, to give her the key to the case, so she can help Dr. Ricci while I am busy. But before I can reach her, there's a clatter behind me.

I turn to find Emma collapsed. The tray is on the floor, drinking chocolate and paper cups dripping and rolling away from her still form.

My hand flies up to my mouth, and then I let out a startled squeak. I rush over to her. She's not breathing. I pull open her mouth. There's nothing obstructing her airway. I check for a pulse. Nothing. There's no injury, no reason for her collapse.

Carmen and Dr. Ricci are both heading this way. "Call 911," I tell Carmen as I move to start chest compressions.

"Perhaps you should let me handle this," Dr. Ricci says. "After all, I am a trained medical professional."

"Yeah, me too." I catch the startled look in Dr. Ricci's eyes before I look down at Emma's vacant ones. This is so not my type of medicine.

And Emma's already dead, declared at the scene when the paramedics arrive.

I don't know how to get in touch with her family. Her parents are on a multi-week Trans-Atlantic cruise. They're probably somewhere off the coast of Spain. Paul was here, looking devastated and sitting alone, after Dr. Ricci told him not to go near the body, but he disappeared as soon as the cops arrived.

Everyone else is stuck here, until the police decide what to do with us. Carmen and Naomi and I start handing out free coffee, but there's nothing else to do except wait. And that's one thing I'm horrible at.

It had looked like Emma had had a heart attack. As far as I know, she didn't do drugs, and hadn't mentioned any kind of prior medical history. And a heart attack in a healthy girl who was only twenty-three means foul play.

I'm going to have to admit to the cops that I was the last person to be alone with her – to have a fight with her – mere moments before her death.

Chapter Four

I'm sitting at a table, nursing my decaf. My friends have all been comforting me, but we've lapsed into silence. We're waiting for the officer in charge of the case. Someone's covered Emma's body with a sheet, but it's hard not to keep looking at the spot where she is still lying. This whole thing is surreal.

Autumn's been trying to comfort me. She's wearing a flowy mustard yellow top, which compliments her skin's undertones. She's curvy-bordering-on-plus-size, and she always dresses to flatter her body type, even when we were teenagers. She is my oldest friend. Which means she knows just what to say to distract me – even manages to get a smile out of me with a joke about doctors and physical therapists. I'm relieved that she's here.

The door opens. I've got my back to it, but I hear the little bell. Autumn gasps in a breath and puts a hand on my arm, her inch-long maroon nails digging into my skin. "Oh. My. Word. Felicity, you are so going to jail."

I look up at the cop. Once I get past the well-tailored suit, up to his face, I do a double take. Arlo Romero. I may not have seen him in fifteen years, but a girl doesn't forget the first guy she ever kissed. Autumn had been there for me in the days after my breakup with Arlo, but she never seemed to understand why the meltdown had happened. She probably still thinks Arlo's justified in hating me.

I suck in a breath. Arlo looks just as kissable now, with warm brown skin and brooding dark eyes and thick black hair I could run my fingers through for days. The decade and a half seems to have filled in his lanky frame with solid muscle, turned him into a man instead of a boy. A lot of people assume he's Mexican, because he's Latino in Texas, but he's actually Cuban. They're even more surprised to learn he doesn't speak Spanish, except for a few halting words to his grandmother. Just him, his mom and his grandma live in Galveston, while most of his family is in Florida.

He looks at me and doesn't seem surprised. Which means he knew I was in town, but didn't bother to come say hello. Which makes sense, considering the way I'd dumped him – in public, at prom. I'd been a teenager, and angry at the time, but I should have done it a little more tactfully.

"How'd he even become a cop?" I ask Autumn softly. Arlo had been a little wild when we'd been together.

Autumn whispers back, "He came back the year after you left. He'd gotten his act together."

Arlo looks over at me, making eye contact. I can't read what he's thinking. At all. His glance flicks over at Autumn. He tells one of the officers, "Separate those two."

Why? Because he thinks we might cover for each other like we're back in high school? I hear a noise of indignation come out of my own throat. I squelch it. I've seen enough cop shows to know that's police procedure. For suspects. From the look on Arlo's face, I really am going to jail.

I give him permission to use my office, and he starts questioning people, one at a time, getting preliminary statements before he decides if he can let us all go. When it is my turn, I feel hesitant about going into my own office, because he seems to have taken over the space so thoroughly. Arlo moves to let me sit at the desk. I'm still so nervous, I pull my hands under the desk to hide the shake in them.

Arlo asks me, "Care to tell me what the fight you had with Emma was about?"

He's already talked to Carmen. I tell him, as tactfully as I can, about Emma stealing money. When he asks how much, I shrug. "Couple of grand."

At least that's what she'd taken the last time. I don't know whether the police would consider $14,000 a large enough sum to murder someone over.

Arlo eyes me. "This is me you're talking to, Lis. You still have your tell. It was a bit more than that, wasn't it?"

I nod. Dang him. He never would tell me what my tell was. That jolt to the past at least stills my trembling. "But she'd promised to pay me back. Which can't happen now that she's dead."

"Which means you had no motive, right?" Arlo sounds like he's trying not to laugh at me.

"Arlo." I can't hide the frustration in my voice. But maybe it means I'm not his main suspect.

He asks, "What do you know about a fight Carmen had with Emma at last year's Island Breeze Bakeoff? Several people are saying it led to a grudge between the two of them."

"The bookstore sponsors a bakeoff?" How did I not know that? I really have been out of town for a long time. Arlo gives me a sharp look. I shake my head. "Obviously, I don't know much."

But it gives me a little perspective on what had been going on with my two assistants.

He moves on to more practical questions. When did I last see Emma? In the middle of the party, and before that outside my office. Who else had a motive to hurt her? I list off the three main suspects I've come up with, Carmen, Kaylee and Paul, though all of their motivations seem weak – except maybe Paul. He'd seemed so distraught after she'd collapsed, which could mean he still has feelings for Emma – or it could have been guilt. Jilted love can lead to irrational behavior.

Arlo gives me a sharp glance at that one. Does Arlo think that maybe I'm talking about how he left town the day after graduation, rather than about the current case?

"Sorry," I say softly.

He gives me an intense look, and I think he's fighting an urge to yell at me. Finally, he says, "Leave the shop as it is, for now. And don't leave town."

I can't tell if he's kidding or not. Could he be harkening back to the way he'd left town? Or maybe telling me he personally doesn't want me to leave? After a breath or two, I decide, nah. There's no way he would be flirting with me after the way I'd treated him. Or that I'd want him to flirt, after the way he'd treated me.

"Can I at least take a few things with me?" I ask.

Arlo hesitates, then nods. "As long as you let Fisk take a look at them first. He's the guy in the Crime Scene windbreaker." Arlo hesitates, bites at his lip, and finally asks me, "What did you do with the ring?"

Pain arcs through my heart. "Your promise ring? What did you expect me to do with it, when everything you'd told me about our future had been a lie?"

I'm not sure I can handle having this fight again right now, when I'm clearly a murder suspect and I just gave CPR to a corpse.

Arlo shakes his head. "I'm still not sure what you mean by that. But I told my grandmother I lost her sapphire. How much did I lie to her?"

I shrug. I still have his grandmother's ring, in a box with all my old stuff from school. It had never seemed right to sell it or throw it out, and I hadn't been about to track Arlo down to return it.

As though we'd just had a normal interaction, Arlo hands me a business card. "Just in case you think of anything else."

I'm still feeling a bit guilty about that ring after I leave the office. I grab the books from the locked case, the money from the day's sales, and my order forms. After these have been examined and swabbed and cataloged, I reluctantly hand over Emma's key to the store.

My friends Autumn, Tiff, Sandra, and Sonya are all standing outside, waiting for me.

Tiff's had her black hair straightened and styled into a bob that matches her professional-looking Real Estate Agent pants suit. I met Tiff through Aunt Naomi, though for some reason the two of them never hit it off. Tiff is relatively new to Galveston, but she's one of those huge personalities that can make you feel like you've known them forever, make you want to step outside your shell and just have fun. And, despite working for the real estate firm for less than two years, it seems like she's sold property to just about everyone.

Sandra and Sonya are identical twins with a lot of dark-haired pale-complected Romanian in their background. They have the same long, straight noses and large, luminous brown eyes, but there are subtle differences in overall face shape that allow me to tell them apart. Although Sonya is a bottle redhead – which makes it easier to keep them straight -- today her roots are showing. I met Sandra at the gym after I came back to the island. I've known them for less than six months but I feel like I could tell them anything and be confident that they won't share it – except with each other. Sandra's a lab tech and Sonya recently opened a yarn shop. I still can't imagine needing a whole shop to sell yarn. How many kinds can there be? But I guess some people can't imagine needing a whole shop to sell chocolate.

Autumn gives me a quick hug. "You okay?"

"For someone who's a suspect in a murder, and got locked out of her own shop? Just peachy." I have my arms crossed. I try to force them to my sides. We're standing on the Strand out in view of everyone. I need to not look guilty.

"Drinks?" Tiff asks. That's her solution to any sort of stress.

I shake my head. Most other times I'd be in for a couple of margaritas and too many chips so I could laugh my troubles away. "I'm still trying to figure out HOW this murder could have been committed. And I need all my wits about me because I've got nothing."

"Why is it your problem?" Tiff asks. "It won't take the police long to figure out you're not a murderer."

I don't have a good answer to that either. Maybe the reasonable emotional response to having an employee die on you *is* to go have a couple of drinks with your friends. I bite at my lip, thinking. "I'm pretty sure I was the last one to speak privately with Emma and, in retrospect, she did look a little ill. But not going-to-die ill. I should have done something."

Autumn taps a finger to her lips. She was a mystery writer, once upon a time. Had a few successful books out too. The real mystery is why she quit writing. But I can see the wheels turning in her mind now. "Emma collapsed in front of everyone. She has to have been poisoned. Who would dislike her enough to think she deserved a death so public and painful?"

I shy away from thinking about Emma's pain. I'm trembling again, trying to keep my brain from sliding back to thoughts of Kevin. At least Emma hadn't suffered in agony for hours, the way my husband had. But Emma's last moments had to have been laced with terror.

"How do you know it was painful?" Sonya asks, tossing back her thick tumble of red hair.

I don't wait for Autumn to explain. "Emma may have been a thief and a liar, but there was something about her I liked. She felt like a genuinely nice person."

Tiff nods. "It all seems surreal. This is a beach town, which draws families on vacation. How could there be a killer among us?"

"And not just in this town," Sonya adds. "in Felicity's shop."

That's the worst of it. There'd been a murderer in my shop. There's been a body on my floor. I can't be comfortable in there again until I understood why.

"Wait a minute," Sandra says. "We don't know for sure there is a killer at all. For all we know, the police will figure out that it was natural causes. A heart murmur. A brain aneurism. It could have been anything."

We all look at her. The lab tech. The most logical mind among us. And the only one not convinced that we'd all stumbled into a mystery.

"What happened with Arlo?" Autumn asks. "He looked like he wanted to murder *you* when he walked in the door."

"That's not funny," Sonya says.

I shrug. "So we have a history."

"You think you two will get back together?" Tiff asks. She's smiling. "I know a couple of people on the police force. I could arrange a little party, give you two time to talk, and maybe find the spark again."

"Not likely," Autumn says before I can put together a coherent response. "Arlo has a serious girlfriend. I saw her over at Sweetie's looking at wedding cake designs." She laughs. "Though whether Arlo knows about that or not, your guess is as good as mine."

"I'm glad that he's found someone," I say. They don't look convinced. "Really, I am."

I'm being honest, but they don't believe me. And I'm not in the mood to try and convince them. I might as well go home and face Aunt Naomi. At least she won't focus on the murder. She'll be ecstatic about my upcoming date with chem-professor Sid.

Chapter Five
Wednesday

I sit bolt upright in bed, shaking away a nightmare that I'm drowning in chocolate, about to be pulled between the grinding wheels of a giant melanger. I throw off my heavy purple comforter. It is six AM, two days after the murder, and I just realized I left my big melanger running, unattended, for all this time. Some people do that, trusting the machine not to have errors, but the manufacturer clearly states you should keep an eye on the process, so I turn it off when no one is going to be there. Carmen and Emma are both trained on how to turn it on and add heat, if necessary, to get the chocolate moving again.

Emma. My chest feels heavy when I remember again that she's not going to be there next time I go to the shop. I really do ache for her family, who have lost much more than a batch of chocolate. But what can I do for them?

The chocolate in the melanger at the grand opening had been ready to temper, which means that by now, it's probably ruined. Just like everything else, given a death in my shop.

But this could make things worse. Chocolate needs to be conched – ground and warmed and massaged – to reduce the particle sizes of both cocoa solids and sugar crystals to somewhere between 15-25 microns. Your tongue will start to feel grittiness at around 30 microns. Less than 15, and the chocolate takes on a gummy, unpleasant mouthfeel. And there's no coming back from that. My melanger holds 30 kilos of chocolate. While that represents a significant amount of cash, it's not enough to break me. I'm more worried about the melanger itself, which was a serious investment. I've heard stories of chocolate makers leaving machines unattended and coming back to find them shorted out. Or on fire.

I'm out of bed, heading downstairs and making coffee reflexively. How long do I have to wait for it to be a civilized hour to call the number on Arlo's card and ask about my shop? He never was a morning person, and I don't know what time he even arrives at the police station.

I manage to wait almost fifteen minutes. During which I down my one allowed cup of coffee and pour the rest out so that I'm not tempted to go back for more. I fill one of the mason jars Aunt Naomi likes to use for glasses with filtered water.

To my surprise, Arlo answers on the first ring, and sounds downright chipper. He says something to someone in the background. "Can this wait until I get to the office? Patsy and I are at Sweetie's having breakfast."

I stifle a laugh. Sounds like she's trying to put the idea of wedding cakes into his head. Good for her. "This will only take a minute. Just -- can you make sure someone turns off the machine with the big grinding wheels at my shop?"

"It's already off." He hesitates. "We drained it. Sorry."

They were looking for evidence. In my chocolate. "And did you find anything?"

He hesitates again. "No. Look, I'll make sure the guys clean the melanger for you."

He'd looked up the proper name for the machine. Maybe he'd become a thorough cop after all.

"What were you looking for, anyway?"

There's silence. For long enough that anxiety starts to build in my chest.

"Can I ask you something, Lis? Let me move somewhere a little quieter." There's a clatter in the background, like maybe somebody dropped a plate in the bakery. I can tell from the ambient sounds that Arlo is moving. He doesn't want what he's about to say to be overheard. Which makes me more nervous. "Physical therapists can't prescribe medications, right?"

"That's right."

"But you know pharmacology." It sounds like his chin scratches across the phone. "Would you have been able to get access to concentrated caffeine?"

I laugh. "I'm not even allowed a second cup of coffee. My GP would kill me." Then it hits me. "Is that how Emma died?"

"The techs found a large amount of caffeine in one of the paper coffee cups from your party. But we haven't found an ampule or a syringe."

I shake my head, even though he can't see me over the phone. "That doesn't make sense. Emma didn't drink coffee. She didn't even like the smell of it. Are you sure it wasn't one of the little sample cups we were using for the drinking chocolate? Emma loves—" I clear my throat as I correct myself, "Loved. The kind we make from our Belize chocolate, with hints of caramel and strawberries."

I'd always been flattered by that, because that bar was my first creation. There's no guarantee that the beans from that same farm will be anywhere near the same next year -- flavor profiles in single-origin bars can be ephemeral – but I'm going to try to keep it as similar as I can.

It sounds like the phone's moved, and Arlo's voice comes from farther away. He must be reading off his screen. He's probably got a transcript of the official statement I made on there too. "It says here coffee residue was also found in the cup."

"Maybe she drank it on a dare? You have to ingest a lot of caffeine for it to be fatal. Unless, of course, you've got a medical condition like mine. I'm sure you've already checked her medical history."

"Yes, we have." He clears his throat. "And it goes without saying that you won't share what I've said, right?"

"Something you weren't even willing to say in front of your girlfriend? I'm not stupid, Arlo."

"I never said you were." Then he changes the subject. "Patsy's amazing with codes and cyphers. She does crossword puzzles in pen. Sometimes I wish I could tell her about cases, bounce ideas off her."

"Sounds pretty serious." I really do need to get him that ring back. It sounds like he might need it.

"Maybe it is. You happy for me?"

"Absolutely."

"Really?" He sounds surprised.

"We both grew up, Arlo. I found someone who made me happy. I'm glad you've done the same."

There's silence on the line for a long time. Then he says, "I'm so sorry for your loss, Lis. You have to know that."

I shake away the heat that those words bring to my nose and the back of my eyes. "Yeah. Thanks." I refuse to cry on the phone. He doesn't say anything else. I try to get the conversation back on track. "Were there any other chemicals in the toxicology? As far as I know Emma was a healthy person. Maybe she took something else that accelerated the caffeine's effect."

"You know I can't tell you that, Felicity. You are still a suspect in this investigation."

Ouch. He'd used my full name. And the tone in his voice now is strictly business. It was Lis when he wanted information from me, but when I ask for a bit of info from him, he practically called Mrs. Koerber.

I find the switch a little infuriating, while at the same time I'm still fighting back the sweet emotion from having him show me sympathy.

We end the conversation. Thank goodness whoever killed Emma didn't have access to my chocolate processing room. That vat of chocolate *would* have been a tempting place to hide evidence. And the one thing I've learned from talking to Arlo is that I'm more of a suspect than I thought.

I make a list in my notetaking app of everyone I can remember being at the grand opening party, including Aunt Naomi and myself. I do a quick Google search on the first few names on the list. The high school principal was at the shop. I find information on her initiatives to get funding for a new science wing and alternative viewpoint articles wanting a bigger gymnasium. Dr. Ricci is receiving an award for some kind of medical technique and will host a follow-up seminar. The girl who works at the bank is getting married. The retired woman who had booked four spots for the hands-on demo is on every social media platform I am – plus some. She has nine grandchildren.

None of this is helpful.

And, except for the fact that the retiree and Emma were both glued to their cell phones and related accessories, none of this connects anyone to Emma.

I hear footsteps on the creaky stairs. They are steep and narrow, probably intended as the servants' staircase when this house was new. There's a more ornate staircase that leads to the front door of the house but that's blocked off because most of the steps were damaged and have been removed, awaiting replacement. Aunt Naomi comes around the corner from the base of the staircase directly into the kitchen.

The house is laid out as a long rectangle with the kitchen at the back right corner. A hallway leads forward into what used to be the formal dining room but Naomi took out the wall separating it from the living room, which had been beside the dining room. Now there's a giant great room taking up the middle of the rectangle, a parlor in the front left corner, and a hallway leading to the entryway and the front door – past that other staircase – on the right. The back left corner has another room, which is completely empty because we don't need the space for anything. This house is enormous. Seriously, there are four bedrooms upstairs.

Naomi yawns. "I smell coffee."

I instantly feel guilty for pouring it out. I hop up out of my chair. "Let me make you some fresh."

My aunt has been working hard on this house. It is going to be a showpiece when she gets it finished – two stories with a wrap-around porch and most of the original gingerbreading. The house is white right now but she's planning to repair the peeling thin wood siding and paint it powder blue. And, when she gets that mahogany banister sanded down and the steps replaced on the staircase, no buyer will be able to resist.

Aunt Naomi leans back against the counter. She has her tablet in her hand. After the whirr of the coffee grinder has quieted down, she says, "I'm glad you're up. I almost woke you myself to show you this. It's – not great."

She hands me her tablet. There's a picture of Knightley displayed prominently across the center of the screen – below the headline: *Craft Chocolate Employee Suffers Chocolate Overdose*.

My chest goes cold. "Where is this from?"

Aunt Naomi reaches around me and scrolls the screen up, where there's a picture of a guy with rectangular black-rimmed glasses wearing a purple shirt and a skinny tie, along with a banner that says *Gulf Coast Happenings*. "This guy's a blogger. He claims it's food and lifestyle mostly, and I think he was trying to be funny."

I scroll down. Hipster guy is *not* funny. Somebody leaked information to the press that Emma died from a toxic amount of caffeine. The article jokes that Emma must have overdosed on too much chocolate. And then proceeds to list off products from my shop that combine coffee and chocolate.

I groan, and try to hand the tablet back to my aunt. "That's not going to be good for business."

But if the police haven't released the information about the spiked coffee, I can't exactly reply on-line to defend myself.

"Oh, it gets worse," Naomi says. "Check out the comments."

The first comment is from a customer who bought a box of truffles. She's asking if Hipster thinks she should return them. Then people start daring each other to come in to try my chocolate – to see if they can handle the rush. Hipster chimes in that I should change my store name to Sympathy and Condolences and put warning labels on the products. Then somebody posts that they came all the way from the Panhandle to check out my shop and see where the girl died from the chocolate, only to find it closed and behind police tape.

Reading each one of these comments sets my heart to hammering harder. "There's nothing wrong with my chocolate."

"I know, honey," Aunt Naomi says. "And everyone else will too as soon as the police find out who killed Emma."

"Don't honey me. I don't think I can take it today." I move over to the cabinet and take out a mug, fill it with coffee, and hand it to Aunt Naomi.

Her eyes are wide, shocked. "I'm sorry. I – are you okay?"

"No, I'm sorry. I shouldn't have snapped at you." I put a hand on her arm. "But, yeah, I'm keeping busy, even if I can't work. I'm supposed to have lunch with Autumn today. And then I should figure out how to respond on my social media to the death of an employee. I've been radio silent since it happened, and that was apparently a mistake."

And now, thanks to Geek Guy, I have an extra mission. I have to figure out which of the other suspects are guilty in order to clear my name in time to save my business. And I have to do it before I get stuck riding the thrill-seeker death-chocolate vibe.

"Oh, Goodness. I wasn't even thinking." She draws me into a hug. I can feel the warmth from the coffee mug against my back. "Today's got to be so hard for you."

And I realize today's Wednesday, the anniversary of Kevin's death. I've been so caught up in dealing with my own crisis this morning that I've completely forgotten about him. Everything comes crashing in and it feels like my chest is going to collapse. I'm grateful Aunt Naomi's there, holding me up. She's the only one I'm not afraid to show my vulnerability to.

I want to go back to my room, and curl up in bed and look at old pictures for half the day. But I don't think Naomi would let me. So I try to focus. Greetings and Felicitations was Kevin's dream too. I can't let some blogger turn it into Sympathy and Condolences.

Knowing that the caffeine was in one of the paper coffee cups doesn't rule out any of those same three obvious suspects:

Paul, the boyfriend Emma just dumped (who I saw drinking coffee, and therefore could have been near the cups), Carmen, who seems to have a grudge against Emma (and who was also the person who made the coffee), and bookstore owner Kaylee, who had a fight with Emma only a few minutes before her death (and who poked Emma's arm in the course of their heated discussion. I can't remember if Emma was holding anything at the time. I don't *think* so. But if she was, Kaylee would have been close enough to slip something into Emma's drink.) But what am I supposed to do with that information?

Chapter Six

I'm supposed to meet Autumn for lunch at the diner across the street from the Seawall. Traffic on the Seawall today is busy, which means parking spaces are few and far between. The only spot I see is a tiny space between two giant pickups. My catering truck is a big vehicle, and I'm not stellar at parallel parking. so I wind up parking behind the diner.

There's a new tree sculpture in the parking lot, carved in the shape of a group of tall skinny sea turtles swimming on a wooden current. The trend in creating the sculptures started after Hurricane Ike, when a local artist reclaimed trees the hurricane had killed, turning the trunks into sculptures still rooted into the ground, turning the heartbreak of the lost oaks that had graced homes for generations into hopeful art. A number of additional artists have followed suit, and you never know where someone might find a new canvas. This sculpture is nice enough that I take a picture of it for my Instagram feed. Maybe I can say something about hope, even in the face of adversity, tactfully enough to not sound like I'm trivializing Emma's death.

I've spent a lot of time thinking about my social media feeds. Part of me feels like I'm showing off, like look at the amazing places I get to go, aren't you jealous? And every selfie makes me feel a bit vain. And at the same time, I worry that it's all going to look desperate, like I'm begging for credibility for myself and for my business. That all those pictures from frozen moments during my days aren't saying anything about my actual life.

Despite that, I still enjoy sharing pictures, especially little discoveries like this new sculpture. And I never wonder if other people are showing off when they post.

I'm still debating what to post about Emma as I enter the restaurant and take a booth in the corner. The place is all green vinyl and white tabletops, with pictures customers have brought in of their pets adorning the walls.

Autumn is running late. After Instagramming the tree, and saying a few words about sorrow and hope, I do a quick Google search for the Turners, Emma's parents. They're easy to find – they recently donated a grant to the hurricane recovery efforts. And the article about it is bigger than their mentions in the coverage of Emma's murder. Mr. Turner is a banker, and his wife is a lawyer. Which makes it even weirder that Emma didn't have money. If she really was in trouble, wouldn't she have asked her parents to help her out?

Vanessa, our usual waitress at the diner, gives me a cup of herbal tea. She knows I won't order anything else until Autumn gets here. We have this standing lunch date every week. Autumn isn't usually this late.

"I like your hat," I tell Vanessa.

It's a slouchy shape, with a bill, and a complicated geometric pattern to the blue yarn.

Vanessa touches the bill. "Thanks! Sonya from the yarn store made it for me."

Interesting, how different people in my life know each other, though I never see them together.

I find myself thinking about Logan again. My phone is just sitting there. And that line about "old habits" was just too intriguing. I have never Googled a guy before. And there probably won't be much about him. I type his name.

Then I delete it. This is stupid. Why can I not seem to get this guy out of my head? It makes no sense – but I can't seem to forget him.

Fine. I'll do the Google search, and then I'll be able to let it go.

I type his name again, and the search field fills in with *Cantu Security Fiasco* as the top potential option. I click on it.

Logan's picture comes up, intense and unsmiling. He's dressed in a black long-sleeve tee, arms crossed over his chest in a way that's meant to be intimidating for what is clearly a posed headshot. It's definitely the right guy.

I imagine him laughing as soon as the camera is turned. Though, I don't know, maybe he really is this scary guy, and the one I met is the mask.

Logan was a big deal with some kind of hotshot private security firm until four years ago. He had been security for a rock star, who had been shot by a stalker – and died on stage. Some of the website hits even display a picture of the girl, collapsed in Logan's arms, and the look on Logan's face is heartbreaking.

I'd felt that same expression from the inside out, caught in my own shock and grief at suddenly losing someone I loved. I'd bet anything that he had been more to that girl than just a hired gun.

On the second screen of hits, I find Logan's site for Ridley Puddle Jumpers. The launch date for his company is the same year as the news articles about the star's death. Which means he's been in Galveston a lot longer than I've been home. I'm not sure how I feel about that. Or why I care.

"What are you looking at?" Autumn is peering curiously down at me.

I jump, startled, and close the browser on my phone.

"No-nothing," I stammer, embarrassed to be caught Googling a guy I have no real connection to. Autumn, at least, hasn't started pushing me to start dating again. And I don't want her to get the wrong idea. "Just killing time."

"Uh huh." Autumn slides into the booth, and Vanessa automatically sets a cup of coffee in front of her. Man. What I wouldn't give to take that coffee cup away from her. I keep reminding myself that Dr. Ricci said it won't be long before I can get off my meds.

I quickly pull up the other window. "These are Emma's parents." In the photo, the couple are wearing power suits, Mr. Turner's tie the same brick red color as Mrs. Turner's blazer. "She lived at home with them. So why would she need to steal money from me?"

Autumn purses her lips. "Drugs, maybe?"

I shake my head. "I don't think she's the type." I look down at my phone. And yet . . . sometimes young people rebel, and the Turners look pretty easy to rebel against. "Of course, if you'd asked me a week ago, I wouldn't have said she was a thief, either."

Autumn laughs and nods her chin at me. "You've decided to solve this case."

"I what? No." But it's no use lying to Autumn. I look sheepishly up at her. "Is it that obvious?"

She looks like she's holding back another laugh. "Come on, tell me what you've figured out so far."

Hesitantly, I outline the few facts I've uncovered.

By the time I'm done, Autumn looks like she wants to say something so badly she's about to pop.

"What?" I ask.

"I'd hate to lead your investigation. I'm just a writer." She catches herself, biting at her lip. "Was a writer. A long time ago."

I nod, hoping that maybe she will finally tell me what happened that made her stop writing. It's something she's been doing since we were kids, and she'd finally started having some level of success. The silence stretches between us. Nope. This is not that moment.

"But-" I prompt, hoping she will at least tell me her thoughts about the murder.

"But, if this case were fiction, and I'd written it, it would be Carmen who had killed Emma."

"Why her?" I ask. "I mean, she definitely makes my list of suspects. There was something going on between her and Emma – and it seems bigger than just a grudge over a baking contest."

Autumn says, "That's motive. So you just need means and opportunity."

"Carmen had opportunity," I say. "She was right there by the cups for half the party. So if the caffeine wound up in one of them, she easily could have been the one to put it there. But the police seem to think it was a controlled concentrated substance. So I don't see how she could have gotten it."

Autumn's eyes go wide. "Felicity, one of Carmen's roommates works neonatal ICU at the hospital. Sometimes concentrated caffeine is used to stabilize preemies."

I blink at her, floored. "How do you know that?"

Autumn blushes. "Research for my last novel, before I moved on to other things."

Autumn now has a shop on Etsy where she sells vintage jewelry. How she makes a living off of that is anybody's guess.

"And about Carmen's roommate?" I prompt.

"She came up to the chocolate shop that time, looking for Carmen. Don't you remember? You were making the caramel, and then we went to lunch."

"Oh." I remember the day in question. Of course, I'd been too busy to talk to Carmen's roommate. Or even meet her. "But why would Carmen's roommate have given her a substance to use to murder someone?"

Autumn shrugs. "I didn't have it figured out. I was just thinking she's the least obvious suspect, because you trust her and believe her grudge with Emma was over something trivial, which in any good work of fiction, means she has to have done it."

I laugh. "The least obvious suspect is you. Or Aunt Naomi."

Autumn shakes her head. "We're not suspects. So we don't count."

She's right. They both had no reason to harm Emma, and no real opportunity to do so. But if it really is Carmen . . . "Her roommate wouldn't necessarily have been in on it. Carmen may have visited her at work, and snatched the dose when her roommate was distracted."

"That's plausible," Autumn says.

"I should talk to Carmen, but I don't know how to interrogate a suspect," I admit. "I won't ask the right questions. Will you come with me?"

"Of course," Autumn says. "Where is she?"

"She said something about going surfing if the weather kept looking like it might storm." Galveston is far enough up the Texas Coast that surfing is not as easy as it is in Padre, or even Corpus. Surfers get excited about bad weather because incoming storms mean good waves, for once. And now, with a tropical storm building in the Gulf, threatening to turn into a hurricane, we've been getting intermittent wind and rain. Surfing in Galveston is for the young and adventurous -- or the dedicated. Which says a lot about Carmen.

Autumn shudders. "I hate the beach here. Brown sand . . . jellyfish . . . tar balls. Give me the Caribbean any time."

"So you're not going to go?" I try to hide my disappointment.

"Oh, I'll go." She downs her cup of coffee and pulls a ten-dollar bill from her purse, which she drops on the table. I eye the empty cup longingly.

The wind's blowing, salty and fresh, when we come out of the diner and make our way to the catering truck. I climb inside and try to straighten my hair, which is out of place, partially stuck against my lip gloss. The temperature is dropping.

The sky is getting gray, and a few fat raindrops hit my windshield. If Tropical Storm Bertha stays on the current course, the weather will get a lot worse than this. But it's far too early to tell. The possible arc the storm might take goes from Lake Charles all the way down to Brownsville.

The storm's name begins with a B, which means this is the second named tropical storm of hurricane season. That name gets recycled every six years, unless the storm turns into a devastatingly destructive hurricane. Alicia. Ike. Rita. Harvey. The mere mention of those names can cause anxiety in someone who's lived a long time on the Gulf coast.

I look over at Autumn, who is buckling herself into the passenger seat. We've been friends for a long time, but something happened here, while I was away in Seattle, whatever it was that made Autumn stop writing. And the fact that she's never wanted to open up about it hurts my feelings a bit.

But she seems happy now, with a business she can run from home, and a ton of friends. And she's been a good friend to me, especially when I first came back home, numb inside my grief and not ready to be a friend to anybody. So really, should I keep resenting her for not wanting to talk about the past?

I try to just let it go as I pull out of the parking lot, driving slowly down the Seawall. I glance out at the water, where a few kids are playing in the waves close to the shore, taking advantage of a few last moments while the weather is still clear. Another side of our love-hate relationship with the Gulf. Kids were doing the same thing the day before the 1900 Hurricane rolled in and devastated the Island.

A line of brown and white pelicans flies by, their bills tucked elegantly.

Compared to the 1900 Great Storm, the tropical storm predicted on the news is nothing.

The East End of the island is wider, and far more populated, this section of the seawall an easy drive from the Historic District. If Carmen is surfing, she's probably farther down, away from the shops, where the waves get better.

"We can tell Carmen we happened to spot her car and wanted to see her surf, since we're all off today." It's not subtle, but it's the best I can think of. With everything my doctors have said about overexertion while I'm on my meds, I can't exactly say I'd randomly chosen to take a stroll down to the beach.

Autumn points. "Isn't that the condos where your grandmother lives?"

I glance over at the tall building, on the side of the road opposite the seawall, laid out wide so that most of the condos have a Gulf view. "Yeah."

I swallow around a sudden lump of emotion. I can't help but imagine Aunt Naomi saying, *You were right there, and you couldn't even stop in for a minute?*

I tell myself that we're on a mission, that there's no time to stop. But honestly, Carmen's likely to be surfing for hours. I love my grandmother – a lot. But I don't *want* to stop by and see her. So I keep going.

I drive slowly, until we spot Carmen's car, a ten-year-old Honda with a surf rack. It's school-bus yellow. I'm going to have to pull a U-turn and parallel park. Which as I've said, I'm horrible at. Perfect, right?

I finally catch a break in traffic big enough to make the U. And there's a section with three empty spots, which means I should be able to parallel park my brick of a truck. I've got all of my attention focused on my rearview mirror, wishing like anything I had one of those fancy backup cameras.

"Stop!" Autumn says loudly.

I slam on my brakes, bracing for a crunch. But I don't hit anything. I check all the mirrors. "What?"

I don't see danger. Maybe a dog had run behind the truck or something.

"Look!" Autumn is pointing ahead of us.

Carmen is running up the cement steps, her hair wet, wearing a rash guard, but she's got on sneakers and is holding her cell phone. She hops into her car and takes off. If she had a surfboard with her, she's left it on the sand. What could have created that kind of panic?

I pull out into traffic, following Carmen's car. I feel ridiculous. Really, how hard is it for someone to realize they're being followed by a catering truck? But Carmen doesn't seem to be trying to lose us. She's driving in a clear path along the Seawall, and though she's speeding – which means we're speeding, which I rarely do – she signals her turn towards the center of the island well in advance.

"Where do you think she's going?" Autumn asks.

"Maybe the hospital?" I guess. That's the direction we're headed. "If she got concentrated caffeine from her roommate, maybe her roommate figured out what she did with it and threatened her."

"Mmmmm," Autumn says appreciatively. "Maybe *you* should have been a writer. That's a good plot twist."

I laugh, even though the situation is serious. If Carmen is a killer, we could be stumbling into blackmail, a second murder in progress . . . all sorts of things I'm not prepared to handle.

"Here comes the hospital," I say, but Carmen hasn't put on her signal or her brakes.

We overshoot the building, and I'm less sure we're right about Carmen. Which makes me feel even more ridiculous about chasing her. Autumn and I exchange a look, equally puzzled.

Carmen pulls up short at a squat white brick building. The sign has a stylized picture of a dog, a cat and a bird. She tries to get out of the car, but she hasn't taken her seatbelt off. She takes a few seconds, struggling with it the way someone does when they're in a panic. She looks up and notices us.

Autumn waves at her.

"I guess I have to park," I say, heat in my face, despite the dropping temperatures.

What are we doing at an animal hospital? More importantly, what are we going to tell *Carmen* we're doing here? We can't exactly admit that we think she's a murderer.

Carmen manages to get herself out of her car, realizes she's forgotten to lock it. We catch up to her in the time it takes her to fumble out her keys. She doesn't even ask why we're here, without even having Knightley in tow.

"We seem to be all the same places today," Carmen says. But she sounds too distracted to realize how odd that is.

"Are you okay?" I ask.

"Not really." Carmen locks the car. "Nobody's home at my house today." Because none of her roommates had their workplaces declared a crime scene. "It's Bruce. My neighbors had to call."

She heads for the vet's front door, as though that is enough of an explanation. It's starting to rain more in earnest. Bruce is Carmen's German shepherd. I feel a tug of fear. I hope he's okay.

Chapter Seven

We follow Carmen into the overly air-conditioned waiting room, which smells sharp of antiseptic and wet dog and something medicinal that might be pet vitamins.

"Carmen!" A middle-aged white woman with purple streaks in her bleached hair stands up from one of the chairs and rushes towards us, wrapping my assistant in her arms. The bald guy that had been sitting next to her stays seated, but casts a concerned look towards the two women. He's at least ten years younger than the woman, but they're wearing matching wedding rings. They're both dressed like they're on their way to a PTA meeting.

"Can I see him?" Carmen grips the woman's arm.

She shakes her head. "They're trying to get him stabilized." She looks over at me and Autumn, shifting her body to include us in the conversation. "Somebody broke in to Carmen's house. We found Bruce collapsed in the yard. It looks like someone fed him chocolate so it would be easy to get to the back door."

"Deb and Harry are my neighbors," Carmen tells us. She sniffs, obviously holding back tears. She's had that dog for going on nine years. "They told me they called the police before they brought Bruce in."

I exchange another look with Autumn. That break-in may well be connected to the murder. And if so, we can scratch Carmen off our list of suspects. There's no way she would poison her own dog just to make herself look less suspicious.

Autumn shrugs. "I said if it was a work of fiction."

Carmen gives her a confused look, but she lets it go.

Deb takes something out of her purse. "I found this near the dog's bowl."

My heart goes cold and I gasp in a breath. It's a chocolate bar wrapper – with an image of Knightley peering sweetly up off of the paper.

Carmen looks at me, suspicion flickering in her eyes. "I've been telling myself all day that it couldn't be you. You're too sweet of a person, and even though you had that fight with Emma, and were the last one alone with her, I didn't want to believe you could actually take a human life. But to poison an innocent dog just to get whatever evidence I accidentally took home-"

"Me?" I squeak. "I've spent all day trying to figure out if it was you."

Carmen and I just stare at each other, until Autumn takes the wrapper and sets it gently on the counter. "I assume the police will want to have a look at this. But it couldn't have been Felicity that brought it to your place, if Bruce was poisoned shortly before you headed here. She went to lunch with me, and then we came looking for you."

I nod. "I went to the restaurant straight from the gym. You can ask Vanessa. I was there for almost an hour." My chest feels hot. How did I go from trying to clear my name to defending myself to my friends in so few minutes?

Carmen looks relieved – right up until Deb pipes up. "The vet said it can take six or more hours for chocolate poisoning to show symptoms. It could have happened early this morning."

Carmen frowns at me.

I frown at Deb. "Then I still couldn't have committed the break-in. My aunt can account for my whereabouts. And I wouldn't have." I look at Carmen. She looks fairly well convinced I'm not a mastermind thief. "You seem pretty sure this has to do with what happened to Emma. What do you think whoever did do it was looking for?"

Carmen shrugs. "I have no idea. I only knew Emma from work."

Deb clears her throat. "That's not strictly true. It didn't go so well that time."

Carmen looks down. "She's talking about the time I asked Emma to house sit and feed Bruce when my roommates and I went to Destin." I remember her asking for that week off, right after she started working for me. I hadn't cared, since the plans were already in place when I hired her. "Emma got a better offer, and after the first day, she forgot, and Bruce spent four days drinking out of the toilet and pooping by the back door. He's not usually allowed to sleep in the house, because he tends to tear things up when he gets bored. So the place was trashed when we got back. Emma acted like it hadn't happened, and I got over it – and then everything went down with the baking contest." Carmen looks up, squaring her shoulders. "I was mad, sure, since I'd paid her to house-sit. But I wouldn't have killed her over it. Especially not months later."

"Next time, ask us. We love to dog sit." Deb smiles, then after a second, she cringes as she realizes what she's just said. We don't know yet if Bruce is going to pull through.

I try to get the discussion back on track. "But you were still mad about the baking contest. What exactly happened?"

Carmen looks at me sharply enough that her dark hair, in its ponytail, swishes around over her shoulder. "Not angry enough to hurt her. The prize for the contest was only like five hundred bucks. I wouldn't have even be mad, except she cheated."

I shrug. We'll never know now if Emma cheated or not. "Would five hundred dollars have meant a lot to Emma?"

"Emma always seemed to need money. One time, right after she started working at Felicitations, she dropped her purse, and a couple of bills fell out, and one of them was marked final notice. But it was for her cell phone. I figured, she lived with her parents, they stopped paying for her phone, so she got another job. Entering a baking contest wasn't like her, but if she needed cash . . . I feel bad for being mad." Carmen grimaces. "I never imagined she'd owe money to someone who would *kill* her over it."

My heart lurches. Could the person I'm trying to find be dangerous? I mean, to someone other than Emma? And now, Carmen's dog? I take a deep breath. I can't just drop this. I still need to know the truth. "Do the police know if anything is missing from your house?"

Carmen shakes her head. "No idea. I came straight here."

"Could either of your roommates be the target?" Autumn asks.

"Maybe." Carmen sounds hesitant. I don't think she believes that any more than I do. "But none of us have anything worth much. And my roommate's little girl's been out of the house. I'm completely paperless, and I carry my laptop wherever I go. It's in the car right now."

"Did you bring anything home after the party?"

"Only a couple of recipe books from the shop. I figured since we were closed, I might as well try out a few new things." Carmen pulls out her phone and shows me photos and notes for the recipe she's been working on.

I can't help but laugh. Some of the recipes farther down in the list are labeled things like, *Better than Emma's Chocolate Cake*. "You were looking forward to competing against her again, weren't you?"

Carmen says, "After Emma won the contest, she Instagrammed about it, at-ing me with her stuck-up screen name in posts where she was gloating about how she'd brought a bit of refinement to the Island where she's 'summering.' Which was ridiculous. Emma'd lived in Texas her whole life. And before she started working at Greetings and Felicitations, she'd had no experience baking anything. She has to have cheated. But she refused to admit it."

I can't imagine anyone killing Emma over a recipe or a recipe book. But what else would a thief have hoped to find at Carmen's house?

And why poison the dog with my chocolate? And then leave the door open when they left? It almost feels like someone is trying to frame me for Emma's murder. Arlo already thinks I'm a suspect, so it wouldn't be that hard to do.

Carmen would have found some other way to frame me, one that didn't involve her dog. Which bumps her down my suspect list. So who should I talk to next?

I'm not about to try to talk to Kaylee. The bookstore owner made it clear last night, when we were all stuck together at my shop, that she thinks I'm the suspicious one.

Which just leaves Paul. I have no way to find contact information for Emma's ex-boyfriend. I look over at Carmen. "Do you know Paul's last name?"

"Dupree." Carmen blushes.

I still think there's more to whatever was going on between Carmen and Emma. Maybe Carmen is afraid Paul's going to tell me. I look through public directory information using my phone. There's only one Paul Dupree.

Leaving Autumn to comfort Carmen, I move aside and call the number. It is answered by an old guy who is obviously not Emma's Paul.

It's a good five minutes before I can find a polite way to get him off the phone.

Carmen says, "I don't think Emma's Paul is from the Island." She'd obviously been listening to my side of the conversation.

"You could have told me that earlier," I say miserably.

"You didn't ask." Carmen scrunches up her nose. "Like you didn't tell me what happened between you and Mr. Tall, Dark and Leather Jacket."

I feel my face go crimson. "Mr. Hanlon?" She could only be talking about Logan. "He's just a customer."

"Don't give me that. I saw the way you looked at him as he was leaving."

"Oh?" Autumn's eyebrows go up.

"So I thought he was cute." I shrug. "Doesn't matter. I'm not ready to date."

Autumn asks, "What are you wearing to the funeral?"

Like she expects Logan to show up there, and wants me looking my best. Which is ridiculous.

Paul might show, though, even though Emma was his ex. He'd disappeared from the murder scene before the police arrived. I wonder if anyone told Arlo he was there. I had been so flustered when he'd questioned me . . . part of me wants to call Arlo again and update my statement. But I'm still irritated that he's considering me a suspect. Arlo should know me better than that.

If I could have some concrete information to give him, that would put me on more equal footing. Trying not to sound morbidly excited, I ask, "They've already scheduled the funeral?"

Carmen makes a face. "One of my roommates works at the funeral home, when she can't get gigs showing her art. It will take a few days for Emma's parents to get back into town, and then they're having the funeral that afternoon. It doesn't sound like a lot of people are coming."

"Emma deserves better than that," I say.

The door leading into the back of the vet's office opens, and a woman wearing a white coat appears in the doorway. We all go silent. The vet's expression is difficult to read. Bruce might be okay. Or he might not.

Carmen moves close to me, and I can feel her bracing herself for the news. She takes my hand, and suddenly, like a year hasn't passed, I'm back in the hospital, waiting for a sympathetic doctor to tell me there's no hope. Heat burns in my chest and in my nose.

Bruce may just be a dog, but he's Carmen's, and she's flooding with anxiety and pain. Besides, he's a really sweet dog. I squeeze Carmen's hand.

The vet smiles – not the megawatt-great news smile, but the softer, reassuring there's hope smile. She says, "We've got him stable. I can't make any promises at this point, but it looks like he's going to be okay."

Carmen makes a soft, relieved noise deep in her throat. "Can I see him now?"

The vet nods. "He's sleeping, but it should be fine."

The door to outside opens, letting in the sound of rain – and Arlo Romero. He spots me and arches a thick eyebrow in my direction. I wait for him to walk over, even as Carmen and her neighbors disappear into the back. Autumn hesitates, starts to say something, then follows Carmen.

"What are you doing here?" Arlo asks.

I'm not about to tell him I've been investigating his case. Especially since I'm about to have to explain how I have no idea how my chocolate wound up poisoning Carmen's dog. I force a smile. "I'm here comforting a friend and employee. And I seem to have gotten here faster than you."

The sour look he gives me fills me with a sense of satisfaction inappropriate to the circumstances. Maybe I do have a little resentment left over from when we used to be together.

"We never did find an ampule in your shop, or on anyone at the scene. Which leads me to believe that the chemical cocktail Emma overdosed on most likely had to be in capsules, designed to be dissolved into that hot coffee. Which brings me back to the one person with a motive who might have been able to prepare such a thing."

I sigh. Is he highlighting my medical knowledge, or my candy making skills? "Or somebody dosed Emma's coffee and left. A couple of people came in just for samples, and a few paid with cash. So my records don't show everyone, and some were there for just a few minutes." I explain how Emma's ex left the minute it looked like the cops would show. "I'm less inclined to think he did it, but really anyone could have-"

"Have you been in contact with Paul Dupree?"

Oh boy. This is going to be a long conversation. But what if Arlo's right? Capsules dissolved in coffee. Who would do that?

Chapter Eight

My hair is drenched by the time I get back to my aunt's house. I have a date later tonight, and I'd cancel if it wasn't something I just want to get over with.

As I towel my hair dry, I keep thinking about the break-in at Carmen's. She'd texted me after she got home. Nothing was missing, as far as she could tell. But that chocolate wrapper meant that whoever had poisoned Bruce had been to my shop, at least once. I have a feeling that person was there when Emma died.

I wish I could get back into the shop, see if they had left any clues. But all I have is that one box of things from the shop that I brought home. I doubt there's anything important in there, but I'm running out of leads. Once I'm sure I'm not going to get moisture on anything valuable, I take the box out of the closet where I'd stashed it.

There's not much in it. I'd taken the cash to the bank, so mainly it is just the books. The three volumes of Jane Austen are on top. I doubt anyone could have tampered with them since I'd put them in the case, but Emma had shown an interest in these volumes. Could she have stuck something into one of them?

I carefully flip through every page, looking for writing or for an object slid between the pages. I find nothing. I do notice, however, that the back endpapers are on a little wonky, on all three volumes. I wonder with dismay if that negatively affects the value. It isn't significantly off, but it looks out of place on otherwise meticulously constructed volumes.

I send a quick e-mail to one of the specialty booksellers I had searched when I'd priced the books, asking if something unique like that enhances or detracts from the value. I get an almost immediate response, offering to take the problem, i.e. the books, off my hands for a couple hundred bucks, subject to "free" authentication.

I delete the e-mail. If there's a bookseller that eager, I guess I shouldn't worry too much about decreased value. But I may need to get these books authenticated. I should have thought about that before putting them up for sale in the shop.

Which gets me thinking. How did valuable British first editions come to be in an old house on an island off the coast of Texas? Knowing that information would make authentication easier, which might save me money, depending on how the experts price their services. Looking into the books' provenance would be a welcome distraction from both my stalled investigation and my unwelcome date. The girl from the estate sale had scribbled me a receipt on the back of her card. I hadn't even looked at the front of it. I find the card in my receipt file. Turns out, the girl's a hairdresser over at PixieCuts. Named Mindi. With an 'i.'

And I happen to have a disheveled head of hair, the afternoon before a date. I peek out the window. The sun seems to be coming out. It couldn't hurt to get a trim . . . and have an excuse to ask who owned the books I'd bought.

I stick the box back up on the shelf in the hall closet – the only way to be sure they're safe from paint and construction debris. Then I call the number on the card. Mindi sounds shocked to hear from me. I have to explain twice how we met.

She says cautiously, "I'm not taking those books back."

I laugh, assuring her that I have no intention of trying to renegotiate and an hour later, I'm leaned back in a chair in a small beige-walled suite in a building where stylists, massage therapists and aestheticians rent individual spaces, with my head tipped back into a sink. Mindi is scrubbing my hair vigorously. I have to admit, it feels good. Which gives me confidence that I will walk out of here with a competent haircut – and a need to explain myself to my usual stylist.

Trying to act like I'm just making casual conversation, I ask, "Whose house was it for the estate sale?"

Mindi's hands tense, and for a second she tugs painfully on my hair. She recovers quickly and says simply, "My grandfather passed away."

"I'm so sorry to hear that." I had half expected her to say something like that. Didn't mean I had anything legitimately comforting to say in the face of her loss.

Mindi shrugs and finishes scrubbing my hair. Before she turns the water on to rinse, she says, "He was a mean old coot, and he didn't have anything worth very much. So I got roped into organizing the estate sale. You might have heard of him. He was on the board of trustees at the hospital until a few years ago, Marshall Klein. You'd have thought he had enough money for nice furniture – I could have used that, you know? But he kept everything until there were holes worn all in it. And he kept everything – string, rubber bands, aluminum foil."

I struggle to keep a straight face. The furniture I'd seen in the office had been early American antiques. If I can't trust her judgment about the furniture, I don't know about her perceptions on her grandpa being a hoarder. After a second, though, the name clicks into place. Marshall Klein. "I met your grandfather once, about twelve years ago," I tell Mindi. "My class was doing a project where we shadowed people at the hospital. You're right. Everybody was scared of him."

Mindi deftly wraps a towel around my head. "It all caught up with him in the end."

She gestures to the other chair, but I sit frozen. "Are you saying your grandfather was murdered?"

Mindi makes a spluttering noise. "Uh, no." She gestures to the chair again. "Heart attack. Because he was too stubborn to listen to anybody. He wouldn't change his diet or let go of the stress."

I walk to the other chair, a little dazed by the coincidence. Emma had had a heart attack. And some old guy had had a heart attack. But it's a silly idea. What's the possible connection between the two of them?

Mindi unwraps the towel and runs a comb through my hair, plastering it down straight. "What are we going to do here today?"

I take a look at her hair, which has a bit too much of the whole Texas-beauty-queen "Big hair" vibe for me. I say, "Just an inch or two off the bottom."

Mindi looks dubious. "You don't switch hair stylists if you're not looking for a change. If you let me take four inches off and give you some layers, it would still brush your shoulders – and there would be a lot more volume." She makes eye contact with me in the mirror. "Nothing like mine. Just a bit of gentle floof."

What have I gotten myself into? I can't tell Mindi I'm only here to snoop into the history of the books she sold me. I mean, I could have taken that approach, but I would have had to start the conversation with that. Now it would look like I'd lied to her.

But I'm not ready for change. The last big change in my life was awful, jarring, and I'm still not over it. I take a deep breath. This is just hair, I remind myself. "Okay. Do your magic."

Mindi starts cutting. I can feel the weight dropping away from my head. Maybe it will look amazing. If I don't turn out looking like Mindi.

I ask Mindi, "Any idea where your grandfather got his books?"

"Why?" Mindi asks. "You need another set of Encyclopedia Britannica from 1967?"

"I was thinking more the fiction. A lot of it seems to be British."

Mindi starts making little detailed snips at my hair. "He spent almost a decade in England, working with some kind of medical engineering company. He came back after some kind of falling out. I don't know the details. It all happened before I was born."

If I had to guess, I'd say Mindi's twenty-two-ish. So that's not difficult to believe. "Then you wouldn't know if he brought a lot of stuff back with him?"

Mindi hesitates, pulling her scissors back away from my hair. "Why? Did you find something cool in all those books?"

I hesitate too. Then I nod. "Very cool."

Mindi snorts out a laugh. "Don't worry. A deal's a deal. I won't ask for it back." She takes a few more snips at my hair. "It's kind of weird though. Some guy called me asking if I'd sold everything out of my grandfather's office, and he seemed really disappointed he'd missed the estate sale."

"That is weird." I still can't see how it dovetails with what happened to Emma. It probably doesn't. There can be more than one mystery going on on an island with a population of over 50,000 people.

Mindi drops the scissors into a container of sanitizer and pulls out a pre-heated curling iron. "You said you have a date tonight, right?" I did say something about that, when I'd been trying to explain why I needed an appointment today. "Let's get you dolled up."

Mindi has given me a cut with natural flow and a bit of bounce that seems to take a couple of years off of my appearance. I can't help smiling in the mirror. I wish Kevin could have seen me at this moment, looking happy for the first time in a long time. He would have called me his sweets and we'd have collapsed in laughter.

So how can I be getting ready to go out on a date with another man? Not even one I like, but still. The sense that I'm betraying Kevin hits me heavily. Naomi keeps saying that he would want me to move on, not live my life with my heart stuck back in Seattle, and my brain thinks she's right. Kevin's love was never selfish. But tell that to my broken heart.

Mindi loses her own smile in the mirror. "Do you not like it?"

"I love it. It's just – life, you know?" This is why I don't visit people. They always want to talk about things. And it doesn't help.

"Bad breakup?" Mindi guesses.

I bring my hands together under the stylist's apron. I have my ring on. I wear it whenever I'm not in the kitchen or in the shop. "Not exactly. But close enough."

Mindi lets me leave without explaining myself further. I may have accidentally found myself a new hair stylist.

I have a little time to get home, and look a little deeper into Marshall Klein, before I need to focus on this date.

Finding information on Klein isn't difficult. The guy even has his own Wikipedia entry. When he'd lived in England, he'd been working in Reading, which isn't far from Steventon, where Jane Austen was born. It is plausible he found the books there and brought them home. Now that Marshall is dead, it is unlikely that I'm going to find out anything more.

The house is empty, but when I finally go up to my room to change, I find that Aunt Naomi has laid out the dress she talked me into buying across my bed. It's green, a few shades darker than Logan's eyes.

Heat fills my face. I mean, than Kevin's eyes. Damn it, this isn't fair. Why do they have to have the same eye color?

I debate for a few minutes, then I leave my ring on the dresser. I've agreed to this date, and it would certainly send mixed signals.

As I'm getting ready, my brain keeps bouncing between building a list of possible murderers and thinking of how to politely tell Sid there isn't going to be a second date. I feel horrible, because he's taking me to a seafood restaurant that's been a Galveston institution since the early 1900s. It's an expensive place that specializes in Gulf shrimp and Galveston Bay oysters using mostly French techniques, but with a few dishes and sauces that give nod to the Cajun side of the gulf coast. I should try to go Dutch on the check, if he will let me.

We're supposed to meet in the restaurant lobby. And I'll be driving up in my catering truck. Life being what it is, it hadn't seemed prudent to take out a second note just to have a more normal-looking vehicle. I'm sure Aunt Naomi would have let me borrow her car – she often does – but I don't want her any more invested in this date than she already is.

The restaurant is on the Island's sheltered side, overlooking calm bay waters. By the time I get there, the parking lot is already full. I wind up parking down the street, so it doesn't matter what I drove up in. I'd worn sensible flats – psychologically, I think I'm already preparing to run away. But I should at least try to have a nice time. I owe Sid that much, for agreeing to go out with him. It isn't his fault I'm not ready to date.

It isn't raining at the moment, but I grab my umbrella from under the passenger seat in case it is pouring when I have to walk back. It's a fancy travel piece that reverse folds to keep you from dripping water on the floor, with a reflective strip so people can see you in the dark. It had been a gift from my grandmother. What would she think of me, here tonight, stepping towards the lobby of a restaurant I'd visited with her a dozen times? She . . . wouldn't be able to understand.

"You're here." Sid is waiting for me just outside the doors. He sounds relieved.

"Yeah. And it isn't even raining." Stupid, Felicity. I stink at small talk.

I've dressed up for this place. Sid is wearing another plaid shirt. I can't help but take that as a bad sign.

When we get to our table, Sid orders wine. Which I take as a good sign. But once he gets his glass, he gulps it down, another bad sign. And then he proceeds to start talking about himself, and the impact he has had on his students' lives in a way that might be charming if it didn't have an underlying thread of arrogance.

If I hadn't already been thinking of an exit strategy, I would be now.

Since he brought up work, I follow suit. "I got into chocolate because I love to travel. I've started getting to see the world, and it changes your perspective. Have you been anywhere interesting lately?"

Sid frowns. "I prefer my own bed, and familiar food. I got up to Dallas last year, but I made it home in three days." Sid drops his fork, and leans over the side of the table to retrieve it. He sits back up straight. "That's a really cool mechanism on your umbrella. I was at a robotics symposium recently where I saw something similar used on a collapsible drone. There were a number of presenters there from Galveston. One of the guys I work with was showing off technology that will soon allow metal to become permeable and then regain its structural integrity. One of our local GPs was discussing his innovation for a painless delivery system for drugs that will make it easier for people with chronic illness to-"

I tune out from the rest of what Sid is saying, and focus on the Snapper Pontchartrain on the table in front of me. The mushrooms and bits of seafood spiced with Cayenne and ladled over the delicate fish are the only thing about this evening I'm actually enjoying. I feel eyes on me from across the room.

I look up.

There is Logan Hanlon, having traded his leather jacket for a suit jacket, about to take what I'm guessing is a group of puddle jumper clients through to a large round table.

And here I am, barely twenty-four hours after telling Logan I wasn't interested in romance under any circumstances, obviously on a date. I look like a huge liar. Heat floods my face and travels down my arms. The green dress must be making my face look even more crimson.

I watch Logan excuse himself from his group. Really? He's walking over here.

I fight an urge to scrunch down in my seat. That won't help anything. "Mr. Hanlon." I try to sound confident. "What are you doing here?"

"I could ask you the same thing." Logan casts a skeptical eye over at Sid, then raises an eyebrow at me. I wish Logan wasn't quite so attractive. "Or should I ask your sister?"

"Aunt," I say, forcing myself not to look down at the table. Logan gives me a questioning look. Duh. He hadn't heard me as he was walking off. "At the shop. I was talking about my aunt."

"So you don't have a sister?" Logan asks.

I shake my head. "Only child."

He studies me, like he's re-evaluating something. I've certainly re-evaluated him since we last met. He's a real, complex person underneath the playful façade he presents to everyone. Seeing him holding that pop star as she died had made him seem more vulnerable – at the same time those articles had re-emphasized that this guy is walking trouble, which is exactly what I don't need in my life.

Sid asks Logan, "Would you like to join us for a quick drink before your meal?"

What? What kind of guy invites another guy to join in on a date?

For a second, I think Logan is going to say yes. Could there be a worse nightmare? Of course, if Logan shows himself to be enough of a jerk to do that, then maybe I can get him out of my head. I keep having to remind myself he's damaged goods, no matter what he looks like.

But then he laughs and says, "I should probably get back to my clients."

The grin he gives me makes me think he's teasing me somehow. Which makes me angry.

Chapter Nine

When I get back to the house, I'm a total wreck. I'm still angry, mortified, and shaking.

Uncle Greg is sitting on the porch, a beer in his hand, watching the storm. His canvas folding chair is back against the peeling white wall and the wide wrap-around porch means he has a relatively dry spectacular view of the coming lightning show. Thunder rumbles as I move up the slick steps as fast as I safely can, my umbrella shielding me from most of the rain.

"So it's getting close," I say as I reach shelter. Uncle Greg isn't due to be home from whichever offshore rig he's currently working. But they send everyone home if there's a tropical storm or a hurricane coming.

Uncle Greg takes another sip of his beer. He has dark hair, with hints of gray at the temples, and hazel eyes. He's wearing a tee shirt with a large fish stenciled on the front, paired with old jeans. "Not yet. Bertha is taking her time, sitting out in the Gulf. I think she's going to take a turn towards Mexico, but Sandpiper never waits until the last minute to evacuate."

Bertha's expected to be upgraded to a hurricane. And the longer she takes to make landfall, the more likely it is for that to happen.

"Personally," I tell Uncle Greg as I prop my umbrella against the porch wall to dry, "I'm glad they're concerned about keeping you safe." I move towards the door, to go inside.

Greg says, "I like your hair."

"Thanks." I haven't seen him in a month, and my Uncle notices my hair is different. He's always been observant. Which means he's being kind, not bringing up the fact that I'm trembling.

When I get inside, Aunt Naomi is sitting at the island, on one of the high stools. She has a plate of saltine crackers, each topped with a spoonful-worth of boudin which has been removed from the casing. Who knows how long she's been nibbling at it, waiting for me to get home.

"Well?" she asks. "How did it go."

I take a seat next to her and grab a cracker off the plate. "In the history of bad dates, mine would make the top five."

"It can't have been that bad." She takes a sip from her glass of lemonade.

"Sid said he doesn't care to see me again." And that wasn't even the worst part of it. "I'd been trying to think of a way to let your chemistry professor down easy because I'm still not ready for a relationship, and at the same time he was deciding I was too flighty because I like to travel, too boring because I don't enjoy doing logic puzzles and math equations for fun, and too selfish because I ordered a chocolate dessert when he'd made it clear he doesn't like chocolate – and might have wanted a bite of key lime pie if I'd been thoughtful enough to order that instead."

I'd realized Sid was horrible at interpersonal interaction, but I hadn't expected him to be that blunt.

"Yikes," Aunt Naomi says. "I'm sorry. He always says such randomly funny things at spin class. I thought you would hit it off, because you have such an offbeat sense of humor."

"My guess is that Sid wasn't being funny on purpose."

"Oh." I can practically see Aunt Naomi re-evaluating every interaction she'd had with the guy as she idly pops a boudin-topped cracker into her mouth. She says, more empathetically and slightly startled, "Oh."

I'm not sure I want to know what she's remembering. "I'm sorry if it causes trouble for your spin class."

Aunt Naomi waves her hand dismissively. "I don't let a little drama bother me. If he even says anything about it. No. We can move on, find you somebody who deserves you."

I sigh, looking down at my hand, bare of its ring. "I told you I'm not ready for love again." Knightley hops into the room. I get down off my chair and scoop him up. He's not usually into cuddles, but this time he lets me hold him. For some reason, this brings to mind Logan holding onto that dying girl. I look levelly at my aunt. "So can we agree, no more matchmaking?"

Several expressions shift across Aunt Naomi's face, too fast for me to understand any of them. "Sure! Fine." Naomi gets out of her chair and pets Knightley on the top of his head before cupping my face in her hands. "Now that you've met someone on your own."

"What are you taking about?" I step back, trying to remove my face from her hands.

She lets me go. "I don't know who that sad, longing little smile was for, but I doubt it was Kevin."

I suck in air, but it still feels like all the oxygen has fled from my lungs. She thinks there was longing in my thoughts about Logan. "Absolutely not."

After all, even if Mr. Dangerous was my type, I'd ruined any chance with him after what had happened at the restaurant. It had been embarrassing, when Sid had put a hundred-dollar bill into the folder that held the check, and then got up and left the building, while I was half way through dessert. Logan had left his party laughing at their giant round table and come over to see if something was wrong, and I had responded by grabbing my purse and my umbrella and bolting into the night, running, doctor's orders or no, all the way to my catering truck.

Logan has to think I'm an inconsistent, lying lunatic.

"Honey, I wasn't trying to upset you-"

And there's the honey again. She doesn't even know the worst of what happened, and my aunt's already feeling sorry for me.

"I need a little air." I hand Knightley to Aunt Naomi and bolt out the door. If it wasn't raining I'd have gone down in the yard to the little bench between the oleander bushes. As it is, I'm stuck at the edge of the porch, looking hysterical in front of Uncle Greg, while lightning crackles in the sky.

"What happened?" Uncle Greg asks matter-of-factly.

"I just went on the worst date ever, to humor Aunt Naomi, and she's already trying to plan me another one." I don't mention what she'd said about me finding someone. I don't want to date an ex-bodyguard who still carries a gun. I don't want to date anybody. "I don't see why she thinks I need a man to be complete."

"That's not what she's trying to say." Greg comes and stands next to me, leaning onto the nearest column, not caring that his back is getting soaked. He gestures with his beer bottle. "Naomi is just worried about you, and she knows that when you had Kevin, you were happy. But love isn't the only path to happiness. And if what you need right now is to work on you, tell her that. All any of us want is to see that you're finding your way out of that dark place you were in right after the accident."

"But my chocolate business makes me happy," I say miserably.

"Your chocolate business makes you busy. So that you can't dwell on how unhappy you are. But the minute you stop working – your smile fades. If it was all that you needed in life, that happiness would last the night."

I look over at him, his warmth and kindness washing away some of the sharp anguish of the night. "How can you figure that out when you're hardly ever even here?"

"I pay attention." Uncle Greg moves back to his chair, leans down and picks up another beer. He pulls off the top and offers it to me. "And I Skype with Naomi a lot. We may not agree on what you need, but we do agree that you need something."

I take the beer. I love the way my aunt and uncle obviously love each other, and are stronger together, without losing themselves. If I ever do find love again, I want it to be like that.

"Naomi told you about the murder?" I say.

"She's already made a list of suspects. She told me she has no intention of letting this Sympathy and Condolences thing stick." Greg puts a hand on my arm. "I told her she needs to be careful. Figuring out the why of a murder is a good way to become the next victim. I'm telling you that too."

"But I'm not-"

Uncle Greg stops me with a raised eyebrow.

"Who does Naomi think did it?" I ask sullenly.

"She's convinced it is that lady who owns the bookstore. She even went over there, and got herself kicked out of the shop for trying to question the employees."

I laugh. I guess I come by my curiosity honestly. "It's interesting you say that. I overheard the craziest bit of gossip tonight about Island Breeze." It was the only potentially useful thing that had come out of my disastrous date.

"Then bring that information to the police." Uncle Greg puts a hand on my arm. "Please."

I'm taking my uncle's advice, which means going to the police station. Despite the fact that I'm heading for a modest square building not far from the port, I find myself dressing up a bit for the occasion, in a dark blue blouse and gray slacks. I want the police to take me seriously.

It has absolutely nothing to do with the fact that I'm going to see Arlo.

Or at least not much.

It's pretty early in the morning, though not as early as when I'd called Arlo yesterday.

When I get downstairs, Uncle Greg is pouring coffee into a Thermos. He's dressed in jeans again, with a day worth of scruff on his face.

"Going fishing?" I ask, though the weather today is horrible. I can already hear the rain pounding the porch roof.

Uncle Greg screws the top onto the thermos. "Bertha's making her move towards landfall, and she got upgraded overnight. Category one." Hurricanes get rated from Category 1 – 5, with 5 being the most devastating. But there is no such thing as a mild hurricane. They all need to be taken seriously. Even if not everyone does. Greg says, "I'm driving to Houston, to check in on Mom in case there's a hurricane evacuation order."

Greg is the one who married into the family. Naomi is my mom's sister. Greg's mom is a bit older than my grandmother and she doesn't drive anymore.

"You're leaving again? You just got here." I open the pantry and pull out a box of protein bars. It sounds like there's a sudden break in the rain. I want to head out before it starts up again. No time for a leisurely breakfast.

There's only one bar in the box. I take it and collapse the box, ready for recycling.

There's a creak on the stairs, and Naomi enters the kitchen. "I'm glad he's going. I'm going to go check on my mom, too. I'll probably stay over there most of the day. You should come." The look she gives me adds the implied, *your grandmother would love to see you.*

"Actually, I'm going to the police station this morning." I look over at Uncle Greg, who gives me a little nod and an encouraging smile.

"Good." He pours the remaining coffee into a mug and hands it to Naomi. I'm not waiting for more to brew. "I'm sure Bertha'll hit farther South. I'll bring back a big pot of my mom's home-made shrimp etouffee as soon as there's an all-clear."

"Just as long as he doesn't bring his mother back," Naomi stage whispers to me.

"I heard that," Greg says.

Naomi shrugs. "I love that woman dearly, but the minute she gets under my roof, she feels like she has to clean and re-organize everything. I know she thinks she's being helpful-"

Uncle Greg stops her with a peck of a kiss on the lips. They look at each other, and he runs his thumb across her knuckles, a quick, reassuring gesture. And I realize that Naomi's bluster is covering up real worry. Most storms aren't that dangerous, and the odds of one making direct landfall here aren't that high. But it has happened. And even if the weather doesn't get any worse, Greg's going to be driving in Houston traffic in the blinding rain.

There's a sudden lump in my throat. I'm about to go out in the rain too. I wish I had somebody to worry about me like that.

The thought of home-made etouffee cheers me up somewhat as I finish getting ready. I have my grandmother's recipes for gumbo and dirty rice and crawfish pie and jambalaya -

- and Sunday rice and gravy. But these aren't the kind of dishes you make for two people, just me and Naomi, so I don't often cook them unless Uncle Greg is in town.

There's lots of local places to get Cajun food and fresh seafood out, though. It's one of the major local cultures – much more so than my dad's Italian side of the family – so it's as "authentic" as a rustic cuisine based on so many individual cooks variations and tastes – and regional differences – and varied access to proteins such as crab and alligator, versus chicken and pork -- can reasonably get. Depending on your restaurant of choice, you can find different takes on gumbo across Galveston, from the thick almost-gravy kind with tons of flour in the roux to the thin near-soup that borrows refinement from Creole New Orleans. I like my gumbo somewhere in the middle, with filé but without okra, because however your mom and your grandmother made it – that's what's going to define gumbo for you. And it's a taste I can't quite find in any restaurant.

And now I want to make gumbo. I may have to stop on the way back from the police station and pick up a couple pounds of andouille sausage. I can invite my friends over to help eat it.

I manage to make my drive while there's a lull, so I'm relatively dry when I knock on the door to Arlo's office. The receptionist told him I was at the station, and she had sent me back. So he knows I'm coming. But he doesn't answer.

Without waiting for a response, I open the door. He's typing at his laptop, his fingers flying over the keyboard. The only sounds in the room are the rapid-fire clacking and the pattering of rain at the window. It's about five times faster than I type. He finishes his thoughts, hits a final key, and looks up. His drawn eyebrows say he's not happy to see me.

How can I explain why I'm here? I'm not sure where to start. My mouth goes dry. It's ridiculous that I'm this nervous in front of Arlo. "I had a date last night," I stammer.

"Am I supposed to be impressed?" He looks amused.

"No. That's not my point." I step closer to his desk, and I drop my voice. "I happened to overhear something in the restaurant."

"Go on." I have his attention, and his dark eyes are scrutinizing me.

"There were three women in the booth next to me. Kaylee from Island Breeze walked past and they started giggling and then one of them said she couldn't believe that's what a criminal mastermind looks like. There's rumors Kaylee's running an illegal gambling ring out of her bookstore."

Arlo sighs. "You're still a suspect, Lis. Pointing the finger at somebody else doesn't change that. In fact, it makes you look even more guilty."

I can feel my face flushing. "How? I'm trying to show you I'm not the one who had something to gain from Emma's death."

I sound angry. And yet, Arlo's face remains impassive. I always hated it when he used to do that, let me get upset, while he stayed stone cold calm.

He gives me a half-smile. "Haven't you ever seen a re-run of Columbo?"

I have, actually, once or twice. Not that I'm going to tell him that. But bumbling detectives aren't my idea of exciting television. I wouldn't have thought it was Arlo's type of show either.

When I don't answer, Arlo continues, "It looks like you're feeding me information, misdirecting the investigation, and counting on our past relationship for you to gain my sympathy and trust. Which the bad guys on that show do all the time. I need you to stay out of this. Whether you did it or not, you're going to contaminate my case."

I take a deep breath, try to calm myself. "You used to know me better than anybody. Do you really think I could be a killer?"

He shrugs. "The girl I fell in love with a million years ago? No. She may have been many things -- self-centered, driven, careless of other people's feelings – but not a killer." I have to stop myself from protesting. Self-centered? People really thought that? Arlo takes a breath. "But people change. And they surprise you. I thought things were going pretty good between us, back in high school. I never thought you were the type to dump someone in public."

I feel myself going crimson. "You have to admit, you gave me enough reason."

Arlo's mouth fish-gapes open. "You're kidding, right?"

I'm confused. "You were dancing with Susie Abernathy." Which had been confirmation of everything Arlo's best friend had told me. Susie had been Arlo's partner on some school project, and Jerome had implied that the library study dates had turned into something more. Jerome had flat out told me that Arlo was planning on asking for the promise ring he'd given me back, so that he could give it to Susie. When I'd come back from the bathroom at prom and seen Susie with her face nestled against Arlo's shoulder, I'd lost it.

Arlo manages to get his mouth closed. His Adam's apple bobs before he speaks. "Maybe it is best if we just leave the past in the past."

"You're right," I say. I take the ring out of my purse. "Maybe this will give you a bit of closure."

"I found closure a long time ago," Arlo insists, though as he studies the sapphire, his eyes take on a softness that makes me questions his words. Some of the serious intensity returns as he looks up at me. "I honestly hadn't thought about you in years, until your little chocolate shop made the news as an up-and-coming local business. And then I told Patsy about how this girl I used to date in high school had made good. She wants to talk to you about custom chocolates, by the way."

I stifle a laugh. Wedding favors, no doubt. Is Arlo really clueless? Or is he waiting for the right moment to buy into the idea?

As Arlo takes the tiny bit of metal from me, he nods towards someone passing in the hallway. "Hanlon." He uses the name as a greeting.

I turn, and there's Logan, looking up from his cell phone. He recognizes me, and there's a curious glint in his eyes. He waves at Arlo. "Romero."

Then he keeps walking.

"You know him?" I ask Arlo.

Arlo raises his hand in a noncommittal gesture. "I think he's somebody's CI. He gave us some good information on a bit of illegal import going on that he happened to spot from his plane. No idea what he's doing back here today."

"It's not a huge police station. That wouldn't be that hard to find out."

Arlo's eyes are on me again, studying my face, probably wondering if I was asking him to find out for me. "How do you know Logan anyway?"

I think I've just jumped even higher on his suspect list, since I'm apparently associating with a seedy element. I hold up my hands in protest. "I'm just doing a chocolate order for the guy. He said he was a pilot, trying to build his business. It seemed like an odd connection, is all."

"Riiiight," Arlo says.

My gaze flicks to the empty doorway. I hate it that Logan's eyes remind me of Kevin. The loss and the pain – but also the kindness. Logan didn't have to come check on me last night, after my date bailed. But he did. People are complex. Logan can be dangerous and annoying – and a genuinely good guy – all at the same time. But what I need in my life is something simpler. Probably something alone. Because I couldn't bear to lose someone again.

Arlo closes the lid on his laptop and leans forward. "There's something going on here, with you, Lis. It would go a whole lot easier if you would just tell me what it was."

I plop down into the chair opposite his desk. I'm not about to tell Arlo, of all people, that I've been daydreaming about

Logan, even though I know it would never work. Even though my heart doesn't feel free to move on. "I lost my husband, and I came home to find a new start. And I'm finding out that maybe coming home again isn't as easy as I thought."

Arlo's face goes somber. "These things take time."

I can't handle that much sympathy, not here, not from someone I used to love and then used to hate. I put a hand on the desk surface. "Please. At least look into the rumors about Kaylee. I'm not trying to skew things. I just want my life to go back to normal."

There's even more sympathy on Arlo's face. "We already have. Months ago, when we first got an anonymous report. Kaylee's not doing anything crazy over at Island Breeze. This supposed gambling ring is six or eight people playing Pokeno until two in the morning, with about ten dollars at stake. We're pretty sure that the report came from Betty Montgomery, who Kaylee says got kicked out of the group for cheating."

"Pokeno?" I ask.

"It's a little like you crossed poker and bingo. I dunno. I never played it." Arlo never was one for games, either of the board or video varieties.

"Did Emma ever participate in their game?" I ask, sure Arlo's going to tell me to stay out of it again.

"No, as far as we know, and nobody tried to place her there."

"Are you only telling me that because you feel sorry for me?" I shouldn't have asked that. I should have just taken the gift information as a sign that maybe he isn't as convinced that I could be a killer as he had thought. But I can't help myself, and the words are out.

Arlo considers me for a moment. "Maybe. Does that offend you?"

I consider it. "Not really." But my brain insists on jumping backwards in the conversation. Why had Arlo said he'd thought things were going good between us right before the breakup? Hadn't he been planning to dump me? Had I missed something? Mis-interpreted everything?

I'm in a fog as I drive to the store, pick up ingredients for gumbo, and drive back to my aunt's house. I think about Arlo the whole way home. The sky has gotten dark, and the rumble of thunder rolls in the distance.

What would my life have been like if I had stayed with Arlo and never met Kevin? Or worse, met Kevin and blew him off? I would have missed out on some of the most special moments of my life. So even if I'd made a mistake with Arlo way back then, it wasn't a mistake in the scheme of my life. But I wonder if I'm the one who needs closure, needs a clearer picture of what Arlo was really thinking back when we'd been together.

I pull my giant catering truck onto the driveway, out of habit parking far enough back that it would be easy to get a car out of either side of the detached garage.

The rain has started coming down again, fierce. I pop up my umbrella and quick-walk towards the porch. The water splashes up and inside my shoes, chilling my feet. I pause under the shelter of the porch, shaking water off my umbrella and imagining what the rain must have done to my makeup.

Kevin had always said I was beautiful without makeup, had kept a photo of me on his desk that he'd taken of me bare-faced and in natural light.

I turn the knob to the front door, so distracted that I don't even try my key, barely registering that it isn't locked. Aunt Naomi must have been in a hurry when she left. Maybe she's more worried about Mawmaw that I thought. But why? I mean, at this point, it's just rain.

Lighting flashes from the direction of the gulf, illuminating the living room oddly as I enter. I try to turn on the lights, but the power's out. I can still see well enough to navigate, with the natural light coming in through the house's many windows, despite the gray sky. I walk through the hall, out of habit, heading for the kitchen at the back of the house. Even though I know it's a bad idea to open the fridge while the power's out, and that without electricity, the ignition on the stove is useless. So gumbo's out, after all.

I find myself flipping the light switch in the hall, even though my brain knows full well it won't accomplish anything.

As I turn the corner into the kitchen, there's a flash of motion from the other side of the island, near the built-in shelves where my aunt keeps her spice jars and row of cookbooks.

I gasp. There's someone in the house, and even in the shadows, I can tell it's not Aunt Naomi.

"Hey!" I shout. My heart lurches. Stupid, Felicity, stupid.

The intruder turns towards me. I can't tell who it is – or even if it is a man or a woman – but the silhouetted figure is holding a gun.

I freeze, bringing my hands up in front of me. The grocery bag falls to the floor at my feet. I can feel my pulse in my palms, rapid and startled and scared.

Without saying a word, the figure gestures with the gun, motioning me towards one of the tall chairs. I move slowly. Trying to sound braver than I feel, I say, "Surely we can talk about this."

"Where is it?" The intruder whispers. "Give it back, and I *might* let you live. *If* you can convince me there aren't duplicates."

I can't identify the voice. I think it is a guy, but it could be a woman with a head cold from all this miserable weather.

"Give what back?" I protest.

The intruder makes an upset, growling noise. Then I hear a single click, likely the gun cocking in the shadows.

My chest goes cold, and my limbs feel like goo. I focus on breathing, on what to say next, to talk the intruder out of shooting me. I have no idea what this person is looking for, so those next words may well be my last.

There's a loud thumping sound, and for a moment, I think I've been shot. But then I realize it's Knightley. He thumps his foot again, and grunts. Rabbits are communal animals, and males are especially protective.

The intruder pivots towards the noise, taking the gun off me. I take advantage of their distraction and dive back into the hallway. It feels surreal, like something that would happen in a book or on TV. But the bullet holes that appear in the wall seem real enough.

I worry that the intruder might turn and hurt Knightley, but I hear the rabbit thumping again, aggressively protecting his territory – and me.

Chapter Eleven

Think, Felicity, think. There's an armed intruder in the kitchen. All I have is my cell phone and my purse.

I'm past the hall, in the open great room. I could go hide in the empty room at the back of the house, or I could head out the front door. There's no way I'm getting up the staircase or across the lawn in time.

Really, my only chance here is misdirection.

I grab the phone and dial 911.

"Please," I say loudly, and as clearly as I can, as I move through the open space of the great room, into the front hall, thankful there's not a clear line of sight through both hallways, and that the intruder seems cautious about following me. It must not be anyone who knows me well if they think I might have a weapon. "There's someone shooting at me in my house."

I mute my phone, so it won't give away my location, but I leave the call open.

I slip open the door to the hall closet, the same place I stored that box of books. My hand's trembling. There's some spare flooring stacked at the back, but not much else, so there's plenty of room for me to hide here.

I throw my purse down the hall. It thumps into the wall next to the front door. I step into the closet and pull the door shut behind me.

I can hear the intruder moving in the hallway, past the closet, towards the front door. I hear the door open and then slam shut again. I let out a breath. But I still don't move from my precarious perch on the flooring. For all I know, the intruder was using the same kind of misdirect I had done, and is waiting for me to reveal where I am hiding.

A few minutes later, when it is hot and humid inside the closet, the power comes back on. A strip of light shines underneath the closet door. The updated central air conditioning Aunt Naomi had had installed kicks on. I'm tempted to come out of hiding. It sounded like the intruder had left, and I'm starting to feel a little bit silly. I put my hand on the knob and my ear to the door, listening. Nothing. Not even Knightley. I open the door and step out into the hallway. Then I hear a creak of the floor upstairs. Someone is still in here.

Sirens sound from down the block, coming closer. Whoever is upstairs runs across the floor, heading for the windows I know are above the porch. I imagine the intruder climbing out into the rain.

Knightley is sitting on the rug by the back door, up on his hind legs, staring out into space like a sentinel trying to sense danger. I've often laughed when he's tried to warn me of "danger," in the past, but this time, my little bunny saved my life. It is reassuring to know I mean that much to him. I wonder if he still misses Kevin. Maybe Knightley's all the more protective because of what we've both lost.

I sit on the floor by him, petting his head and back. You can't explain death to a rabbit. Knightley had just known that my husband had left home one day – and never come back. He'd been a fluffy, warm presence for me in those early days, and I'd spoiled him with parsley and bananas – his two favorite treats – to keep him close.

But what if *he* is afraid of losing *me*?

Sitting with Knightley calms my heart rate. By the time the police officer knocks on the door, I might well have imagined the whole thing, if not for the bullet holes in the sheetrock. I'm expecting Arlo, but they sent a woman who introduces herself as Officer Beckman, wearing the traditional uniform. As I'm showing her the damage, and blocking out for her what had happened in the kitchen, I spot Aunt Naomi's keys and purse still sitting on the counter.

My chest goes cold. "Oh, no."

I had assumed my aunt had left the house just after I had.

"What's wrong?" Officer Beckman's hand goes to the gun at her hip.

I gesture at the purse. "What if my aunt was upstairs when the intruder came in? Why else wouldn't she have come running when sirens started blazing in the driveway?"

"Stay here." Officer Beckman says.

I ignore her, following her up the stairs. I point out the room that corresponds to the noise I heard overhead. It is Naomi and Greg's bedroom. She pushes the door open. The window at the room's far end is open, letting in the wind and rain, soaking the carpet. Naomi was planning on pulling the ugly green-gold carpet out anyway, and sanding the floor underneath. If something happened to her – I don't know if I'll be able to take it. I follow Officer Beckman as she looks around the bed, in the closet. Nothing.

Together, we make our way through the whole house. Attics freak me out, especially in old houses like this, so I let Officer Beckman look up there alone. I go into the guest bathroom – my bathroom. There's really nowhere else to look. The shower curtain is closed. I flinch as I open it to find the blinding white tub. There's no sign of Aunt Naomi. Anywhere. We check the detached garage. Her car's still there. We even look in the trunk. Nothing.

Officer Beckman puts a hand on my arm. "Just stay calm. Maybe she left the house on foot. Could she have gone to visit a neighbor?"

"It's possible." I take a deep breath, trying to calm my heart rate. I try to pick up Knightley again, but he's having none of it. He still looks agitated and nervous from his run-in with the intruder. "But could she have been kidnapped?"

"That's unlikely. If someone had tried to take her out of an open window into the rain, there would have been some sign of struggle."

A banging sound echoes from outside, on the other side of the house. I follow Officer Beckman out onto the wraparound porch. There's Aunt Naomi holding a hammer. Miles, her son's friend, is holding a wood plank in the space where one had been missing on the side of the porch, while Naomi centers a nail.

I look behind me, and Miles's car is in the driveway, behind the car the cop was driving. He must have pulled in, and assumed I just had a regular visitor. Who just happened to be a police officer.

The incongruity of finding my aunt safe, doing something so normal, sends me into a fit of giggles.

Miles looks up. "Mrs. Koerber. Who's your friend?"

Naomi follow his gaze. She looks a bit more startled to see me with a cop. "I didn't expect you back so soon. Is everything okay?"

I shake my head. And then I run up and hug her. "Where have you been?"

Naomi leans into the hug and pats me on the back. I can feel the confusion in her touch. "I was next door salvaging wood, while Miles ran to the hardware store."

Officer Beckman asks, "Did you see anyone suspicious while you were over next door?"

"Not really." But then her eyes go wide. "There was a car that went tearing up the road. It looked like it came out of the driveway across the street."

"What kind of car was it?" I ask.

"It was a black Lexus. I couldn't see who was driving, but I can't imagine there are a whole lot of those on this island."

We explain what happened inside the house.

Aunt Naomi looks from me to Officer Beckman and back. "Are you saying I might have seen whoever shot at you?"

Officer Beckman asks, "Are you sure you didn't get a look at the driver?"

Miles laughs. "In this rain?"

Naomi gives Miles her hammer. "I need something to drink."

I'm pretty sure she's done as an amateur sleuth.

We follow her back into the house.

Aunt Naomi turns to me and says, "I was planning on going to your Grandmother's, take care of a few upgrades. You don't have to go over there, Felicity. I know this has to have been traumatic."

Her voice breaks on the last word. The hand holding her glass of water trembles.

My heart goes out to her. This is her home that was violated, her cookbooks scattered on the floor. I notice my laptop, still sitting on the island, undisturbed and closed.

There's a knock at the front door. I go to answer it. Arlo is standing on my doorstep. He's hot when he's all broody and angry like that. Not that I have any business noticing.

Without greeting him, I say, "Now do you believe I didn't kill Emma?"

He shrugs. "It would be rather elaborate for you to have staged this. But on the other hand, did anyone else actually see this intruder?"

I roll my eyes. Yep. Heat extinguished. "Do you want to take a look at the bullet holes?"

"Sure." He steps ahead of me into the hall. He looks back. "Do you happen to own a gun?"

I can't tell if he's serious or not. I guide him over to the wall. He leans down and takes a closer look at the holes. Then he calls to Officer Beckman, "Meryl, did you find any bullet casings?"

I shudder. Somehow, that makes the whole experience real. I got shot at. I could have died. The intruder here was probably the same person who poisoned Carmen's dog. Maybe even the same person who killed Emma. Those bullets weren't a bluff.

So how did that add up with the threat? Give something back, and maybe I would be allowed to live. That was a lie to get me to cooperate. I would have been dead as soon as the person got what they wanted.

"There's one in the sink, and another rolled up against the fridge." Officer Beckman says from the kitchen. "Which leaves two more missing. I left them where they were, so you could have a look before I bag them."

And yet . . . Emma's killer – if that's who it was -- had waited until everyone had left the house before breaking in here. The same at Carmen's. I get the idea that this is a person who will kill – but prefers not to. Either that, or maybe they just don't like fuss. After all, I had managed to contact the police, and am happily still alive. Which doesn't help me narrow down the suspects at all.

"We have only your voice on the 911 tape," Arlo says. "Did this supposed intruder say anything to you?"

He really believes I made the break-in up. More Columbo-esque manipulating the information. "He – or she – I'm still not sure -- asked me to return something. But I don't know what it could be. Maybe Emma took something, and this person decided she must have given it to either me or Carmen. Was Emma's place broken into too?"

Arlo sighs. "Would you stop asking me for information."

But he says it in a tone that makes me think no, it wasn't. Or, at least Arlo doesn't think it was. After all, nothing had seemed missing from Carmen's. Just someone had seen the dog and the open door. And nothing had been disturbed here, except the cookbooks, which had fallen when I'd startled the intruder, and the window, which had been left open in the wake of a hasty exit. With Emma's parents out of the country, someone breaking into her place would have been able to take a more leisurely pace. And not knowing what Emma's room was supposed to look like, how could the police determine if anything was missing?

This might be about recipes, given that cryptic comment about not having duplicates. Emma had won a baking contest.

Carmen had brought home a box of recipe books. And the intruder had been examining the cookbooks on my aunt's shelf. But what recipe could be worth killing someone over? If someone's not willing to share a recipe, you can just find something similar on the internet.

And if it has something to do with the baking competition, why involve me? I do bean-to-bar chocolate, not baked goods. I'd never enter a baking competition. And my laptop is on the kitchen island, undisturbed. I'd be more likely to have something unique stored on my hard drive than in book form.

None of it makes any sense.

Arlo asks, "What are you doing this afternoon?"

The question throws me. Arlo's in a serious relationship. So he's not asking me out on a date. Is he inviting me to help with the case? The thought leaves me oddly elated. Because who would have imagined me – the girl who doesn't do dangerous – to actually be excited about solving this thing.

It's become about more than just clearing my name and shutting up the Sympathy and Condolences blogger. I want to figure the puzzle out. And if I can do it while Arlo keeps me out of danger, so much the better.

I shrug, managing not to sound excited. "I'm supposed to go help my aunt at my Mawmaw's."

And yeah, it probably would be good for me to go see my grandmother. Now that I'm in a different frame of mind, maybe I won't dissolve into a crying wadded-up dishtowel, like last time.

"I want you to come with me down to the station."

"Okay." I nod, trying to hide the smile forming on my lips. So there for his Columbo-esque theory that I'm concocting an elaborate plan to impede his investigation.

But then he adds, "I want to have you tested for gunshot residue."

How? How was I ever together with this guy? I hope that whenever he gives that ring to Patsy, she sees him for the jerk he is and throws it right back in his face. "Do I need a lawyer?"

"That depends," Arlo says. "On what we're going to find on your hands, and how many answers you have for my questions."

"I'm the victim here. I'm the one who got shot at, and threatened." I go back into the foyer and pick up my purse from where I chunked it at the wall. It smells like maybe my perfume spritzer broke in there. Then I march right back past Arlo and up to my aunt. I tell Naomi, "I need you to have a lawyer meet me at the police station."

"My dad's a lawyer," Miles volunteers. "And if I tell him it is for a friend of Wyatt's, I bet he will waive the initial fees."

"That would be amazing," I tell him.

"She's not officially being arrested," Arlo puts in. "Just being questioned as a person of interest in the case."

I tell my aunt, "He wants to have me tested for gunshot residue, just in case I shot up that wall myself."

"What?" Naomi casts a panicked look over at Arlo, who is waiting patiently, arms crossed, in the doorway. She whispers, "Is he trying to get back at you for dumping him?"

"Looks that way," I whisper back, loud enough that he's surely heard.

Chapter Twelve

About two hours later, I get back into my catering van. At least Arlo had given me the dignity of driving it to the police station myself, instead of shoving me into the back of his black and white SUV.

Miraculously it has stopped raining, though that won't last. Everyone inside the police station had been glued to the Weather Channel. It looks like Bertha has turned again, heading more solidly for Corpus. We'll get a lot of wind and rain, but mandatory evacuation is seeming less likely.

I put my key in the ignition, but I don't turn it on. I just stare at the hanging layers of brown fronds at the bottom of the palm tree I'd parked near. My first thought is to go home and take a hot shower, make some cocoa and disappear into a book.

But I keep thinking about that startling white tub, and how certain I had been that I was going to find Naomi there. I shudder. How am I supposed to go back to the house, with the person who had threatened to kill me still out there somewhere? The police didn't believe me. They're not about to send somebody to watch the house. Unless it's surveillance. On me.

I lean forward, resting my head on the steering wheel. Arlo had seemed surprised when I had come up clean for gunshot residue. But he hadn't apologized.

My phone buzzes with a text message. *That offer for drinks still stands. Or iced tea. Whatever you need right now.*

It's from Tiff, obviously. Naomi must have told her about me getting dragged to the police station. Which means that by now, all my friends know.

Tiff texts again. *Maybe you could come to my place. Watch one of those cheesy old movies and make nachos like last time. The electricity is on over here, and Ken won't mind.*

Ken is Tiff's husband. She'd moved to the island when their dating had gotten serious. I'd actually been a last-minute bridesmaid addition at their wedding when Ken's sister had gotten sick.

Moisture bites at my eyes, but I didn't cry inside the police station and I'm not about to start crying now. But that doesn't mean I'm ready to answer that text. Because as much as I'd like to go to Tiff's instead of going home, I could be putting her in danger.

My phone rings. It's Autumn. I'm afraid she's about to try and talk me into meeting up with the group. But that's not it. "I was at an entrepreneurial leadership event today, and they seated me next to a Collections Conservation Librarian. The man was hot. Seriously, girl, hot."

"That's great." I try to hide the tears in my voice. "Did you ask him out?"

Autumn laughs so loudly I move the phone away from my ear. "Maybe I would have had the nerve if he wasn't so beautiful. But I wanted to make intelligent conversation, so I started talking about your books with the lop-sided endpapers. He asked me to find out if those endpapers were a printer's error, or a later repair. If they're a repair, it could negatively affect the value of the books."

"I have no idea." And, I have more important things on my mind than the value of a couple of books – or Autumn's love life. Ordinarily, both those things would interest me greatly. But someone *shot* at me. And the cops don't care.

"Felicity, don't leave me hanging. I've got this man's number, and nothing to say when I call him."

"I'll look into it." I get her off the phone before I have a complete meltdown.

I open my glove box looking for a tissue and I find all the order forms for my chocolate. I'd shoved them in here when I'd taken the money from the shop to the bank, meaning to call all my clients and let them know their orders would be delayed, which I still haven't managed to do. I guess subconsciously I've been hoping that this will all blow over, and I'll be able to get the orders done without being late.

There's Logan's order for Ridley Puddle Jumpers, right on top. It had been the last one I'd taken before everything fell apart. And it hits me. Logan. He'd come here, started a new business and a new life, but once upon a time, he used to be a bodyguard.

I think about him coming back to the table to check on me at the restaurant. That protective nature seems to still be in his blood. I've got money – the lawyers after Kevin's accident had seen to that. But I have no idea what Logan would say if I tried to hire him. He might be offended that I'd looked up his past. Or that I'm offering him money for something he's not doing anymore.

But I'll never know unless I ask. His information lists a single phone number, which I assume is a cell phone. I call it. It goes straight to voicemail. I leave an awkward message. "Hi Logan! Um, this is Felicity from the chocolate shop. I, uh, I'm in a bit of trouble, and I have a business proposition for you."

Yeah. I wouldn't call me back.

But Logan sends back a text message. *Busy doing maintenance on the plane. If you want to talk, meet here. Gate Code 7761.*

He's added a location, which my maps program says is a warehouse-like hangar. It's out of the way. Private. In a movie, it'd be the kind of place where a minor character goes to disappear. And yet, going out there feels safer right now than going home.

I text Tiff that I have an appointment, and I send her the location, so that *someone* knows where I'm going. She asks if she should come with me. I tell her it isn't necessary.

I'm nervous about talking to Logan. This is going to be even more awkward in person. But I started this – it will be even weirder if I drop it without even talking to him. The worst he can do is tell me no, right?

I start my catering truck, and plug in the route – which takes me out onto the less populated side of the island. There's water on the roads from so much rain, but it is draining. The air strip has been cordoned off with a tall chain link fence, and a gate with a box like you see at some apartment complexes.

I hate those. Half the time they don't work but this one is well-maintained. I drive through the gate, as soon as it has opened wide enough, onto a pockmarked private asphalt street. There's a single hangar at the far end of the road, and a flat dent in the low plant life that I assume marks an air strip that I can't quite see. I drive over to the hanger and park.

The hanger door is open. Loud, European-style techno music echoes from inside. As I get closer, I can see Logan dancing to it as he removes a tire from his plane. He sees me watching, but he doesn't look the slightest bit embarrassed. He puts the tire down on a counter, where he's got his cell phone plugged into a set of speakers.

He turns the music down. "You sure got here fast." He picks up a different tire, trying to keep working while we're talking, and places it on the counter next to the old one. He picks up a tool and starts removing the old tire's rim.

I watch his hands. I need his full attention. "What I want to talk about is urgent. To me at least."

After all, it is my life at stake here.

He puts down the tool, and turns to study me, crossing his arms over his well-muscled chest. He's wearing the type of tee with a couple of buttons at the neck, which emphasizes his chiseled jaw. He's waiting for me to say something, and suddenly I can't.

I look past him at the plane. It looks small. "How many people can you fit in that thing?"

He looks confused. "Four, including me. If you're looking for a charter, the Cessna's going to give you better views than anything I've got over at the airport. But the weather's still iffy for flying today, which is why I'm in here doing maintenance. So if it's urgent, I'm afraid I'll have to disappoint."

I shake my head. "I don't need a plane. What I need is a bodyguard."

The smile falls from his face. "I don't do that anymore."

"Please," I say, even though it feels hopeless. "At least consider it. I don't know who else to go to. One of my employees died in my shop on Monday, yesterday somebody poisoned the other one's dog, and today I got shot at. These are not the kind of things that usually happen in the life of a craft chocolate maker."

He's starting to get his smile back, like he's waiting for the punch line, but when I don't offer one, the smile fades again. His eyes, which I'd found so kind, look cold in a way Kevin's never had. "I'm sorry. I don't think I could work for you."

"Why?" I look down, at one of the tires still on the plane, all puffy like a doughnut.

"Because I don't trust you."

"What?" The word is out of my mouth before I can stop it. But really, I've hardly interacted with this guy. What could I have said to make him not trust me?

He points down at the ring on my finger. "I don't like it when people's stories don't add up. First you tell me you're not interested in love. And then I see you out on a date with some dork. And then you're accepting a ring from some cop. Seriously, your love life is your business, but you're all over the place. For all I know, you made up being shot at, too."

"I have a perfectly logical explanation for all of that." I can tell that logic appeals to him. His tools are meticulously laid out in the hanger, clean, with nothing out of place.

"Really?" He moves over to an area in the shade, where there's a green and black geometric rug on the floor, along with a beige sofa, a mini fridge, and a giant black beanbag chair. He takes a mineral water from the fridge, and as an afterthought offers me one too.

He plops onto the beanbag chair, looking at ease, but never losing his board-straight posture. I sit on the edge of the sofa, leaning forward least I sink into it. I have a hard time talking about all of this with my family. How am I supposed to explain it to someone I hardly know?

"It's not Arlo's ring." I take a deep breath. "I'm a widow. I don't wear a ring when I'm working with food, so you didn't see it at my shop, and I took it off for the date – which was entirely my aunt's doing – because it felt weird. And I wasn't taking a ring from Arlo. I was giving him one."

Multiple expressions flit across Logan's face, settling on a mix of sympathy and curiosity. "Why?"

I look down at my hands. "It's a long story. We have a history. And not a good one."

"Which is why he sees you as a viable murder suspect."

I look up. "How do you know that?"

"Word gets around." He takes a sip from his mineral water. "But you didn't do it?"

"No!"

His expression is appraising. "You can be honest. I've dealt with worse."

"Well, I haven't." I stand up from the sofa, ready to have the last word and then walk back to my catering truck. "I'm an ex-physical therapist who was married to an engineer. We had a good life, and both of us helped people for a living. Even people who came in to my practice at their weakest, their most broken wouldn't have-"

Logan holds up a hand. "I'm sorry."

"Excuse me?" I blink, trying to track the change in the conversation.

"I'm sorry. You are obviously still raw from the loss of your husband. I shouldn't have been so blunt. I know what it is like to want to start over, to reinvent yourself. I never lost a loved one, but I did lose a client once. It was . . . difficult. I wasn't able to find the murderer afterwards, either, so she never got the justice she deserved."

I can't decide if Logan is lying to me – or to himself. I sit back down. "I've seen the news articles, and the look on your face in the pictures. And it wasn't the look of a man who's merely lost a client. If you're demanding honesty here, you owe me the same."

Logan's cheeks color, somehow making him look even more attractive. "I've never told anyone I was in love with Mari – not even her. How can you look at a picture and know that?"

"Because I lived that same moment. Kevin got crushed by a bulkhead that collapsed, on a ship that he had designed. He was still alive when they got him to the hospital. And I couldn't help thinking, maybe if we hadn't stayed up so late the night before, or if I hadn't been distracting him all that week, trying to plan a sailing trip, it wouldn't have happened." And that's something *I've* never told anyone before. It's weird, having this frank of a conversation with a near stranger. It's the kind of talk you couldn't have on a first date, when you're trying to hide and put your best self forward.

Logan's eyes are wide, with remembered pain and shock. "Mari was a pop star. She was above me in so many ways. But I should have told her how I felt, that my feelings might be clouding my judgment. I should have stepped aside from her detail – but I was afraid I'd never see her again. And I should have insisted she cancel the concert. There'd been a threat. But she wanted so badly to perform. And I was overconfident."

"It wasn't your fault," I insist. "Any more than that sailing trip is really why Kevin died. The investigation turned up shortcuts my husband hadn't authorized that had been taken in the construction." I lean forward again, this time with purpose. "I read the articles. No one blamed you."

"I blamed me." Logan gestures around himself at the plane hangar. "I put myself in exile. You shouldn't look to me for help. I'm unreliable."

I tilt my head. "Who do you recommend I go to? The police aren't going to help me. I can pay, enough to cover whatever you need for your plane." We've had this moment of connection. After that, I have to hope he believes he'd feel at least a little responsible if I wind up dead. "If you can help me, just for a few days, then if Emma's murderer is still on the loose, I'll figure out a more permanent solution."

"Just for a few days," he repeats softly, and I can see he's taken with the idea. Maybe it's a way to make up a little for his past failure. Maybe he thinks I'm cute and wants to spend more time with me. I don't care why. After a moment, his face takes on a determined grin. "But if I do this, you have to listen to what I say, even if it sounds stupid. And you can't get mad if I go digging into your past or your finances or anything."

"Okay," I say. "But what about your fee?"

He waves a dismissive hand at me. "Whatever you think is fair. We can figure that out later. Once you're safe. I can fly you to the mainland, and then get up to speed on the case."

"But I have some information-"

He stops me with a look. Right. I just said I'd listen to him. Obviously, I'm not very good at that.

"I appreciate that," Logan says. "And we will get to it on the plane. We'll take the biggest thing I've got at the airport. With bad weather on the way, you'll probably be more comfortable inland anyway. The radio just announced that Bertha has been upgraded to a class two, and they think it might hit closer to Matagorda."

My heart lurches. I'm not about to go off with Logan alone like that. But I don't want to tell Logan the idea of being alone with him intimidates me. Because I'm attracted to him. And, since I'm still in mourning, I don't want to be. No. I need to make a different argument. "Whoa. I'm not leaving the island. How can I find out who took shots at me if I'm not even here?"

He hesitates. "I'm not going to kidnap you. But I highly recommend you consider that your employee was killed in view of thirty people at your shop."

I nod and take out my phone. "My friend Tiff wants to go for drinks this afternoon. We'll be at a restaurant where everyone knows us. She'll probably bring along half a dozen people." And I won't be bringing danger into her condo. "I can stay there while you do your reconnaissance."

"I guess that will work." Logan picks up his cell phone and unplugs it from the speakers. "But you've at least got to give me some concessions here." He gestures with his phone as he makes each point. "Leave the GPS on on your phone. And don't tell anyone you've hired me. The killer might see you as more of a serious threat, with a closing window of opportunity."

"Not even my friends?"

Logan checks something on his phone. "Not until I've established who they are."

What the heck have I gotten myself into here? "What about my aunt? She's going to be shocked if I'm bringing a man back to the house."

At first I think he's going to say no again, and my face starts heating with pre-emptive embarrassment. But then he says, "Unless you suspect your aunt killed Emma, I think it will be safe to explain the situation."

Chapter Thirteen

By the time I get to Chalupa's, all of my friends are a margarita ahead of me. They have a round table at the back of the restaurant. Tiff stands up and gives me a hug. "You okay?"

Autumn says, "More importantly, did you get any clues? You were in the same room with the killer. Again."

Tiff gives her a sharp look. "You promised. We're going to have fun before we have to leave the island."

Autumn says, "Nobody's evacuating."

Tiff looks at me. "Naomi said she's packed everybody's go bags. That's the last thing you do before you evacuate, right? And before she could leave, you got hauled into jail." Normally, Tiff is the one who brings the party with her when she enters a room. But this is her first hurricane season on the Island, and she looks nervous.

"Don't go by Naomi," Sonya says. "She's super prepared,"

"You're supposed to have go-bags packed way ahead of time, anyway," I say. "Y'all have go bags, right?" I sit in the empty chair between Sandra and Sonya.

The twins look past me at each other.

Finally, Sandra says, "I keep meaning to get to that."

I feel heat building in my cheeks. So I'm a rule follower, and I'm prepared. Sue me.

Tiff notices me watching her and asks, "What's the difference between a mandatory and a recommended evacuation? Ken says we won't go unless it is mandatory."

Autumn tells her, "Recommended means they're less sure we're in the storm's path. A lot of people here won't leave, even if it's mandatory, because there are so many times they ask for evacuation, but the storm fizzles, or misses the island, or just isn't strong enough to worry about. But if you stay, the city won't guarantee basic services or rescue options, so you're pretty much on your own."

Sandra shakes her head. "They do their best never to make it mandatory. That has a ton of legal implications. You should tell Ken you want to go if evacuation is recommended."

Autumn says, "Can we talk about how Felicity got shot at?"

I turn to Autumn. "I'd rather not talk about that part. All I learned is our killer may drive a black Lexus. And that whoever it was sounds like they may have a cold."

Tiff gives Autumn another look, this one more defeated. Tiff is all about organizing parties and building people up. She has a hard time *not* working to make people happy. "If you need info on a car, I have a friend who can get us into the DMV database. I helped her get a condo, so she owes me."

Yep. She doesn't have it in her to withhold the information, even if she'd rather spend the evening on in-jokes and meaningless chatter.

I consider the offer. Logan didn't say I couldn't keep investigating the case. As long as I stay here in public, where I told him I'd be. "Make the call."

Five minutes later, I'm looking at three names. It's all the people with a recent-model black Lexus sedan registered to them here on the island.

David Parker

Rebecca Jones

And Emma Turner.

I turn to Autumn. "So if this were a book . . ."

"Then it would turn out that Emma wasn't really dead, and that she is, in fact, stalking you."

I gesture down at the list of names. "It is more likely that someone she knows has her car. But I never saw her drive a Lexis.

She was always in a beat-up Ford Focus. Is there any way to find out how long she had this car?"

Tiff calls her friend back. "The registration got transferred the day before Emma died."

Could that be what Emma had been so desperate for money for? But why would she risk her job and her reputation to buy an expensive car, when she already had a reliable mode of transportation?

"You would have thought she'd have brought it to the grand opening to show off," I say.

"Maybe she did," Autumn volunteers. "Maybe she was waiting for the end of the party."

"Or maybe," Tiff suggests, "She knew you'd be mad if she bought something extravagant after saying she didn't have the money to pay you back, so she decided to keep it under wraps for a while."

"Maybe," I murmur. But if Emma had arrived in that car, it wasn't in the parking lot when Arlo had finally let us go. Sure, Arlo had kept me and a few of the others longer, questioning us, but there was only one person who could have broken into a car and made off with it undetected: Paul. He'd left before everyone else, when the police had been focused on what was going on inside the shop.

I ask Tiff, "Does your friend have access to the DMV records for the whole state?"

"She can probably get that information." Tiff taps her chin with her index finger. "I guess."

"Ask if she can find contact info for Emma's ex-boyfriend. Paul Dupree. And not the 90-year-old retiree. This guy's in his early twenties."

My phone rings. It's Arlo. The first words out of his mouth are, "What did you do?"

"I keep telling you I didn't do anything."

"Well, Logan Hanlon sure did. This guy you say you hardly know showed up at the police station and demanded to see Emma's file. He's got friends with serious clout. After I told him no, I got a call from my superiors, suggesting I cooperate with him."

I move the phone a little farther away from my ear, and I leave the table, acting oblivious to my friends' curious stares. There's a little cubby not far from the restaurant bar, where there used to be a pay phone. I close the door. "Yes. I may be responsible for that. I hired him as private security. He must think that includes solving the case."

I wait for Arlo to yell at me. But I've left the guy speechless. For once.

After a while, I begin to think that I've lost the connection. "Arlo?"

He exhales heavily into the phone. "I can't even find evidence Hanlon existed before he took some high-profile private security gig four years ago. That suggests this guy is way above taking you on as a client. I mean you're a baker on Podunk Island, for Christ's sake."

"Chocolate maker," I interrupt. It may not be relevant to the point Arlo is making, but for me, it is an important distinction. Even if it does just make me a different variety of nobody.

Arlo hesitates. "Sorry, Lis. Chocolate maker. But I'm trying to tell you – Logan Hanlon doesn't belong flying prop planes on this island. He's running from something, or hiding from something. And whatever that is, whenever Hanlon's past catches up to him, that might put you in even more danger."

I take this information with a grain of salt. After all, Arlo sounds jealous – though whether it is because Logan seems to have taken the case because he likes me – which can't be farther from the truth -- or if it is some kind of professional thing, I can't tell. "I know what he's hiding from. He told me. It is a case that made all the papers. He's calling Galveston his self-imposed place of exile."

"I really wish you hadn't involved him."

I sigh into the phone. "What was I supposed to do? Somebody tried to shoot me today. It's not like you were offering me protection."

"I'm not heartless, Lis. You passed the residue test, so I had somebody watching you to make sure nobody else showed up. You wind up hurt, and I'd never hear the end of it. Hanlon got the guy called off."

"I don't know what to say," I tell Arlo.

"Is Hanlon with you?" Arlo asks.

"He told me to stay in public, with friends, while he gets up to speed."

"Some bodyguard." Arlo chuckles into the phone. "Hasn't been on the job for five minutes, and he already leaves you alone."

I explain that it was my idea. I wind up sounding like an idiot.

Eventually, Arlo sighs and says, "Lis, if you really think you're in danger, you should listen to the people you're asking for help." He pauses and his voice takes on a hopeful tone. "Unless you're just playing this guy to take suspicion off yourself."

I need a minute to get my composure back after I hang up with Arlo. Otherwise, the girls at the table are going to ask more questions about Arlo and Logan than I feel capable of handling right now.

Miles comes into the restaurant and makes a beeline for me. "I take it you're investigating what happened to Emma."

"Well yeah," I admit.

He nods. "Good. I just talked with one of my friends who went to school with her. He said she'd acted odd in junior year. It's been years now – I don't know if I should go to the police, or if I'm asking for trouble for no reason."

I feel like he's way ahead of me in the conversation. "Wait. How did you even know I was here?"

Because if it's that obvious, maybe Arlo's right, and I'm not safe.

Miles pulls his phone out of his pocket and shows me a circle with my initials at the center of the screen. "You're still sharing your location from the other day. Want me to show you how to turn it off?"

"Don't worry about it." I move towards the wall near the cubby, and Miles follows, out of the line of traffic. "So what did you find out."

"My friend was an office aide where Emma went to high school. Emma missed a whole month of school Junior year. When she came back, she claimed she had mono, but she didn't, but she never got in trouble for it. Then she started skipping French and Precalculus, and wound up failing both classes for the year. That's odd, right? Why just those two classes?"

"That is odd," I agree. "Any idea what she was doing?"

"No, but I'm looking into it."

"I don't think that's enough information to take to the police." I gesture down at his phone.

"I know," he says. "That's why I'm still asking questions."

I nod. I'm doing the same thing. "Don't do anything that could get you in trouble. The person who killed Emma is dangerous."

Miles looks straight at me. "I don't know why, but I felt a connection to Emma when we met."

I could tell him why. He's a teenager, and she was gorgeous and needy.

He continues, "I need to know what happened to her."

"Be careful," I say. Because what else am I going to tell him? I'm investigating this too.

"Of course, Mrs. Koerber." Miles pockets the phone and heads out of the restaurant.

By the time I get back, Tiff has a print map spread out on the table. She carries them by the dozen, with her real estate logo at the bottom. It's the whole region surrounding Houston. She's circling an address in Kemah, over on the bay side of the mainland.

"No good," I tell her, sliding back into my seat. "I'm pretty sure that's the octogenarian I spoke to already."

"Well, the next closest is a guy who lives in San Antonio."

I lean closer to the map. "Carmen did say Paul wasn't from the Island. That's like a four-hour drive, but maybe he has friends here to stay with."

Sonya has started crocheting at the table. I think she's making a hat. "That kid you were talking to. You know he comes into my shop sometimes?"

"Miles?" I did not know that. Because I don't do yarn arts.

She nods. "He knits. He comes with his mom to the Tuesday yarn circle. Then they go get pizza after. He's better at it than she is."

"That's really cool," Sandra says. "I wish I'd had that kind of relationship with our Mom at that age."

"I still don't have that kind of relationship with mine," I say. Mom tends to take over projects. My phone rings. I'm expecting it to be Logan, but instead, it is a call from Carmen. I lean back and answer my phone.

Carmen's hysterical. "El está muerto, Felicity. Muerto."

"Who's dead?" My Spanish isn't fluent, but I'm working on it. It is an important skill for a chocolate maker who wants to create goodwill with South American cacao farmers, the ones I will deal with most frequently. But Carmen must be flustered to address me in Spanish, because her English is fluent.

She switches to English, but she's not making any more sense. "At the beach. In the surf. I came to get the stuff I left out here earlier. I called the police. I – I didn't know who else to call."

Carmen doesn't have any family in Texas, as far as I can tell. And her roommates don't seem to be the most reliable people. I'm not sure whether or not to be flattered that when she's in trouble, I'm the one she calls.

"What can I do?" I ask.

Autumn is looking at me around Tiff, her eyebrows asking all kind of questions about what's being said on the phone.

Carmen says, "I just don't want to be here alone. Not after – that."

I hesitate. I promised Logan that we would stay at the restaurant. But Carmen needs me. I look at my friends. I also promised not to tell them I hired private security, so I can't ask for a second or third opinion. I tell Carmen, "Turn on your Find a Friend. We're heading your way."

I turn towards Sandra. She's the only one of us with a vehicle than can hold five people. She pulls out her keys. "You're getting the tab for this one. I didn't even get to drink my G&T."

That's why I love these four people. They're there for me, no questions asked.

I pay, and we pile into the car. I feel a sense of déjà vu as we make our way down the seawall and Sonya U-turns into a parking spot behind Carmen's car. The only difference is that it is raining now. Carmen must have been trying to say that she'd come back out here to gather up the stuff that she had left scattered on the beach when she'd hurried to check on Bruce.

I can see her, a small figure in the rain, standing by a surfboard, facing the water.

We all open our umbrellas as we make our way carefully down the steps. The rain slows to a drizzle, pattering against the fabric.

She notices us coming, turning to face us, but she doesn't move from the spot where she's standing.

I make my way out onto the sand, which is wet and clumpy and getting into my shoes. Most of the beach is underwater, with waves lapping up within ten or twelve feet of the base of the steps, way above our usual high tide, a sign of the incoming storm. I pick my way carefully over to Carmen. This part of the beach is a mess, dotted with stubble of plants and bits of trash, and old seaweed.

I hold my umbrella up over Carmen. "Aren't you cold?"

"Not as cold as that guy." She points to what I had taken for yet another clump of seaweed and debris, just past the edge where the waves are hitting. "Storm surge down the coast must have brought him in here." She shudders.

I shudder too, just thinking of the storm surge. Bertha just made landfall right at Matagorda Island, close enough to us to leave the waves here tall and glassy, high enough to be breaking over the jetty on either side of this section of beach. The water at the end of the jetties keeps striking the rocks with such force that it is bouncing into the air, which is a little scary, considering what the beaches here usually look like.

The worst thing is that Bertha has begun to stall. That's dangerous, because if the storm had just proceeded inland, it would have weakened and lost strength. But it looks like Bertha will be bouncing back out into the Gulf, which means she could sit there and regain strength – and then she could tear her way up the coast. The weather reports keep showing probable trajectories. We could be in the path. But we won't know for a while. Which is why hurricanes are so frustrating.

Sonya unfolds a knit wool blanket she's carried down with her and drapes it over Carmen's shoulders. So, okay, there are some advantages to owning a yarn store. Sonya says, "Fisherman's wool is the best for this weather." Then after a pause, "Do you want to tell us what happened?"

Sonya is so good at being gentle with people. Her twin Sandra has already moved over to examine the body, from about two feet away, without touching anything.

While Carmen explains to Sandra, I take a closer look. The misshaped lump is wearing a boot. I don't need to look any closer than that. I hear Carmen say, "Murder." Then she falls silent.

I put a hand on Carmen's shoulder. "It's probably not a murder. Galveston has lost a lot of people to the Gulf. For all we know, he's been missing since Hugo. Or fell off one of the offshore rigs."

Carmen shakes her head. "I know him, Felicity. Sort of. At least I think it's him. He always wore a distinctive necklace, and the body has on the same one."

I shudder. "Who is he?"

Carmen says. "My roommate's little girl was staying with her ex-husband. Ryker's a total deadbeat. So about two weeks ago the guy just disappears, never picks the kid up from daycare or anything. Child protective services got involved, and my roommate just got custody back."

"Is this the roommate that's a nurse?" I ask.

"Yeah." Carmen takes a deep breath. "I found Ryker. I'm afraid the police will think that I had something to do with it, since they already questioned me about Emma. Several people saw me near the body. I couldn't just leave. That'd be more suspicious." She gestures up, and I can see a half dozen people standing near one of the staircases, huddled under umbrellas. How could they even tell from that distance that what Carmen had found is a body? I think Carmen's being a little paranoid.

I look back at the waves, pointing out at the water. A fish jumps about ten feet out. Probably a mullet. Probably confused by jumping up into the rain.

"How could you have possibly arranged to be there when a body washed up on a beach?" Autumn insists.

"She's right. They won't think that," I tell Carmen. Though it is odd. She's been at the scene of two murders in the same week and has had a conflict with both victims. In theory, she could have suspected the storm surge would wash the body in and came to remove something she didn't want the police to find. I feel a moment of relief – Arlo won't be able to ignore the possibility that he has stronger suspects than just me. I've downgraded Carmen on my own suspects list, after everything that happened with Bruce. Though everything else says she's the most likely person to have done it.

Tiff is standing at the edge of our group, staring at the jetty. Every time the waves cover the structure, she flinches. She's probably never seen the beach like this. I start to move over to reassure her.

"Felicity!" Logan calls, running down the steps, sure-footed despite the rain. I'd hoped to be back at the restaurant before he came looking for me.

"Oh, great." I sigh. He looks upset.

"What?" Carmen asks, looking from me to the rapidly approaching Logan.

"Long story," I tell her. "Here."

I leave her the umbrella and move to intercept Logan. I hold out a hand and pre-emptively say, "I'm sorry."

His frown echoes through me, making me feel truly sorry. "Why aren't you where you said you'd be?"

I hear sirens echoing from above us. The police will be here in a minute. I glance back at Logan.

"Did you do something wrong?" Logan asks. He must be reading the guilt in my face.

"No. But Arlo keeps accusing me of trying to steer his investigation, and we just found – I mean *Carmen* just found -- another body."

Logan looks amused.

I huff out a frustrated noise. "This is serious. Somebody died."

"Which is exactly why you aren't supposed to be here." He still looks amused, though his tone is serious. "You're supposed to be staying safe so that you're not next."

I shudder, though part of my discomfort is from standing, having a conversation in the rain. "Do you really think the two deaths are related?"

Logan looks over to where my friends have gathered around Carmen, all of them staring from a safe distance at the bundle on the beach. The humor is gone from his face. "I don't know enough to tell. But if they are, that means you have more than just an isolated murder on your hands. You have someone willing to kill without compunction. Which means you are in more danger than either of us thought."

I swallow. "This guy's death was probably just an accident."

A car door slams. I look up, expecting to see the police. But it is a lone figure, peering over the edge of the seawall.

My phone rings. I don't recognize the number. I get so many junk calls that I don't usually answer numbers I don't know. But I feel the need to answer this one.

It's Paul, Emma's ex. "Can you tell Carmen I was here? She sounded panicked when she called, and all alone, but it looks like she found some friends to come out for her after all."

I peer up at him, can feel Logan's gaze following my own. What is Paul's connection to Carmen? And why is he so determined to avoid any contact with the police? But what comes out of my mouth is, "How did you get my number?"

His laughter comes over the line. "It's on your web site."

"Fair enough." I've been trying so hard to get ahold of this guy. And now that he's got my number – I've got his. "Look, can we talk?"

"Later," Paul says. "Call me and let me know that Carmen's okay. She's been through a lot in life. I'm not sure if she could handle being arrested."

"How do you know so much about Carmen?" I ask.

Paul hesitates. "After I broke up with Emma, Carmen and I went out a couple of times. But I started having second thoughts about dating somebody who worked with my ex. But it's not like I was getting back with Emma or anything. So don't go thinking that Carmen had motive."

Paul hangs up on me and gets back into his car.

Logan looks even more amused. "Well, Miss Marple?"

"You are aware that Miss Marple was like eighty years old."

"I was not aware of that," Logan says. "But she's my sister's favorite sleuth. Dawn is always telling me I should read more." He runs a hand across his chiseled jaw. "But what did that guy tell you?"

"Paul is Emma's ex. He was pretty high on my suspects list. But after talking to him just now -- if Paul's our killer, he's an extremely good liar."

Logan says, "You shouldn't discount that possibility."

I tilt my head. The rain is clearing up again, but I must still look bedraggled, so that's not as cute as it sounds. "Aren't you supposed to tell me to stop investigating? So that I'll be safe?"

"Don't you think it is a little too late for that? It seems like my role is more keeping you safe while you're doing it." He gestures towards my hair. "And part of that should be keeping you from catching your death of pneumonia. I understand you're prone to asthma, and other lung issues, so you should be doubly-careful."

Logan snags Autumn's umbrella – she seems all too willing to hand it over – and he holds it over my head as he ushers me towards the stairs. He's one step away from carrying me up them. And part of my mind thinks that's an intriguing idea – the treacherous part that keeps forgetting I'm supposed to be in mourning every time I look into Logan's laughing green eyes.

But I can't leave Carmen here alone. Especially not after what Paul just said. I balk, turning back towards the beach. "I'll be fine. It isn't even cold out."

Though there is that freshness in the air that you get when the barometric pressure is still falling.

About that time, Arlo shows up in a jeep he's driving slowly across the sand. He parks near us and gets out. Arlo gives me a raised eyebrow. He looks at Logan standing behind me and hesitates, like he's going to leave it at that and keep walking. Maybe the Governor told him Logan was to be completely hands off. But Arlo hesitates, and bites at his lip. Then he says, "Here at another crime scene, Lis?"

"I wasn't even here when this guy washed up on the beach. I have a whole table full of witnesses that were with me at Chalupa's when Carmen called."

"We were just leaving," Logan says. "I think you'll find your victim was asphyxiated. Which probably means he drowned."

How can Logan tell that? I hadn't even seen him take a close-up look at the body.

Arlo puts a hand on my arm, gently stopping me from walking away from him. "I have something for you."

I blink. "Oh?"

He reaches into his pocket and takes out a key. Emma's key. He hands it over. It is warm in my palm. "We've finished processing the crime scene. We didn't find anything incriminating, so you're free to re-open as usual."

"Thanks!" I clutch the key. Maybe now, I can get my life back to normal. Well, normal-ish. Considering the bodyguard trailing me. Still. I can't help but quip, "This never happens to Columbo, huh?"

Arlo frowns. "You know I can take that key back, right?"

"Then it would obviously be personal," I say. "And you wouldn't want to have to explain that." But my bluster is gone. I need to get my business back in order before my dream – mine and Kevin's -- slips away. "Seriously, Arlo. Thank you."

He shrugs. "I'm still not convinced I'm not missing something here. But you know, I don't have that one more thing to mention yet."

Chapter Fourteen

I'm in my catering truck, still drenched and bedraggled, driving down Seawall Boulevard, heading back towards all the businesses, and passing the jetties positioned at intervals that help break up the waves. At the top of the seawall, we're so far above the beach up here, what happened to Ryker seems so far away, it's almost like a bad dream.

I stop for a red light. I look in the rearview mirror at Logan's black Mustang. He's following me home. It hits me what I've really done, letting a total stranger into my life.

Nervous butterflies dance in my stomach.

I look up. My light is still red. I take out a brush and do my best to smooth out my hair. The rain has finally stopped again. A black car crosses in front of me. A black Lexus.

My heart rate increases as I fumble to call Logan with one hand, while I hit the blinker with the other.

"Is everything okay?" he asks. "A right turn isn't en route back to your house."

Never mind the fact that he's mapped out the route back to where I live. "I see a black Lexus."

"Do not follow it."

I take the right turn. "But we don't know what happened to Emma's car."

I hold up my phone and take a clear picture of the car's license plate. There's a squeal of tires as Logan forces his Mustang into the space between my catering truck and the Lexus. "This is dangerous, Koerber. If you want to be guarded . . . that's the opposite of what you keep doing." He slows down, forcing me to tap my brakes. "Besides, it's obvious you've never tailed anybody." I'm not about to tell him about my comical attempt to tail Carmen earlier today. "You're way too close, especially in such a conspicuous vehicle. Back off, but try not to lose me. And if I stop, don't come any closer. Promise me."

"Promise," I say. And I mean it.

We take a couple of turns and wind up back on the seawall. The Lexus does a U-turn across traffic to pull into a parking spot near Pleasure Pier, the amusement park and restaurant district that replaced the Flagship Hotel after Ike blew a hole in it. There's no way either Logan or I can stop discreetly.

"Just keep going," Logan says. "Slowly."

I try to get a look at who is getting out of the Lexus as I pass it. It's a short Asian woman, with her whole family, which includes four adorable kids and a sandy-haired white guy with a short beard.

Logan pulls into the parking lot of a restaurant a couple of blocks away. I follow. We both get out, and face each other in the parking lot.

"That can't be the right Lexus," Logan says.

I compare the license plate pic with the info I'd gotten from the DMV. I show my phone to Logan. "No. That's Emma's car."

Logan checks his gun and puts it back in his holster. "Stay in your van and lock the doors."

"Oh come on," I protest. "They're here with a bunch of kids."

He looks like he's seriously regretting having taken this gig. "Come on." He grabs my hand, his grip just this side of a vice. "Act like we're a couple. But do not leave my side."

We walk quickly up the block, slowing when we get to the entry to the pier. The couple and their kids are still standing in line to get in.

Logan waves at the guy. "Hey!"

The guy glances behind himself, looking for whoever Logan is so happy to see.

As we get closer, Logan says, "You're Emma's friends, right?"

The woman's smile gets big and warm. "That's right. I'm Tam Binh and this is Stewart." She gestures down to include the kids. "We're the Mixed Plate Travel Blog."

"What does that mean?" Logan waves down at the kids. He's cracking a smile, and I can feel his grip on my hand relax a little.

Stewart says, "We go places with the kids and try restaurants that are kid-friendly, and show how them being mixed race and mixed palates is actually an advantage. We home school, of course."

"That's a cool concept," I say. "Travel with a purpose always feels richer." Sudden tears bite at the back of my eyes. I'd had so many trips planned with Kevin where we weren't going to be just tourists. I blink them away.

"Hey, you okay?" Stewart asks. From the look on his face, you can just tell he's a dad, used to dealing with skinned knees and bad days.

But he can't fix my problems. "Yeah. Sorry. You must have patient kids if they're willing to wait for you to photograph the food before y'all eat. It takes me forever to get photos set up with good enough lighting for social media."

Tam Binh rolls her eyes. "You have no idea. They can be patient – sometimes. But blogs only show a polished view of your life, and sometimes it's just how you wish it had happened. I've photographed dishes on other tables before, because Stewart Jr. there likes to put his hands in the mashed potatoes."

Logan laughs. "Kid after my own heart."

Mine too. They seem like such a caring family.

Stewart Jr., standing with three older sisters, blushes. He's been listening to us talk about him. He mutters, "The camera eats first."

I can't help but laugh, the tears of moments before now at bay. "That must get exhausting."

Stewart ruffles his oldest daughter's hair. She bats his hand away, but she's giggling. He says, "Some days. But it's worth it. And the blog is this amazing record of the places we've been, and of the kids at different ages. And we have so many friends now – people we've met in real life. People send cards to the kids from Australia and Kurdistan and France. And they invite us to stay with them, to eat at their restaurants, to help their grandmother make tamales or perogies or kolaches."

"You have to be careful, of course," Tam Binh says. "Especially with where we take the kids."

Logan asks, "So is that how you guys wound up with Emma's car?"

"She offered to let us borrow it, since she prefers to ride her moped when she's on an island. We're supposed to bring it back on Monday, when we tour the chocolate shop she came to Texas to help open."

I bristle. Whatever lies Emma told these people, she worked for me. She wasn't doing me a favor. Logan's hand clamps down on mine before I can say anything.

He says, "You haven't heard the news."

Tam Binh looks uncertain. "We don't usually waste time with local media. You understand."

"Emma's dead," I tell her.

Tam Binh's mouth drops open. She pushes her kids behind her, like she's protecting them from the bad news. "Emma Giselle is dead?"

I start to correct her, but Logan squeezes my hand again. It's getting annoying, but he's right. We need to dig into this alternate identity, and as open and friendly as they seem, the Mixed Platers are less likely to give us more information if we tell them Emma was lying to them. Tam Binh really does seem cautious.

They don't seem to have much other information for us anyway. The whole rest of the time we're talking to them, Stewart keeps blinking and saying, "So how are we supposed to return the car?"

Finally, I tell him, "If you decide to stay on the island., bring it back by the chocolate shop on Monday. I'm the owner. I'll give you that tour." And then I'll figure out how to return the car to Emma's parents. "But you might want to head out while travel is still relatively easy. Bertha has turned back out over the Gulf and is getting stronger again. They're saying it may head back this way."

"I don't think we're ready to leave," Tam Binh says. "I'm really into history, and this place seems steeped in it. Maybe you can share some of it on Monday."

"Sure!" Assuming, of course I can get my shop ready to be open to the public by then. I don't know how much of my stock the police would have damaged or confiscated. I wonder if I'm allowed to charge them for that, once I'm proven innocent.

"You're a bean-to-bar chocolate maker?" Stewart says it with reverence, looking at me like I suddenly turned into a rock star. "It must be amazing to travel the world with such purpose. I mean, we just go places to eat and talk. But you . . ."

There's no way we're getting the conversation back on track after that. But it is really nice to have my work recognized. "I'll show y'all some pictures when you come for the tour. And some of them are up on Instagram."

Stewart opens the app on his phone. "What's the account handle?"

When we finally get back to the house, all I want to do is shower, change into comfy pajamas, and start Googling Emma Giselle. But I won't be able to wander around in my PJs for a while.

Logan grabs a duffle out of the back of his Mustang and carries it with him into the house. He drops it near the back door. It is dark blue, with a white baseball stitched onto that and the word Twins on top of that.

I raise an eyebrow at it. He grins back. "Sue me. I'm a homer. I'm from the other side of the state, but that still makes it my team."

I know nothing about baseball. Where does that mean he's from? He doesn't elaborate, and I feel too ignorant to ask.

He insists on going in ahead of me, and clearing the whole first floor. I'm afraid he's going to terrify my aunt, but she's not downstairs.

I go inside and call up the stairs, "Aunt Naomi?"

"It's about time you're home," Naomi calls back. "Be down in a minute."

Logan has gone back by the door to grab his bag. He crouches down, holding out a hand towards Knightley, letting the rabbit sense him without trying to touch him. "Who's this little guy?"

Good move. Knightley is timid when it comes to strangers, and he's already had one upsetting encounter. "That's Knightley. I named him after the hero in one of my favorite books."

"A literary bunny." Logan laughs. "What book?"

Knightley hops away from the sudden sound, retreating into his cage, where he feels safe.

I move over to the fridge and grab a sprig of parsley from the crisper. "Here." I eye Logan skeptically. "It's from Emma." No recognition. "By Jane Austen." Nope. Nada.

"I never had much time for reading. Always too busy being my dad's son." He says it like I should know who his dad is. Logan holds out the parsley, and suddenly he has Knightley's attention. Knightley hops over, letting Logan pet him while he munches on the parsley. The little sellout.

Aunt Naomi walks in. She's looking down at her tablet. "Felicity, that blogger's at it again." She looks up, notices Logan. "Oh, hi."

"Hi." Logan grins at her. He pets Knightley one last time, then straightens and extends a hand to my aunt. Man, he's tall, especially compared to her. I'm blushing, though I'm not entirely sure why.

Naomi scrunches up her nose. "Have we met? Your face is familiar, though I can't quite place it."

Logan studies her. Then recognition lights in his eyes. "You were there at the chocolate shop's launch party. I came by to place an order."

Naomi makes a sound like she's choking on nothing, then cuts a glance at me. Uh-huh. She's realizing she missed this guy in order to set me up with Sid the Dork. For a moment she looks happy for me.

But her eyebrows go up as she takes in the duffle bag at Logan's feet.

Really. She has to know me better than that. I was married for eleven years. I expect commitment. And if I ever give my heart away again, it's got to be as strong as what I had with Kevin. And this guy – he may be cute, but if he's never heard of Jane Austen, he's not even in the running.

"Logan's my new-" It sounds so cheesy to say bodyguard. "Private security. He's going to be staying here until we figure out who tried to kill me, and what they're so desperate to get back."

"I hope it's not a problem." Logan looks at the floor, then up at my aunt. "I'm good with whatever sofa you have handy."

Aunt Naomi puts a hand on my arm. "Thank goodness! I've been putting off calling Greg because he'll want to come home to protect us."

"And that's a bad thing?" Logan quips, but he still looks uncomfortable.

I tell him, "That means bringing his mother back with him, in case the storm turns last minute and we have to evacuate after all. She tends to take over."

Aunt Naomi nods. "Now I can call Greg and tell him we're safe."

"If you might also be in danger, you might want to reconsider. I've agreed to protect Felicity, which means whenever she leaves the house, I'm shadowing her." Logan looks down at the floor. "I'm sorry, but I'm not equipped with a full team."

"Such an honorable guy." Naomi wraps Logan in a hug, kisses him on the cheek and then snaps a selfie of herself standing next to him before taking the phone into the next room. "Y'all have no idea how jealous Greg is about to be."

I follow her. "Wait. The blogger you were telling me about. What's happened now?"

Aunt Naomi sighs. She puts her tablet behind her back. "I'm not sure if you want to see this."

It's not like that will make the bad news go away. I hold out my hand. "Better I see it now than hear about it from someone else later."

I take the tablet and open the cover. There's a picture of me, on the beach, standing next to Carmen, while behind us, Logan is clearly examining Ryker's body. How did I not notice him doing that at the time? And who the heck took this picture? They must have had a lens a mile long.

But that's not the worst of it. Hipster Guy is reporting more of his Gulf Coast Happenings. *Clients Jump Ship after Chocolate Killer Spotted at The Scene of Another Crime*.

How? How could he have gotten this up that fast. For a second, I wonder, what if the blogger is actually Paul? And the profile pic is a fake? Everyone else has a couple of identities right now. And he was at the Sea Wall, at approximately the angle this picture was taken from. But that doesn't feel right.

The first line of the second paragraph catches my attention. *The Bergamot Hotel announced today a new partnership with Sally Annie of All My Chocolate, a craft chocolatier out of Colorado. This will kick off with a gourmet chocolate dinner next month with Sally appearing in person, and will continue with a standing offer of complementary bon bons in each upgraded guest room.*

What in the absolute heck? That was supposed to be my gig. With mini bars instead of bon bons. It's my biggest client. I was going to announce the deal at the end of my grand opening party, after the bar making demo. Because my new Sierra Nevada 60% – the very chocolate people were set to be decorating – were supposed to be the signature bars at the newly renovated hotel. Light roast and sweet, the Sierra Nevadas are perfect for most palates.

Hipster guy continues, *This standing order had originally been offered to Galveston's own Felicity Koerber, of Sympathy and Condolences – I mean Greetings and Felicitations. But with Felicity's shop the scene of a murder, the hotel has rushed to cut ties.*

I let out a squeak.

"Everything okay in there?" Logan is standing in the doorway, leaning against it like he's already at home here.

"Not really." I take out my phone. "But not the kind of danger you can help with."

"Are you sure?" His eyes look troubled. Those intensely green eyes with the thick dark lashes. I melt inside, and try not to let it show. He's big and strong, and playing at being my protector. And that makes him just as dangerous as whoever tried to kill me. Because letting myself get attached to him would be a total mistake. And not just because I'd be rushing to heal from Kevin's memory.

I look away, down at the phone. "I need to make a call."

He nods. Then he looks at Aunt Naomi and gestures at the fridge. "May I?"

"Help yourself."

I vaguely register Logan rummaging through the fridge and coming out with eggs and cheese and veggies as I dial the number of my contact at the Bergamot.

Taylor answers, her voice chipper and professional. I'm guessing she didn't look to see who it was before picking up.

I tell her, "I just took a look at a blog post, and I wanted to find out if what they're saying about All My Chocolate is true."

There's dead silence on the other end of the line. For a long time. "Felicity." She sounds flustered. "I know I should have told you. But you were shut down . . . and my manager is personal friends with Sally, and-"

"My shop's opening back up again tomorrow." I hear the note of desperation in my own voice, but I can't stop myself. "Taylor, I promise you, I didn't do anything wrong."

"I know that," Taylor says. She sounds sympathetic. "But, Felicity, my manager's not willing to be connected with a scandal."

I feel like she's punched me. "I understand."

She's still stammering apologies when I hang up. I wander into the living room, looking at the pictures Aunt Naomi has hung on the wall. There's one from when the whole family last got together, for a huge crawfish boil. Kevin's in the picture, looking mostly happy, but slightly disturbed. He never could get the hang of crawfish, and some of my cousins used to think it was fun to gross him out by sucking the brains or whatever out of the crawfish heads.

It almost feels like Kevin's just been party to the conversation on the phone, like that look on his face comes from the thought that someone might be believing these rumors, ruining the business started in his memory.

"Was that as bad as it sounded?" Logan hands me an omelet. It looks amazing. But I'm not the slightest bit hungry.

"Yeah." I take the plate, just holding it. It's not fair. I didn't do anything wrong. I certainly didn't kill anybody. And the scandal could well tank my business. If that happens, then I've wasted a year of my life, wasted Kevin's insurance money, disappointed his memory, and failed at my new dream.

The plate is trembling in my hands.

"What do you need, right now?"

There's a man in my living room, saying the perfect thing to comfort me.

But he's not the right man. Not the one I've missed night and day. Not the one I belonged with.

I hand him back the omelet. "I'm sorry."

I bolt from the room, taking the stairs two at a time as I go up to my bedroom and close the door. I let out a little squeak. Someone has been in here, probably while Aunt Naomi was home. And they tossed the place. Not the whole house, just my room. My clothes are in a jumble, on the floor in front of the dresser. The mattress is half off the bed, and the open closet door reveals a jumbled tangle.

Oh boy. This is going to be awkward. I race back down the stairs. "Logan?"

When I tell him what's wrong, Logan sprints past me, up the stairs. He has a gun in his hand. "Stay here."

My heart jumps. I don't think the intruder is still in my room. But Logan Hanlon is about to get a close-up look at my rather plain collection of underwear. I give him a few minutes, then head upstairs, intent on ushering him out of my room so I can tidy up.

I find him standing at the window, taking a look at the lock. "I'm going to call a friend of mine. We'll get some alarm equipment installed before you go to sleep tonight."

"Thanks." I surreptitiously grab all my underwear off the floor and shove it back into my dresser drawer. "But wouldn't it be easier just to board up the window?"

He laughs, a deep, throaty sound. "Let's consider that Plan B if my friend doesn't come through."

He picks something up off the floor on the far side of my bed. It's a picture frame. I tense as Logan studies Kevin's face. Finally Logan looks up at me. "He had kind eyes. I bet he was a good guy." He moves back around and hands the frame to me.

"He was." I move over and put the picture back on my nightstand. I wonder if Logan noticed there are a few superficial similarities between him and Kevin – both tall and broad-shouldered, with green eyes. "My one and only."

Am I saying that to Logan? Or reminding myself?

People keep telling me Kevin would have wanted me to move on. But I don't think Kevin would have liked the idea of someone like Logan replacing him. Logan has too dark of a sense of humor, is too rough around the edges – carries a weapon. I don't think he and Kevin would have been friends.

So what does it mean that I'm attracted to somebody I don't think Kevin would have liked? It feels like failure, when my entire goal this past year has been to honor Kevin's memory. To pay tribute to the love that had sustained me my entire adult life.

"Hey, what's that?" Logan points at a wooden box on the shelf I'd installed above my dresser. Old houses don't have a lot of storage. The box is open, and some maps are sticking out. One of them is badly torn.

"Oh, no." I rush over to the maps, pulling out the hand-colored depiction of Brazil. There's not going to be any fixing it.

Logan is looking at me like I've lost it. "Tell me that's not a treasure map."

"No. Of course not." I smooth out the edge of the ruined paper. "Kevin and I used to collect maps. All the places we were going to go together. And ones for the places we'd been." I hand him the map of Brazil and pull out the one of the Hawaiian Islands. Thankfully, it looks like Brazil was the only one that had gotten torn. "This one's Maui. From our honeymoon."

Logan looks trapped, like he's not sure what to say. I don't want him to say he's sorry. Or that he's sure it's all for the best. Or any of the other meaningless platitudes people keep throwing at me over the last year. He looks down at the map in his hands. "I'll take a go at repairing this one later tonight. I'm pretty good at that kind of thing."

This response takes my breath away. Out of all the people over the last year, Logan's practically the only one who's gotten what I needed him to say. I have an urge to wrap my arms around him and hold him close. But I don't. Instead, I mumble, "I'll clean up in here and take a shower. I want to get to the shop early tomorrow, and see what kind of damage I'm looking at."

Logan doesn't look like he's going to leave me alone for a minute, with the ease the intruder used to get into my space. He finally nods. But I get the idea that he'll be waiting for me in the hall.

Chapter Fifteen
Friday

The next morning, Logan is standing behind me as I unlock the back door to the chocolate shop, using Emma's key. That key is so solid and straightforward, unlike everything about Emma herself, as I'd learned last night, when I'd been sitting in bed Googling Emma Giselle while Logan had been downstairs repairing the torn map. Now, it's my first time back in the place where Emma had died.

Logan is skeptically eyeing a pair of half-shuttered windows on the other side of the alley. All the uneven doors in the narrow throughway – part of what I see as charm and love about coming to work – seem to be making him nervous.

"My neighbors are all very nice people," I tell Logan as I step ahead of him, into the building.

"I'm sure they are. Still. Wait at the doorway. And close the door." He moves around me, opening cabinets and peeking into the chillers before moving from the kitchen into the chocolate making area. It unnerves me the way he checks the gun under his jacket before going through the doorway.

I'm supposed to handle this situation? Without coffee? I had needed to see my shop, to reassure myself. And what I see is mostly reassuring. There's flour spilled on the floor, and on the shelf where the sealed jars are kept, but most of it is still in the jars. I thought Arlo told his officers to make sure they cleaned up after themselves, but I guess you can't force people to be careful.

All my kitchen supplies seem to be in order, but I need to wash everything. Who knows what happened in here while I was gone. I make a list on my phone of what I need to do in here.

The containers of sugar sprinkles, which Emma had lined up in the other room according to bright and cheerful color, are now empty and piled into the sink. For some reason, that's sadder than anything else that's happened.

I have no idea why they would have suspected the sprinkles. It's as much of an enigma as why Emma Turner, small town Texas girl, had felt the need to create the on-line persona of Emma Giselle, foodie socialite who travels the globe.

I mean, on one level I get it. There's not a lot of glamor in the Gulf Coast. Galveston is known more for stubborn history than for gorgeous beaches. One example: the hurricane in 1900 that put the island completely underwater hadn't prompted Galvestonians to abandon their ruined city. Instead, they'd raised the island by seven feet by pumping in sand off the seabed and adding a seawall, plus all those jetties to keep the whole project from washing away. And then later, we built a museum to celebrate our triumph over the Gulf.

But triumph isn't Instagram-worthy. Even the prettiest cars here rust out and get covered with seagull poop. It's quaint. It's touristy. It's not trendy.

Other generations of teenagers had dreamed of getting out of their small towns, long before this one gained instant access to what it is like inside other peoples' lives – or at least the illusion of what other people want you to think their lives are like. I had been comfortable with the small-town pace, but I'd been in class with a ton of kids who couldn't wait to graduate and move to New York or LA – or at least Dallas. Admittedly, that may have had something to do with joining theater club with Autumn, and with my brief stint with journalism as a schedule-convenient elective.

But I'd never known of someone so ashamed of where they come from that they not only wanted to be somewhere else – but wanted to be someone else when they got there. Where is the authenticity in that? How could you ever be comfortable when no one knew who you really were, what you really were, no matter how much outward success you attained? It would be like constantly traveling, constantly putting on performance art, with nowhere to really live, where you could take off your dress clothes and be comfortable in baggy sweat pants.

Emma had obviously thought the lies would make her happy, if she got enough approval from random strangers on the Internet. Likes and hearts. Could they really be that much of a driving force? When what people were liking was patently fake?

And when it might hurt people in the process. Emma had fabricated pictures of herself in famous spots around the globe, and posted them on a blog that spins a story of a vagabond who has rejected the values of her ultra-rich parents to look for authentic experience -- and to help out small business owners. Like me, apparently. Who knew?

Emma had posted a picture of her, me and Carmen working at the warehouse space I rent for Felicitations out in Waco, transporting beans to the chocolate factory ourselves, because the transport company I usually use had flaked. We weren't about to let that make us miss our deadline for orders.

Only, instead of telling that story, Emma has slanted it so that it looks like Carmen and I are doing the grunt work of hauling around the heavy bags – while she smiles for the camera I hadn't even noticed. Her narrative implies that she's helping us learn how to better our production.

I'd be angry about it – if she wasn't dead. It is hard to hold a grudge against someone who had died even as I'd tried to breathe air back into her lungs. And who obviously had a gift for Photoshop. Some of the pics on that blog, showing her in different regions of the country, were dated in weeks when she was working for me.

I step into the space where we process chocolate. I'd known the melanger would be empty, but it's still heartbreaking that I've lost all that work. But staring at the granite wheels of the machine won't change anything.

I force myself to take stock of what hasn't been lost. The molds and other supplies in here look more or less in order.

I move through into the bean room. I have a lot of beans already sorted into a covered bin. I hesitate about using them, but I can't afford to throw everything out, and they don't look like the cops did anything odd. I get the roaster going, setting it for the time and temperature I figured out during the experiments in Aunt Naomi's kitchen, tweaking the settings to play up the pecan notes in the beans a bit more.

"The office looks more or less intact," Logan says, coming into the room from the hallway side. "At least your computer's there. And the stock in the front looks pretty much like I remember it from when I came in the first time. Except for the big bin in the center."

"What?" That bin has my Guayas River bars, the Ecuadorian Arriba beans so floral, with notes of spice, the pride of what I've been able to create. I rush out into the store. The bin is empty. Why had the cops taken every single one of them? Surely, a random sample would have been enough.

"Maybe someone got hungry?" Logan quips.

I give him a sour look and take out my phone. I dial the police station. When Arlo comes on the line, I say, "How could you!"

"How could I what?" Arlo sounds confused. Or maybe he's just done so many questionable things, that he's not sure which one I'm referring to.

"Destroy all of my Guayas River bars. Isn't it bad enough that you emptied the chocolate I was making, but-"

"Lis," Arlo interrupts. "We took two of each of your products to randomly sample. That's it."

"Then why is the bin empty?"

"Hold on." I hear the faint echo of clacking, as Arlo no doubt pulls up a report. "I have no idea. There's nothing here about a suspicious bin of chocolate." He hesitates, then obviously trying to lighten the mood, says, "Maybe someone got hungry?"

It wasn't funny when Logan said it. I sigh. "Arlo."

"Do you suspect a break in?"

I shrug, though of course he can't hear me over the phone. "Why would someone break in and take nothing but chocolate?"

"I don't know." Now it's Arlo's turn to sigh. "Don't go anywhere. Fisk and I will be there in half an hour to take your statement."

He's bringing his crime scene guy. Because my shop is a crime scene. Again.

While we're waiting for the cops, Logan helps me to count the remaining chocolate bars on the shelves, and the stock of truffles in the coolers in the kitchen, as well as the few truffles left in the glass case that forms the counter. Just like Arlo said – two of each product are missing, no more, no less. And I'm short a bag of cacao beans, and a sack of isomalt.

We move back to the front of the store, making sure everything looks like it is back in order. Logan's peering at the inventory list. "Which one is your favorite?"

"My favorite what?"   I feel like I missed the first part of his question. For all I know he's asking my favorite baseball player. I did look it up: The Twins are from Minnesota. Which makes his accent make sense.

"You made all of this. Which one of these chocolates is your favorite?"

"That's like asking someone about their favorite child." Not that I would know about that. Kevin and I hadn't been able to have children. The doctors had said it was him, but I'm not sure I believe that. So I'm still not holding my breath that I'll ever have kids. I've come to terms with that. But I'm an only child, with a cousin who's an only child. Which makes my Mawmaw sad, since she grew up with a huge extended family gathered around the table on Sundays back when she lived in DeRidder, Louisiana. It's yet another reason I have a hard time managing a visit.

None of that is appropriate to share with Logan.   Instead I say, "My favorite is whatever I'm currently working on. Take those beans roasting in the back. I picked them for the flavor notes that I want to develop. There's a fruity sweetness like cherries, and a nutty undertone at the same time." I hesitate. "I don't want to tell you things you already get. How much do you know about craft chocolate?"

"Not much," he admits. "Just enough to know what I like. I went to a couple of tastings with a former girlfriend. But that was closer to home."

"And what do you like?" That comes out breathy, like I'm not talking about chocolate at all. Stupid, Felicity, stupid.

He arches an eyebrow, but answers the question. "I'm more of a beer person than a wine drinker. I like chocolate with oaky or citrusy notes. I've tried a bar that had malted barley in it, and I've had ganache infused with beer."

"Oh?" I'm surprised. "But the chocolate you ordered is sweet and rich." The exact opposite of what he just said he likes.

He makes a what-can-you-do gesture. "That's what high-end clients expect. I don't dislike that kind of chocolate. It's just not what I prefer."

"Try this. If you had any of the cupcakes at the grand opening, it's the chocolate Carmen used in them." I hand him one of my bars made of beans from Chiapas, Mexico. I'd bought them as part of a split shipment, and I think these beans had appealed to me because of my mental state at the time. I'd needed grounding, and something that tasted richly of the Earth had satisfied a longing deep inside me. The natural honey note that counterpointed it, ever so lightly, had been as fragile as me.

I study Logan's face as he opens the wrapper, breaks off a square of chocolate and pops it into his mouth. He closes his eyes, and for a moment a look of intense happiness takes over his features. He opens his eyes, blinking those thick lashes. "Felicity, this is amazing. There's really nothing in here other than cacao?"

"A bit of sugar. But that's it." I feel myself flushing with embarrassed excitement, a magnification of what I usually feel when someone really gets my chocolate. Chocolate has been the subject of so many novels, including romance and magical realism, that play cacao into something causing intoxication. Writers keep trying to imbue it with these mystical qualities. But they don't need to. There's something about real-world chocolate, that way it melts at body temperature on the tongue and releases feel-good chemicals in the brain, that even industrial chocolate hits people's emotions. Enhance it with flavor profiles you know a specific person likes – and of course, you'll inspire moments of bliss like what I just saw on Logan's face.

It's nothing super-human. So why is that blink of Logan's eyelashes burned now in my brain?

Carmen comes in. She raises an eyebrow at Logan, then looks at me and mouthes the word, "Nice."

I shake my head subtly at her, trying to regain a sense of distance after the sheer physicality of watching Logan enjoy my chocolate. "Carmen, you remember Logan Hanlon. He's assisting me with security until we sort out this thing with Emma."

She looks disappointed that there isn't a more romantic take here. "Aren't we opening the shop this morning?"

"Not until we look over everything, and make sure it's clean and still in good shape after the cops went through it."

"Let me grab the glass cleaner," Carmen says. "I'll do the cases and the door."

"Thanks. I'm going to re-wash all the dishes." I move back into the kitchen. Logan's checking out the front windows, like he's thinking about installing alarm systems again, so I leave him to it.

My phone buzzes. I have a text from Autumn. *Did you check on those endpapers? I want to call this guy before he forgets who I am. I've been doing some research, and there's no record of a print run with lop-sided ones.*

Sorry! I text back. *I'll get to it!*

I should have gotten to it last night, but I had been too nervous to think straight with Logan in the house. His presence on the sofa downstairs had kept me up half the night.

Moments later, when I've just gotten suds going in the sink, Carmen walks in with an odd look on her face and announces, "Emma's killer is a guy."

"Why?" I turn off the water and dry my hands.

"Come see."

I follow her into the men's restroom, where we store some of our cleaning supplies. She points to the counter between the two sinks, where there's a clear boot print, made out of something that looks like flour. It probably is flour, considering where we are. I look up. There's a vent above the sinks. Whatever this mystery person has been searching for, they've got to be pretty desperate at this point. "You don't suppose the cops could have done that?"

"Nope," Carmen says.

"Yeah, me neither."

"So it had to be a guy," Carmen repeats.

I study the boot print. How did someone get from the mess into the kitchen with enough flour to still make a boot print when their foot hit the damp counter? They must have spilled the flour in the kitchen, had it all over them. The print itself is not huge. "It could have been a woman with large feet."

"Like Kaylee." Carmen giggles. "She's like a size ten."

I think back. I've never studied the bookstore owner's feet. But maybe she does wear boots. "We shouldn't wash anything in the kitchen, in case our intruder left fingerprints in the pantry."

Carmen looks down at the glass cleaner in her hand. "Good thing I didn't wipe anything down yet."

The three of us sit down at a table to wait for Arlo. Logan takes the seat that puts his back to the wall. Carmen takes the one that puts her in front of the window – not that there's much to see with the miserable weather. I take out my phone and start calling my regular clients, to re-assure them that the shop is back open, and their orders will be delivered on time.

Thankfully, most of them are fine with that. I only have two cancellations, people who, like the Bergamot, are afraid of being connected to the scandal. But some of the others express sympathy and support, talking about how horrible it is that I've been put through all of this. Those clients leave me with relieved tears glittering in my eyes.

Maybe this is all going to be okay.

Then I get an incoming phone call, which I answer because it could be a client calling back. Instead, it's a guy, young, gruff and laughing into the receiver. "Hey, my friend and I are throwing a huge party at his club in Dallas in a couple of months. We've already got Death's Door coffee, and Dark Night whiskey. We were wondering if you could make us some 100 percent dark chocolate, with a Sympathy and Condolences label. You know, something that includes the line, *Careful, this chocolate could kill you.*"

I stiffen, my heartbeat increasing as he talks. My first instinct is to hang up on him. But as he lays out the details, this sounds like a huge contract, even bigger than what I'd been offered at the Bergamot. It sounds like massive brand exposure too. But – would I be selling my integrity? Selling the hopefulness of mine and Kevin's dream? I swallow hard. "How attached are you to the *This chocolate could kill you* line?"

"We're not married to it, if it's a deal breaker. We heard good things about your products, even before Ash started blogging about you. We're looking at bringing in talented people from all over the States and parts of Europe."

To Dallas, Texas.

"I'm flattered," I say, before I can stop myself. "But it would be a big shift for my brand. Can I have a minute to think about it?"

"Sure," the guy says. "Call me back at this number. I'll be here till three."

Carmen, who's been eavesdropping shamelessly, says, "You should totally do it. Take what that blogger jerk said, and turn it into an asset. Your labels are all supposed to be greeting cards anyway. You of all people should know that sometimes happy cards aren't appropriate."

Surprisingly, Logan nods. "This could be an opportunity for you to heal, in more ways than one."

"Y'all, I don't know." What would Kevin have thought of the idea? Would he have approved? And how would I have felt if someone had given me bitter chocolate when I was in my darkest moment of need? If it had been deeply flavorful chocolate – with notes of cherry and pecan – I might actually have appreciated it.

It takes me a second to realize that I've just described the specific scent of the roasting chocolate lightly perfuming the room.

"I'll volunteer Bruce to be on the label photos," Carmen says, putting a hand on mine. "Chocolate did, after all, nearly kill him, and he's a big fan of irony."

"Your dog likes irony?" I ask, at the same time Logan asks, "Who's Bruce?"

Carmen smiles, ironically. "Of course he does. He's my dog."

We all start laughing, and the release, after all this tension, feels so good that I just can't stop.

Not even when Arlo walks in the door. He scowls, looks down at himself to make sure nothing is out of place. "What?"

"Carmen's dog has a sense of humor," I say. But I don't think I can explain it in a way where Arlo would get the joke. "Never mind. You had to be here."

Arlo takes a deep breath, which seems to derail him from being irritated. "This place smells good."

"Felicity's roasting beans in the back." Carmen says.

Fisk comes in and surveys the situation, all of us standing there, looking kind of dopey, just appreciating a smell. "Someone broke into this place, took all of their favorite chocolate bars, then left?"

"Not exactly," Carmen tells him. "There are also a couple of boxes of books missing. I never got around to unpacking them, and the shelf's still empty."

I look at her, and she nods. I shrug at Fisk. "I didn't even notice. I was more upset about the chocolate."

Carmen and Fisk head over to the other side of the store.

I call after them, "Don't forget to show him the boot print!"

An alarm goes off on my phone. I look from Logan to Arlo. "Excuse me a moment. I need to go check on my roaster. The beans keep roasting until you get them cool, and I don't want to lose *another* batch of chocolate."

"I did say I was sorry about that," Arlo insists.

I head to the back, as I watch Arlo sit down at the same table with Logan. Oh, boy. That probably won't end well.

The roaster I use is a drum style that rotates the beans in something half akin to a clothes dryer, while getting them up to a high heat. I use the roaster's mechanism for grabbing beans to test – a long handle with a cup-like end that will catch a few beans as they tumble past. I withdraw it, take a couple of hot beans and winnow them in my hand. I crush them together, creating a pile of hot cacao nibs in my palm. I pinch a few together and taste them. I've decided to do a heavy roast on these, and they're almost perfect, tasting like they smell. Nibs surprise some people. They expect them to be sweet, like finished chocolate, when they actually taste more like nuts with a chocolaty aftertaste.

I drop the rest of the nibs into three tasting cups.

After another two minutes, I pull another sample and taste again. This time, they *are* perfect. The flavor will continue to shift a little, finishing right where I want it. I turn off the roaster and dump all the beans out of it into a deep-walled tray that sits permanently next to the roaster, with vents to let cool air blast through it. I use a wooden stirrer to rotate the beans so that they cool evenly, and when I'm satisfied with the process, I shut everything off and take the tasting cups back out into the main room.

Fisk is still busy talking to Carmen, so I hand tasting cups to Arlo and Logan, and set the third one on the table. I explain what they're tasting.

"How do you know how the nibs are going to taste?" Arlo asks.

"Chocolate making is chemistry. Understanding the processes lets me predict flavor." I can't help but smile right at Arlo when I say, "There's a lot of chemistry when you study medicine. I guess my degree's good for something other than making me a suspect."

These nibs were meant for the hotel order that got cancelled. I taste a few myself, thinking how I'm re-interpreting them with the heavier roast. Maybe for Logan's corporate clients . . . or for the possible Sympathy and Condolences offer. If I decide to do it.

At this point, I honestly don't know if I want to.

Arlo looks at me. "I'd like to speak to you for a moment. Alone."

We both look at Logan, who starts to get up from the table. Arlo looks a bit smug about it.

"No," I say. Both Logan and Arlo look at me. "Logan, you don't have to move. Arlo and I can talk in the office."

When we get into the office, Arlo closes the door behind him. It is a tiny space. It had once had a window facing out onto the sidewalk of the Strand, but that had been bricked in by a previous owner. You can still see the different colored bricks filling a rectangle above my desk.

I sit down at the desk, trying to gain a bit of psychological control in the situation. I put my hand on the handle of the top left drawer, the brass ring cold against my palm. There are a few things of Kevin's in this drawer – including his diving watch and his camping knife. Things I want to use someday on my travels, when looking at them doesn't hurt so bad.

"What did you want to say that you can't say in front of Logan?"

"I want your take on what happened in this shop. Without coaching."

My mouth drops open. "What are you implying?"

Arlo settles carefully into the folding chair that's the only other seat in the room. "I'm just wondering if it was a coincidence that he showed up in your shop the day of the murder. Whatever happened, it seems to focus on you, Carmen and Logan."

"I never met Logan before that day." I open the drawer a few inches, then close it again. "Admit it, Arlo. There's nothing tying me to this murder. Right now, you're grasping for straws."

"Maybe." Arlo shrugs. He leans toward me, making intense eye contact. I'd forgotten how beautiful his warm brown eyes are up close. "Just so you know, Hanlon was wrong. Ryker Brody had a heart attack before he went into the water. Similar appearance, which explains Hanlon's mistake, but the guy didn't drown."

"Am I supposed to be shocked by that?" I'm not sure what to think, actually, but I say, "I don't have any super-special attachment to Logan."

"You're putting a lot of trust in him. And he's not perfect." Arlo looks down. "It worries me that you're putting him in charge of protecting you."

Arlo's dating somebody else. He's not allowed to act like he still has feelings for me. That isn't fair.

"What right do you have to be worried about me?" My breathing sounds heavy in the shocked silence that follows.

He shrugs. "None. I just don't want to see anyone get hurt. Especially not my star suspect."

"You really think I shot up my aunt's house and then stole my own chocolate? What did I do with it?" I jut out my chin, and gesture around the cramped space, with the broken metate still on top of the filing cabinet.

He reaches over without having to get up and pulls open one of the filing cabinet drawers. It's full of old, scratched chocolate molds. I'm saving them for an art project I may never get around to. Arlo raises an eyebrow. "They could be anywhere if you had a reason to want to get rid of them. This supposed theft could be that one more thing I've been looking for."

I huff out a noise of indignation. "I'm proud of that chocolate. There's nothing wrong with it. And that's not my size boot print in the bathroom."

I'm blustering. But what if whatever the housebreaker had been looking for would have been small enough to hide in a batch of wrapped chocolate bars? Or process into the chocolate itself? Could Emma have put drugs or something in the melanger when I wasn't looking? If the intruder had taken the chocolate, did it mean that they had finally gotten back whatever Emma had taken, and would now leave me alone?

"You'd better hope so," Arlo says. But he's talking about the chocolate not being tainted. "We still have our samples of those bars, and I just had someone at the office send them off for more in-depth testing."

I sigh. "This is getting old, Arlo. What will it take to get you to drop it?"

Arlo shrugs. "A more viable suspect." He leans forward. "Speaking of which. How much do you know about Carmen's personal life?"

"She didn't do it." I'd been down that road. Carmen's not a viable suspect.

"She found the second victim, and she was acting odd when I questioned her. She knows something she's not telling. That makes her suspicious."

"Arlo, what she knows is the victim's identity."

"So do we," Arlo says. "Ryker Brody, 25-year-old unemployed musician."

"Ryker's ex-wife is Carmen's roommate. Carmen told me the two of them were fighting over custody of their kid." I bring my hands to my forehead, massaging my temples. "Carmen was probably worried that she'd wind up on your suspect list." I hesitate. I may be upset at Arlo, but he's still a cop. I need to tell him what I've uncovered. "Or that her roommate would. The roommate works at the hospital, and could have had access to concentrated caffeine."

"And you're just now telling me this? I swear, Felicity, if you start messing with my mind again, I will throw you in jail for obstruction, and I don't care if I get reprimanded later."

"Messing with your mind?" I stand up. But no. It's my office. I'm not storming out. I sit back down. "When have I ever done that?"

"Oh, I don't know, back in high school. When you sent me all those notes."

I blink. "What notes?"

He squints at me, his dark brows furrowing like accent marks. "The cryptic suggestions that I change little things about myself. I did everything you asked, and you still dumped me."

I shake my head. "I never sent you any notes. I dumped you because of Susie Abernathy."

He still looks confused. "Why?"

"Because I was dumping you before you dumped me. I found out what you were planning. I don't know why you're so mad about it."

"What was I planning?" He repeats the words slowly.

I hesitate. "You were going to ask for your ring back to give it to Susie. That's why I kept it."

Arlo's voice goes soft. "Who told you that?"

"Jerome." My voice sounds weak, uncertain. I'd made some pretty rash decisions based on the word of one person. And Jerome had drunkenly tried to kiss me that one time at Autumn's graduation party. I'd chalked it up to impaired judgment – but what if Jerome had actually been into me? Would he have been capable of coming up with such a devious plan?

"And you believed that jerk?" Arlo scoots towards the front of his chair, searching my face for the truth. "You know he stole my motorcycle?"

"You think he'd lie to break us up?"

"It seems to have worked, didn't it?"

"I guess." I try to remember the days after the breakup, which had mostly been a fog of heart-broken lethargy. The devastation had lasted pretty much until graduation – even if I'm starting to realize I had partially brought it on myself. "But if Jerome had hoped to be there in the aftermath to swoop up me up for himself, he was sadly disappointed."

Arlo manages a laugh. Which is more than I can do. I had really broken his heart. Me. When he hadn't been disloyal at all.

"I'm sorry," I tell him. "I might have come to my senses if you hadn't left."

I don't mean it as an accusation, but his sharp intake of breath means he takes it that way.

"What was holding me here? Everyone thought I must have really screwed up for you to drop me like that. And then my grandmother died – and you didn't even show up for the funeral."

I blink. "I didn't know."

His eyes go wide. "How could you not know?"

He doesn't believe me. I can see it in his face. He thinks I've been lying to him about everything, still thinks I'm lying now.

My heart is beating fast, and I feel fragile inside, like I might break. "I-" I shake my head. "I have no excuse. I was so broken after losing you. I felt like I had been sawed in half. I wasn't paying attention to anything."

"And then you met Kevin." He says it simply, like I'd closed one chapter in my life and opened another and never given it a second thought.

"He was on the island to attend college. He was older than me, and seemed to have his life and his goals together. I thought you had betrayed me, so I was looking for someone who would never hurt me. I was looking for forever."

"I could have given you forever, Lis. I had wanted to."

Arlo and I are so close now, I can smell the soft citrus scent of his cologne, accenting the hint of chocolate in the air. I could see making a truffle that way, with just a kiss of citrus. His lips are soft and tempting, and I can remember the taste of them. My breathing is coming faster than I'd like it to. But this isn't right. We're different people now. Whatever we once had, it's been replaced.

And yet I can't move. Arlo and I are still in the held breath of revelation and shock, and I'm acutely aware of his physical presence and our closeness in this room.

I turn my face away.

Arlo's in a relationship with someone else. Even if he would let me kiss him, it wouldn't be right.

Besides which, I'm still grieving. So I would hate myself doubly later.

The moment passes. If it was even a moment for Arlo, and not just my imagination, and suddenly the closeness in this room feels cloying and awkward.

Arlo smiles, and I don't think I'm imagining the note of sadness in it. "Look Lis, I hope you find someone new who makes you as happy as Patsy makes me."

That stings, the way it echoes what I'd told him earlier. Even though he meant it kindly. "I had love, and I lost it to a stupid accident."

"I'm not talking about the past." Arlo cuts his eyes towards the door. "Assuming you actually are innocent, you need to find a way forward. And if your way forward is tall and wearing a leather jacket, I just hope you're not making a mistake."

I take a deep chocolate-scented breath. Opening my heart again feels dangerous. But the way Arlo just looked at the door leading out into the shop terrifies me even more. Apparently, Arlo's cop instincts are telling him there's something up between me and Logan. And that's a possibility I'm simply not ready for. I shake my head. "That's not a mistake I plan on making."

He looks surprised. "I'm not sure if I should believe that any more than anything else you've been saying, Miss Star Suspect."

But he at least looks ready now to consider whether I might be telling the truth about everything.

Chapter Sixteen

Logan and I are getting lunch at the same diner where I had met up with Autumn. I have decaf coffee today instead of herbal tea. I usually don't like the brands of decaf restaurants tend to use, but today has been extra stressful and what I've got in my cup today is better than I remember.

I tilt my plate, gesturing towards my fries. The cooks here always give me too many.

Logan takes one, maybe just to be polite, because he says, "I'm more of a tater tot man myself. I still make my mom's recipe for hotdish, but I hate canned soup, so I make the cream of mushroom from scratch."

"What's hotdish?" I'm more curious that he mentioned his mom, but I don't feel comfortable asking details. I know so little about this guy, and I'm trusting him with my life.

He looks a little hurt, honestly. "I don't know how to describe it. You take meat and vegetables and throw them into a casserole dish and put a layer of tater tots on top."

"Like shepherd's pie," I venture.

"Not at all." Now he looks like he's about to laugh. "Look, I'll make it for you tonight, if there's time. But I warn you it's not pretty." He looks down at his phone, getting back to work.

We've already looked at the feed from both cameras inside my shop, at the front and back doors. The back-door camera didn't register anything. The front door camera just showed a flash of motion, before going dead. Logan shows me another video clip. This one is from a camera showing the outside of my shop. I don't know how he got access, and I don't ask.

A figure approaches the door, but it's in a nighttime portion of video, and my front door is at the very edge of the screen. The figure never turns towards the camera. It could be Kaylee. Or it could be a guy with a modest build. Heck, the video is so blurry, it could be me.

If we show this to Arlo, he'd say it *was* me.

I throw up my hands. "Fine. If Arlo wants a better suspect, let's give him one."

Logan eyes me from across the table. "If you're suggesting framing someone, that you'll have to do on your own."

I start to squeak out a response, but the waitress is heading over this way to top off my decaf coffee. There are a number of people I know in here. Aunt Naomi's plumber is over at the counter, drinking coffee by himself. My doctor is at a table by the window – even my former hair stylist, who still doesn't know she's not my current hair stylist, is sitting on the other side of the restaurant. I'm more terrified that she's going to look over here and realize I have a completely different haircut than I am that any of them will notice us and get the wrong idea about me and Logan.

Vanessa tops off my cup, and gives me a very significant wink. Yes. I get it. My bodyguard is very hot.

I drop my voice and tell Logan, "Of course not! Innocent people don't frame people. I'm talking about figuring out who actually killed Emma. I think we need to take a look around her room."

Logan gets up and moves over to my side of the booth, so we can talk more quietly. "Felicity, the police already did that."

I am acutely aware of the warmth from Logan's body, he is sitting so close to me, trapping me between him and the window. "I know that. But they didn't know about Ryker at the time, and they still don't know about Carmen and Paul being sort of together. I don't think Arlo even believes the two deaths are connected, but I have a gut feeling that Ryker's the key to all of this."

And if I can get into Emma's room, I can also take a quick look to see if she stole anything else that belongs to Greetings and Felicitations. It's frustrating how much of a liar Emma was, and at the same time how impossible she was to dislike.

I take a deep breath. I am getting too worked up. My heart keeps racing unpleasantly for a few seconds at a time.

"Will Emma's parents let you in?"

"They won't get home until the morning." They had left me a message that they wanted to come in and talk to me. Seeing as I was the last person to speak to their daughter, and all. I can't believe I'm even thinking of violating their privacy. I have no way of getting into their house anyway. And if I did, I might not even go through with it.

"Hey, are you okay?" Logan studies my face, which I can only assume has become pale and sweaty.

"Are you sure this coffee's decaf?" I try to laugh, but I feel the way I did that one time, early in my treatments, when I had ignored my doctor's orders and knocked back a couple of Vietnamese Coffees in the same day.

Logan snatches my cup off the table and peers into it. "How can you even tell?"

"You can't." I try to lighten the mood. "Maybe I should have hired a food taster."

His face goes red. "That's not the kind of threat I know how to guard against. I want you to take my advice to get out of town. I can fly you somewhere safe."

I smile as confidently as I can. "I'll be fine."

Logan gets up from the table and takes my cup over to Vanessa, who takes it and heads for the back.

Dr. Ricci is heading for my table. "Are you feeling okay?" He sounds almost like he's excited to get to play the hero, since I didn't let him with Emma. He starts to reach for my wrist, to check my pulse.

Logan is back at the table, hovering protectively. He steps between Dr. Ricci and me. He says flatly, "Somebody switched the decaf and full leaded pots back there. It's not likely an accident. The pots are different colors."

Dr Ricci's thick eyebrows arch upwards. "How much coffee have you had."

"Maybe three cups." This feels awkward. It shouldn't be this big a deal. I shrug, trying to make it seem offhand. "I'm sure it was an accident. It's not like people are shooting at me again or anything."

Logan crosses his arms over his chest, emphasizing his built biceps. "People rarely shoot at someone and then just give up."

"But I don't know why someone would want me dead. I still have no idea who broke into my aunt's house, or what they want me to return to them. The voice sounded weird, like a woman trying to project a gravelly voice – but it could have been a guy faking tones going the other direction."

Dr. Ricci looks shocked. "You really have no idea who that intruder was?"

I shake my head. Seriously. Gossip travels at the speed of light on this Island. "There was a break-in at the chocolate shop too. I'm hoping they found whatever they were looking for and will leave me alone."

Logan half-laughs, but Dr. Ricci coughs, like he's choked on the spit in his own mouth.

Logan says, "You can't count on that."

"It seems like you've got someone here to look out for your safety." Dr. Ricci puts his hands in his pockets and beams at Logan. "Good thing too, to catch that kind of mix-up. Maybe it would be safest if you stop drinking coffee altogether."

"I'll take that under advisement," I say.

"Good." Dr. Ricci smiles. He waggles his eyebrows in a gesture that says *You should hold onto this one*. Meaning Logan, who hopefully can't see the gesture. Even my doctor likes the idea of me and Logan. "You should probably lie down for a little while. If you feel worse instead of better, go directly to the hospital."

"I'll track her vitals," Logan offers. "I can grab a portable blood pressure monitor."

Dr. Ricci's eyebrows go up again. "Aren't you just unexpected." He turns back towards me. When he pulls his hands out of his pockets, I get the impression there's something different. Had he been holding something before? "I still never did get a chance to look at those rare books."

"I'll have the store open for a while tomorrow. Come in then."

"Let's call it a date." Ricci turns and heads back to his table.

Logan drops back on the bench next to me, and this time, instead of feeling trapped, I feel protected. He waves away Vanessa when she tries to bring me a new cup of decaf. "What was that in that guy's hand?"

I pick up a French Fry. Surely that's still safe to eat at least. "I don't know."

He casts a skeptical glance at my fries, but doesn't try to stop me from eating them. "I didn't like the way he was holding it. Like a weapon."

"He's a doctor, Logan." I'm afraid my bodyguard is getting paranoid. Or maybe feeling in over his head, since he's taken a client who could be taken out with a cup of coffee. "He probably holds everything assertively."

"Which books were he talking about?"

I'm beginning to wish that I had never decided to sell books. I should have just stuck to chocolate. "I have a selection of books that I've picked up on my travels. Maybe he's interested in one of those. Because I don't see him in the kitchen using one of the cookbooks to make chocolate cupcakes, and he doesn't strike me as someone who's into Jane Austen."

"Are you worried that the book he wants might have been stolen?"

"I doubt it. The travel books are in the locked case, and that wasn't disturbed. Which is weird, right? Whoever broke in had no problem with the front door. They have no problems picking locks. Why take the less valuable books, but leave the case alone?"

"I don't know," Logan admits.

I glance around. Half the people in this restaurant keep glancing over at me. "I'm feeling a lot better. I wish people would stop staring."

Outside the window, I can see Dr. Ricci getting into a black Acura, so there goes medical help if I need it.

Logan waves Vanessa over and asks for the check. Despite the fact that he's working for me, he drops a bill on the table to cover it. "Come on."

He offers a hand to help me out of the booth.

"Where are we going?" I let him help me up, trying not to think about how nice his hand feels supporting mine. I have a brief moment of horror that maybe Naomi bribed him to take me to my grandmother's. I'll go on my own, thank you very much. When I'm ready.

He leans close to me and says very softly, "To Emma's. That's what you wanted, right?"

My heart jolts. I hadn't expected him to agree to go. And sneaking into someone's home is not exactly the kind of thing I normally do. I think I'd hoped he would talk me out of it. But I can't say that without sounding stupid.

When we get into his Mustang, I say, "Aren't we supposed to wait for the cover of darkness or something?"

Logan starts the car. "You'll look a lot more suspicious showing up at Emma's door in the middle of the night. If it's anything other than custom locks, I can have us in in thirty seconds." He looks over at me. "Are you sure you're feeling better?"

"A bit." I take a deep breath, trying to gauge how I'm doing. "My heart rate's still high, and I feel a bit rubbery. But I can rest on the way over to Emma's."

But I'm too jittery and wired to actually rest. I'm glad Logan didn't want to wait hours before heading out to do something productive. I try to relax, which is difficult when we're heading to Emma's to do something illegal. I'm going to have a heart attack on the front steps, when you couple the caffeine with my rising anxiety.

Logan stops in at a drug store and makes me come in with him while he buys a wrist-style blood pressure monitor. He is seriously worried, and makes me take a reading in the car. It's high, but not dangerously so. He starts the car up again and heads for Emma's.

"Are you ready for your first B&E?" Logan's tone says he's teasing me.

"I thought you said we were just entering. But if you're going to start breaking things . . ." I'm bantering again. I shouldn't be doing that. It's not fair to Logan. Though he seems to have no problem with it. "I thought my security guy would be trying to talk me out of this."

"What? Because my dad's a cop? And my sister's a cop? I didn't wind up the smashing success I am by following the rules." He's made it clear he thinks of himself as anything but a success. His sarcasm is obviously covering a source of pain.

I hesitate. "I don't know anything about your family."

"I assumed someone would have told you." He clears his throat. "One of the biggest pastimes in this town is gossip."

I blink, confused. "Arlo said he couldn't find any evidence you exist before you took that security gig."

Logan glances at me, surprised, before returning his eyes to the road. "You screw up bad enough as a cop, and the records tend to get sealed. But that doesn't stop people from theorizing on the Internet. Even if they got it all totally wrong."

My face goes hot. I don't want this guy to know I was prying into his past. But I'm trusting him with my life. I need this to make sense. "Logan, I Googled you. I didn't find anything either."

He sighs. "Look under Michael. I used to go by my middle name, because the guys on the force used to tease me about the Gilmore Girls."

"But that means they actually watched the Gilmore Girls," I point out.

"I know, right?" He smiles, though he doesn't take his eyes off the road. "I prefer the Wolverine jokes."

"Because that Logan's a hero?"

Logan shrugs. "Maybe. But after I screwed up the case, I wound up with dangerous guys looking for me. I sweated it out in Europe for a couple of years, until someone else scooped them up. The gig with Mari was supposed to be my second chance. But then I messed that up too." He pulls up to a stop light. He looks at me, searching my face. "Now do you see why I was shocked you'd hired me?"

"Maybe."

"Do you regret it?"

Should I regret hiring Logan? He's had two huge failures, with the implication that people have died as a result of both. And Arlo had as much as said he thinks Logan is a bad bodyguard. If Logan fails again, I'm the one who could wind up dead.

But I trust Logan. There's logic behind everything he's done so far. And I haven't felt in danger since I hired him.

My heart is still beating too fast, but I manage to slow down enough to make my response sound serious. "Absolutely not. Everybody deserves a third chance." I put a hand on his jacket. "Besides, you already saved me once already. Death by coffee would have been too sadly ironic."

He smiles, and his eyes crinkle in a way that melts me inside. I've got to get a higher melt temperature. After all, Logan just confirmed my original assessment: he's too dangerous to be a real part of my life. Especially considering the look on his face when he'd talked about his years in Europe.

The light changes. Logan moves us forward. "I wouldn't be offended if you decided to replace me."

"Who am I going to get in the middle of a hurricane?" I quip.

"I could make some recommendations-"

"I was kidding." I study him as he drives, his earnest eyes, his strong jaw. "Just tell me you've learned from your mistakes."

"Oh, yeah. I'm not going to presume again that I know better than people I'm working with. And I'm never going to let myself fall in love with another client."

Wow. I'd thought some of his banter had been bordering on flirtation. And I was worrying about having to let him down easy. But apparently, that's just Logan being friendly.

"Fair enough," I say, but the words sound funny, obvious I'm trying to hide feeling let down.

"Aren't you at least going to Google me again?" Logan asks.

"Why?" I lean my face against the window's cool glass. It is sprinkling rain outside. "You said they got it all wrong."

My phone rings, startling me. It's Arlo.

"Just curiosity," Arlo asks me. "But did you know Ryker Brody?"

Whatever Arlo's trying to do, it isn't idle curiosity. "No, I didn't."

"How about Emma? Did she know him?"

"I have no idea. Why don't you check her phone? You guys took her purse." Wait. Could whatever the intruder keeps looking for have been in Emma's purse? "Just curiosity," I ask Arlo, "but what did she have in there, anyway?"

"Ah ha, nice try, Lis. I'm the one investigating here. Just answer my question."

"No, Emma never mentioned Ryker Brody. I never heard the name before he washed up on the beach. Why is that important all of a sudden?"

Arlo hesitates, maybe deciding whether or not he is giving too much away. "There's only two things that could have happened to Mr. Brody. One, he went for a swim, had a heart attack in the water, and wound up at the bottom of the Gulf. Only, he's in his twenties, and his medical records don't show any prior issues. So more likely, someone killed him and dumped his body in the Gulf. Which is strange enough in itself. But that's the second person under thirty to have a heart attack in two weeks. And this guy turns out to have a six-million-dollar life insurance policy payable to someone whose number *is* in Emma's phone."

"Who?" I ask breathlessly.

Arlo laughs. "I told you, I can't just give information. I probably said too much already."

Fine. I hang up with Arlo.

But I still hear the echo of his laugh. I just – I don't like feeling like the villain in his life. I was young and irrational, and I broke his heart, and he's still not over it, not completely. I don't know how to make that right. I don't even know if that's possible.

But here in the car with Logan, I can't exactly break down and cry. I have to do something constructive. Maybe if I can figure out who killed Emma, I can at least bow out gracefully from Arlo's life. And at least leave him knowing that, even if I am a villain, I'm not a criminal.

I call Tiff. She has a friend in the insurance industry, and like Logan said, the main pastime here is gossip. It takes all of about five minutes for me to find out that the mystery policy was taken out in benefit of Ryker's new girlfriend – Monaco Ryan, which does not sound like a real name.

Chapter Seventeen

"We're here," Logan says.

I've never been to Emma's place before. I had no idea what to expect, but this is nicer than most homes in the neighborhood, many of which are tiny and poorly built. Emma's is a two-story historic-style home with bay windows that make up one front corner. Not a true Victorian like the one Aunt Naomi is fixing up, but more recent construction with nods to the past. The vinyl siding is pale pink, with tall gray shutters. There's a carport to the left of the house, in front of a detached garage.

Logan parks the mustang under the carport. It doesn't look like anyone has been out here to do storm proofing.

"I feel like we should drag the patio furniture into the garage," I tell Logan.

"You shouldn't lift anything until your blood pressure goes down." He gestures to the monitor in my lap. "We can't do that anyway, not if you don't want anyone to know we were here."

I shudder. "Arlo already thinks of me as his prime suspect. The last thing I need is to get arrested. He'd start accusing me of destroying evidence."

Logan looks troubled. "You know that anything we find here can't be used as evidence, right?"

"I'm fine with that," I tell him, even though I hadn't realized it. "I just want to follow any clue that will help me clear my name."

"Then be confident, but quiet, and let's get in and out as quickly as possible." He takes his keys out of the ignition and reaches over me to open the glove box. He slips on a pair of cotton gloves, and tosses a pair to me. I wonder exactly what kind of guy I've hired. I mean, why does he even have these?

As he pulls a couple of small metal tools the size of nail files out of a flat back case, he notices my hesitation. "Are you feeling okay to do this?"

"I'm still a little shaky, but I'll be fine." I open my door and get out of the car. I just can't believe I'm about to start digging through a dead girl's things. Like I said, I'm not a rule breaker. Or am I now? Does the fact that I'm not backing out of this change how I think about myself? Challenge my need for order? For boundaries? I'm seriously overthinking this.

I follow Logan up to the house's front door, where, as promised, he unlocks it. For a second, I feel a sense of un-named anxiety. And then it hits me. That security video from the shop had shown someone with an equal ease with locks. But putting a name to the feeling makes me realize how silly it is. After Logan had opened up to me, I can't really see him skulking around and shooting at me.

"Wait here," Logan says. He goes in to clear the house.

I feel conspicuous, standing where Emma's neighbors can see me. I step inside, closing the door behind me. I can hear Logan moving through the space. Right next to me, the wall is covered with photographs, many of them Emma at different ages. In some of them, she's standing smiling with her parents.

They must be grieving horribly right now.

I've been thinking so much of the implications of her death, of the puzzle behind it, that I haven't processed the reality that Emma's actually gone. Her funeral is tomorrow, mere hours after her parents return.

"Okay. You can come on up." Logan's voice is coming from the top of the stairs.

I climb the stairs slowly, trying not to stress my body any more than I have. Then I step past him, towards an open door. Emma's room is elegant, with everything done in neutral tones. She has a queen-sized bed with a satiny comforter made of blocks containing six different textures. I'm fascinated by this whole other side to the girl I had thought I knew.

Her laptop, hot pink in contrast to the rest of the room, is sitting on her desk. This could be easier than I thought.

I point at the computer. "Why didn't the cops take that?"

"They probably just cloned it." Logan takes out his phone. "Like I'm about to do."

Logan opens the laptop, and quickly bypasses Emma's password. He scrolls through her files, copying everything onto his phone. "I'm not seeing much here. I didn't expect anything obvious. The police have already been through this room."

"You trust them?" I'm joking, trying to belie my own nervousness as I go through Emma's dresser drawers – with a lot more consideration than that intruder had used when going through mine.

"Well, yeah." Logan takes the question seriously. "I have friends in local law enforcement in Houston, and the cops under Arlo's command have a reputation for competence and thoroughness. I've met Arlo multiple times. I don't know what the issues are between you two, but I like him."

"I don't think he likes you," I tell him.

Logan smiles. "I know. Can you blame him?"

For someone who doesn't think he has skills, I find it alarming how easily Logan cracks the password to get into Emma's e-mail, which doesn't seem to have a lot of sensitive information, just a bunch of group mails about an upcoming wedding. The groom's name sounds vaguely familiar – like maybe he's a TV chef, I think. There are a few e-mails from people in Hollywood, turning her down for something. And she has a ton of coupon subscriptions.

I ask, "What's in her trash folder?"

Logan clicks over to it. There's an e-mail from Kaylee, demanding Emma pull down a blog post. I pull up Emma's alter ego's blog on my phone. I do a search inside the site, but there's nothing about Kaylee.

I tell Logan, "She must have taken the post down. Whatever it was."

I open the desk drawer. There's a yellow manila envelope, on top of a stack of file folders. I open the envelope, and find receipts for a two-thousand-dollar bridesmaid dress, a plane ticket to Paris, and what adds up to a good chunk of the expenses for a bridal shower. I gasp. "These dates match up to the transfers of funds Emma had stolen from my shop. She was stealing from me to go to a wedding."

I can't decide if that is more or less upsetting than when I thought she might be paying back dangerous people who were threatening her life. It certainly makes me sad. Emma had had a life off-line. She had had a real-world boyfriend, at least until recently. And a real family. I think about those pictures downstairs, with her smiling on family vacations or posed in a studio between her parents. There's nothing with her family or with Paul on her social media. She's always alone, or with random groups of people. Sometimes, the same people -- the friends she'd been proud to belong with. And she'd felt the need to steal to impress them. There's something tragic about that, and about the way her life ended before she could see through all the falseness.

I examine the next document under the receipts.

"Hey, what's this?" I hold up a slip of paper with Paul's name on it.

Logan takes it from me. "That's paperwork for Emma having bailed her ex-boyfriend out of jail." He points at a date. "A week before she died."

The two of them were broken up way before then. I scrunch up my nose. "I really will have to have that follow-up chat with Paul."

The only other thing in the envelope is the paperwork for the Lexus.

"Felicity, there's nothing here pointing to Emma having been in trouble. Or to a motive anyone had for killing her."

"I know." We really should get out of here. But I don't move to leave. "I have to see what kind of bridesmaid's dress costs two thousand dollars. I should at least see what I've been paying for."

I open the closet and pull out the conspicuous garment bag. I unzip it. There's a pale purple satin dress. It's beautiful, but it doesn't look *that* different from the one I had worn to Tiff's wedding. And that had cost all of three hundred dollars. I lift the dress up to look at the hem work.

A thick white envelope falls out of the garment bag, landing silently on Emma's thick carpet.

I pick it up and unfold the two separate sets of contracts inside. As I read through them, things start falling into place and I find myself getting more and more excited. "Logan, I figured out what would make Emma so desperate to keep up her fake persona that she'd go broke buying a car. There are a lot of zeros on these pages. And that wedding that she was going to – I think it's to solidify a guest list of her own. For her show."

These are contracts Emma has signed for a book deal *and* for her own lifestyle show on a major network – under her alter ego's name. She's got a fake ID in here too – including a passport. Which is way beyond just writing under a pen name.

"Ryker's insurance policy was probably paying out to a fake name," I say. "Do you think this is the connection? She needed the fakes, and reaching out to get them put her in touch with dangerous people?"

"Possible."

Downstairs, the door opens. People start walking up the stairs, talking softly.

Logan strips the gloves off his hands and gestures for me to do the same. He whispers, "I thought you said Emma's parents weren't coming home until tomorrow."

"They aren't."

The voices are getting louder, as they come down the hall. "Sargent Romero said to look for anything connecting the two victims."

"It's the cops." I push Logan towards the room's separate bathroom. "This is my problem."

The door opens just as I close the one to the bathroom. I freeze, my hands up. "Hi, guys."

It gets awkward, as soon as the two officers start asking me what I'm doing here.

There's the sound of running water. Logan steps out of the bathroom. "She's with me. We came by to stormproof the house."

By the time we leave the police station over two hours later, I'm pretty sure Arlo likes Logan even less. And he's not a huge fan of me right now, either. He wanted to hold me on suspicion of murder, but apparently Logan has a virtual Get Out of Jail Free card.

And I'm more confused than ever. I'd almost wanted Arlo to put me in jail. I'd felt like I deserved it, looking at him again and knowing how much I'd hurt him. It's stupid. By the time they're thirty-two, who still has chemistry with their high-school sweetheart? I know maybe two people who'd married someone straight out of high school and are still together. So . . . why do I feel like we could have been one of those exceptions?

Arlo didn't even care that we'd found the contracts. If he believes they had anything to do with Emma's death, he's hiding it well. If he's still thinking about me and how badly I'd screwed up any hope we'd had for happiness, the way I've been thinking about him and how cruel I'd been, he's hiding that well too.

But I'd spent the time Arlo had left us waiting productively distracting myself -- texting people, and making a plan. I can try to fix something, at least. And at least the rain has paused.

"Where are we heading?" Logan asks as we pull out of the parking lot and turn back towards the Seawall.

"I finally got ahold of Paul. And if he doesn't have the information we need, I think we should swing by the bookstore."

I feel like I've gained so much self-confidence since trepidatiously trying to question Carmen. Can that have been just a few days ago?

Logan nods. "Where are you meeting Paul?"

"It's actually back the other way. He wants to meet at his dad's junkyard."

Logan slams on the breaks, stopping the Mustang in the center of the road. "Absolutely not. Seriously, Felicity, do you *want* to die?"

"No. But I want him to feel safe too."

"Paul doesn't feel safe anywhere the police might show up because he's a car thief." That had been clear enough from the file Logan had gotten access to.

I run my hand across the dash. "I thought it would be okay since I have you with me. I'm not stupid enough to go somewhere that remote by myself."

"And I'm not Superman. It would take a whole team to make a location like that safe." His face is unyielding, an element of authority in it I've not seen before. "Change the meet."

I text Paul, explaining that I've been advised to meet on neutral ground.

We wind up at McDonalds.

By the time we make it through the doors, Paul's already standing in line, and he waves us over to join him. "Want anything, Mrs. Koerber? My treat."

"We already had lunch," I protest, since fast food is not my thing, but he looks disappointed, so I say, "Maybe some fries?"

Paul, who's about my height, keeps glancing up at Logan.

"Paul, this is Logan," I finally say. "He's private security."

Paul shakes hands with Logan. He nods down at their hands. "Does it hurt when the claws come out?" I get Paul's need to make a joke. He's probably never seen anybody traveling with a bodyguard before. Heck, *I've* never seen anyone with a bodyguard before either. And I'd never imagined I'd need one.

But I know Logan's not a fan of the Wolverine references. He responds by withdrawing his hand, crossing his arms over his chest and looking intimidating.

By the time we get our trays and find a table – Logan chooses one in a corner, where he puts both himself and me against the wall – Paul looks nervous. Which isn't want we want.

Logan points with the straw sticking out of his giant strawberry shake. "You are a hard man to find."

Paul runs his fingers across his eyebrows, emphasizing the notch. "I'm going to school in San Antonio. I want to do something different with my life."

"Good choice," Logan says. "There's not much of a future in auto theft."

I give Logan a warning look, then turn to Paul, and say diplomatically, "What are you studying?"

"Computers. I have an interest in electronic security." He looks down at his tray, then makes eye contact with me. "It's not what you think. I want to make a better life for myself, and for my son. I don't want him to be tempted when Grandpa tells him how to make a quick buck."

"You have a son?" Logan sounds skeptical.

Paul takes out his phone and shows me the lock screen pic. It's him, holding a little boy up like the kid's flying. The kid's maybe four. "I got married when I was nineteen. I thought it was forever, and it sure seemed like it when Sebastian came into the picture, but my wife got other ideas." He shrugs. "You adapt."

"By finding Emma. And then Carmen." It sounds harsher than I'd meant it.

Paul nods. "There was a time when I thought Emma might be the one."

Logan asks him, "Why'd she dump you?"

"I called it quits with her," Paul says, a bit defensively. "Some of Emma's friends thought she was someone she wasn't, and she'd taken to stealing bigger and bigger things just to keep up the pretense. I told her that she needed to let her friends at least know who she really was. That it was strangling her being a fake, and I couldn't stand to watch."

Logan gestures with his cup again. "You don't have a lot of room to talk. You're telling everybody you want a better life, but a week ago Emma bailed you out after you'd stolen another car. They only let you go because they think you can lead them to the larger auto theft ring."

"That was a favor gone wrong. You see why I have to find something different?" Paul asks. "Emma liked bad boys, but she wasn't bad herself. Which is why it didn't work out between us. She didn't have it in her to be a jerk, so what these so-called friends thought mattered too much to her. She didn't have money like them, so what? They needed to like her for her, or they weren't her friends."

"Did you know that she was stealing from me, in order to impress these friends?" I ask.

Paul nods. "Emma said she intended to pay that money back, after she got back from Paris. She said she had something big in the works, that was going to take care of all of it. Her philosophy was always, 'fake it until you make it.' I hadn't talked to her in a while, until that night she bailed me out, but apparently that philosophy finally worked."

"Was that why you were so desperate to talk to her at the grand opening?" I remember thinking maybe he'd been stalking her. "Did you want to get back with her now that she's made it?"

Paul shakes his head. "No. I told you, I wasn't going back. Emma told me she needed the money back from the bail right away. She had a plan to entertain some blogger friends who had dropped into town unexpectedly. But I didn't want Carmen to see me with Emma and get the wrong idea."

"You don't think Emma might have stolen or borrowed money from the wrong people? That's a common way to wind up dead." Logan asks.

Paul's chin juts out. "She wouldn't have tried to do that on her own. If she'd wanted a . . . loan . . . she would have asked me, because I know people."

"That doesn't make sense," I say. "If she wasn't involved with shady people, who would have had a reason to murder her?"

We all look at each other, stumped. As the silence drags on, Paul starts eating his burger. After a few bites, he puts it down. "It all comes back to the chocolate shop, right? Could the killing have been random, to get the shop closed? Or could the real target have been Carmen – or even you?"

I gulp, my mouth suddenly grown dry. "But who would have a reason to want to kill me?"

Logan makes an ironic noise, deep in his throat. Because, right. I'd seen a need to hire private security.

Who in this town might have a reason to want to ruin me? Or to want me dead?

I've been operating from the assumption that I was targeted because the person who broke into my home thought I had something Emma would have given me. But if she was killed by mistake, that theory wouldn't work.

Paul has to be wrong. The only person who'd been overtly unkind to me since I came back home was Kaylee. But even she didn't seem *that* angry.

Arlo's upset at me, but he's hardly the kind of person to kill two people just to frame me for their murders.

I shake my head and pick up a couple of the greasy fries. "That doesn't make sense either."

But could I have upset someone badly enough for them to want me gone, and not even know I'd done it? I shudder.

Chapter Eighteen

Logan holds the door for me. I take a deep breath, and then step into Island Breeze. The door chimes as Logan crosses the threshold and lets it swing closed behind him.

This thing keeps coming back to books, just as much as chocolate – the boxes of books that went missing from the shop, the books Carmen said she took home, even the fact that the intruder at my aunt's house had scattered the books in her kitchen. And – I'd entirely forgotten what my new hairdresser had said about the guy showing up the day after the estate sale asking about the very books I'd bought. Or at least about the room that contained them. It wouldn't have seemed odd if Emma, who had been so desperate for money, had wanted to steal the volumes. Or if someone who knew she needed money had asked her to steal them – and then gotten angry when she'd failed.

The bookstore is cluttered, in a welcoming kind of way, with overstuffed stacks that go all the way to the ceiling. The parts of the walls I can see are red brick, and there's a little area off to one side with a cluster of tables. I haven't been in here since I came for one of Autumn's signings, eight or nine years ago. If Kaylee owned it then, I don't remember seeing her.

"Hi there," Kaylee says, as she comes around the corner, pushing a cart piled with even more books. But then she sees who we are, and the smile dies on her face. "Oh."

Kaylee's wearing a short-sleeved sweater made out of the same distinctive yarn Sonya had been crocheting with when we'd gone to Chalupa's. Is Kaylee on Sonya's good side too? How is it that Kaylee and I have gotten off on such the wrong foot?

"Can we talk?" I ask. "Just for a minute?"

Kaylee picks up a book off the cart. "I don't think so."

There's something so cold about the way she's holding that book – for a second I really think she might be the killer, and that she had indeed gotten Emma by mistake.

I shake off the feeling. She's not a murderer. Probably. But she did have an issue with Emma. "I just wanted to ask about that blog post Emma wrote." I swallow my nervousness against a dry throat.

Kaylee's face goes pale. "I thought she took that down."

"She did." At least I think she did. "But I want to know if you're still mad about it."

Whatever *it* is.

"Well, yeah. At least I was. Until . . . you know." Kaylee puts the book back on the cart. "But Emma had her blog under a pen name, so she, of all people, should have understood a person's need for anonymity. Can you imagine what it would be like if my children found out I'm Kay Sinclair?"

I suck in a breath, trying to hide my surprise. Seriously, I must have misheard.

"Who's Kay Sinclair?" Logan asks.

"A rather prolific romance author," I tell him, trying to reconcile the beautiful prose of one of my favorite contemporary authors – one who writes empathetic, open-hearted characters – with the chilly response I'd gotten from Kaylee. "And at times, a rather racy one."

Kaylee nods. She turns to Logan, since I seem in the know about her secret, and he doesn't, and explains, "Emma had talked about it in her blog – which thankfully, nobody I know read. I got her to take it down. But then she tried to name-drop me to my agent. Becky called me to ask if I had really recommended she'd take a look at this random girl's lifestyle and entertainment manuscript. I confronted Emma about it, the day she died. Emma said it didn't matter. She'd already accepted representation with another agent, and had sold the book."

"That's what the fight was about, then," I say. "At the store. When you poked her in the arm."

Kaylee nods. "I was angry."

"You poisoned her coffee to get back at her?" Logan asks.

"No! Of course not." Kaylee blinks and points at me. "She did." I can practically see it register: if I'd killed Emma, then what was I doing, trying to figure out if anyone else had a motive. "Didn't she?"

I let the accusation go. I ask Kaylee, "Did you ask Emma to steal the volumes of Sense and Sensibility? Or did she offer to take them, and ask you to set a price?"

Kaylee's thin, perfectly plucked, brows furrow. "Did someone steal them?"

Well, that's a no.

"Not exactly. But a number of books have come up missing."

But what if someone had approached her about stealing them? And not just because first editions are valuable? What if the books in my aunt's house are the key to a puzzle code? Or a cryptic treasure map? Or someone's hidden will? Or . . . something?

"I don't take stolen merchandise," Kaylee says, gesturing at the mostly used books around her. "It's not like I'm desperate for money." If she really is Kay Sinclair, she's one of the most successful romance writers in the country, so that's probably true. "And I don't know anyone else who wouldn't just pay you for the books, if they wanted them. The only reason I can think for someone stealing books is if they didn't want the books to be able to be traced back to them. Or if they're broke."

I'd looked at the Sense and Sensibility volumes. There hadn't been anything unique about them. Except for those wonky endpapers. But – Autumn's mystery man had asked if those endpapers might have been a later repair. What if it's not a repair -- what if there's something written on the other side? The key or the code or the will. It's unlikely, but now that I've got it in my head, I can't escape the nagging *what if*?

"Logan, I think I should get home. There's something I need to take another look at." I remember how delicately he'd repaired that torn map. "And I will need your help."

"Hey," Kaylee says. "If you want to be polite, you could at least buy something."

So I do – the latest Kay Sinclair.

She doesn't offer to sign it.

Back at my aunt's house, I open the closet door. The box with the books from my shop is gone. My heartbeat rises again.

"Aunt Naomi!" I call.

Logan's hand lands on my shoulder. He guides me away from the closet, into the living room. "You should sit down for a minute. You just went all pale again."

"But the books . . . if someone broke in again . . ."

"I'll look for your aunt."

I sit on the leather sofa, right in the middle. That's always been my favorite spot in any living room, ever since I was a kid. In the middle of the conversation, in the heart of everything. Until recently. My favorite spot since coming to my Aunt's house is the overstuffed blue chair on the far side of the room.

I feel awkward sitting where Logan left me, and still nervous. My heartbeat's high. I might have been in trouble from the caffeine earlier, but I think I'm just scared now. I hear Knightley drinking loudly from his water bottle, back in the kitchen. *Click, click, click* of the little metal ball.

"She's not here," Logan says, as he comes back into the room. "But neither is her car."

I try calling. Which I should have done right away.

Aunt Naomi picks up on the first ring. "Felicity! Are you okay?"

"I'm fine."

"But you're practically sobbing into the phone."

"I think whoever killed Emma broke in again. The books in the hall closet are gone."

Aunt Naomi laughs into the phone. "They're not gone."

"They aren't?" I'm confused. Relieved, and confused.

"I'm sorry. I didn't realize there was anything important to you in there. I'm redoing that closet, with more shelves. I'm at the store right now."

"So where did everything go?" I'm starting to get my heartbeat back under control again.

"I stacked it in that empty room in the back."

I'm up off the sofa, heading for the room.

There's the box. I open it. There are the three books, safe and sound, still guarding whatever secret those covers hold.

I hand Volume 1 to Logan, open to the back.

He takes it. "What am I looking at?"

"I think those back endpapers are replacements, or that the original sheets got re-glued."

"You want to take these off?" Logan examines the edges of the paper. "This could destroy the books' value."

"I know that." I think about how excited I'd been when I first found these books. *Sense and Sensibility* had been Kevin's favorite Austen. It had felt like these books were meant for me – and yet I hadn't hesitated to plan to sell them. What does that say about me? "If they're ruined, I'll keep them."

Assuming I still want to, after we see what's inside.

Logan holds his hand out for the other two books. "I'll be careful."

"I'm hoping you can keep those endpapers in one piece," I tell him. "In case I'm wrong, and there's nothing on the other side."

"Do you have a paring knife?" he asks.

We go around to the kitchen. I hand Logan the knife from the block, and he takes it over to the island. He slides the knife between the edge of the paper and the cover, cutting through the glue that binds them together.

Something tugs at the bottom of my pants leg. I've been watching Logan so intensely that I jump, bumping Knightley, who's down on the floor, begging for attention. I reach down to give him a few apologetic pets behind the ears, but I keep my eyes on Logan. Knightley starts chinning my shoe, reminding the world that I'm his, a sure sign that he's happy and comfortable. I'm glad one of us is. I stand up, to watch Logan's progress. There's nothing visible inside the back cover of the first volume. He's moved on to the second book.

The knife moves faster than it should, and Logan freezes. "I almost cut the paper. I don't think this was glued on all the way."

He edges the knife around the outside part of the paper, making small cuts in the glue, opening out the endpaper from the cover.

"There's something else in there." I pull out a thin piece of paper. It's a hand-written ledger page, covered with letters and numbers with about twenty entries, but no key or way to make sense of them. The handwriting is blocky and generic.

"Look at this." Logan points to the middle column. "That has to be payments."

The last entry is RB -- 20000 – HFBKGSMR. If Logan thinks it's a list of names and payments, that means RB received 20000. For something.

"So if someone's been desperate to get this list back, that means my hairdresser's grandfather was probably blackmailing them." I look to Logan for confirmation. "Right?"

Logan blinks. "Your hairdresser's who?"

Once I explain who my hairdresser's grandfather was, and how I'd acquired the books, Logan agrees. "But we don't know who was being blackmailed. Or why this person would have killed Emma for failing to retrieve the book." Logan peers at the paper, as though the answers will suddenly appear.

"Or meant to kill me for having it." I swallow dry panic. "After all, Emma could still have had another go at the books, so getting rid of her seems premature."

"That is another possibility, yes." Logan makes eye contact, those green eyes sharp and intense. "Can I just say again that getting out of town may be the best way to deal with this? I can fly you to Los Angeles, which has better beaches than here. And doesn't have a hurricane getting ready to crash into it."

"We still don't know where that stalled storm is heading," I point out. "Besides, I thought you said you couldn't fly in this weather."

"I'd make an exception." He looks at the window, which is still boarded up, then opens up an app on his phone called ForeFlight, which shows a complicated map. "But you'd have to make the decision soon. Probably within the next couple of hours. The weather has cleared up for now, but as soon as Bertha gets on the move, it won't stay that way."

I consider it. I have a chance to fly away from all of this, now that I know how dangerous what I've gotten involved in really is.

Logan snaps a picture of the list. "I'll forward this to Arlo while you pack. Then once the police handle this, you'll be safe to come back home."

"I haven't said I'm going anywhere." I take the list from him and fold it up again. I tuck it into my purse. "If I don't open my shop again for regular hours soon, I can kiss my business goodbye. And I'm so close to putting all of this together. There needs to be justice for Emma. And for Ryker Brody."

And it hits me. Ryker Brody. RB. The last entry on the list had been RB – 20000. Which could mean that someone had been paid $20,000 to kill Ryker Brody.

And it doesn't take a genius to figure out who would have wanted Ryker dead.

When Mindi had been doing my hair, she'd mentioned that her grandfather had had a heart attack. Which seems to be going around lately. The whole scenario starts to unfurl in my brain. Whoever our killer is – let's go ahead and call her Carmen, since my surf-loving assistant is the only person who connects all of this -- she finds out that this old guy has a copy of her hit list. She's facing blackmail. So she kills him, assuming that the list will be somewhere easy to find. Somehow, the guy gives her a hint about *Sense and Sensibility*, and it takes her a minute to figure out what that means, and by the time she does, the books are gone. She could have easily paid some guy to contact Mindi about the estate sale – or she could even have someone working with her.

I show up with the books at the store. I'd assumed Emma was the one who moved the box with the volumes in towards the back door. But it could have been Carmen, intending to take them before I discovered the altered endpapers. But then I'd locked up the books, and maybe she figured I found the list, and was trying to taunt the killer out into the open. So I have to die. She knows I'm not supposed to have caffeine. If she'd managed to slip me that overdose instead of Emma, it would have been chalked up to natural causes, or at worst an accident.

But she kills Emma by accident. I don't know how she made that big of a mistake, though. Or why she would frame me by poisoning her own dog. It's the loose thread to all of this that's still worrying me.

But, whatever happened, she's a killer for hire, who -- according to the lines on the ledger -- has quietly offed at least 23 people without getting caught. Having realized I'm not giving up the investigation, she manages to get those two coffee pots switched at the café. She knew Logan and I were heading there for lunch.

It should be simple enough to find out if she was in the restaurant at some point before we got there. If she wasn't, that alone might prove her innocent.

I'm not ready to present all of this to Logan, though, so I go into my office and make a quick call to the café. Vanessa confirms that Carmen was there for breakfast, hours before Logan and I showed up. So even if she'd switched the pots, the error might have been corrected, or the coffee refilled before it even got to me. Unless she'd done something more creatively devious?

Chapter Nineteen

I get Logan to drive me across town, and now I'm worried that Carmen's roommate won't be home. I'm convinced she's involved with Ryker's murder. Because logically, who else would have wanted him dead?

Bruce is in the tiny front yard, lazing in the sun in the one dry spot provided by a slightly sloping sheet of metal someone is half-done turning into a sculpture. The house is one-story brick, with Southwestern styling. It's a nice neighborhood, which probably explains why Carmen needs two roommates to live here.

Bruce wags his tail. I've met him enough times, he remembers me. He doesn't even bother getting up until Logan and I get close to the door. Then he comes over and stands by us, obviously hoping to get inside when we do. I still don't want to believe that Carmen would be cold enough to poison him, just to strengthen her alibi. But if she's killed over twenty people, who knows.

A hand written sign says *Please Do Not Ring Bell!*

I had sent a text to Autumn while we were on the way over here, telling her she was right, after all.

Now she texts back, *About the books having a later repair? I knew it!*

It's not the right time to correct her. I knock on the door.

A dark-haired white woman, maybe a year or two younger than Carmen, answers it. She wipes a hand across sleepy-looking grey-blue eyes and glances down at her phone. Behind her, there's a little girl playing with a video game controller, oblivious to anything going on outside the flat screen. The room is cheerful, with a striped cloth sofa, a rocking chair and a solid red easy chair. The floor is ivory-colored fake wood, and there are riotously-colored paintings on the wall.

I'm a little bit flustered, because I have no idea what the person I'm looking for is named. I ask, "Are you Carmen's roommate?"

When she nods, I add. "Are you the nurse or the artist?"

"I'm the nurse. Violet's asleep." She moves forward, blocking the doorway, instead of inviting us in. She glances up at Logan. "Carmen's not here. I can tell her you stopped by, Ms. . . . "

"Koerber. I'm Carmen's boss. But it's you I wanted to talk to . . ." I trail off, implicitly asking for her name in return.

"Tasha." Her gaze flicks to the little girl, then back to me. "Do you have any ID?"

I pull up an interview of me from the local paper, with my name splashed across it, and me smiling, fanning out bars with Knightley printed on them, the chocolate shop in the background. "This help?"

Reluctantly, Tasha lets us in. She's still perusing the news article, when my phone lights up with another text. I can see my phone well enough to read, *Or was I right about the killer's identity?*

Tasha's eyes go wide. She hands me back the phone. "I'm not sure this is a good time."

But that guilty look told me all I need to know. She has to be the person who paid Carmen to kill her husband. Maybe even the one who gave her the concentrated caffeine to do it with.

"Where'd you get the $20,000?" I ask.

Tasha backs away from me. "I don't know what you're talking about."

Though it's obvious that she does.

"I think you do," I insist. I point at the little girl. "And I get it. Ryker was being a jerk, and you didn't want to lose your daughter to someone who wouldn't love her the way you do. But she's going to want to know what happened to her father."

Tasha's face goes bone white, and her expression crumbles. She crumbles. "No," she insists, but the word comes out more as a wail. She looks at me like I'm the life raft, and she's drowning. It's a little frightening, actually, like she might pull me under.

I say, "Please. Whoever killed Ryker has also killed other people – probably including Emma. Did you ever meet Emma? She looked a little bit like your daughter will when she grows up."

Tasha glances at the child, then back at me. I can see her anguish. And I can see that she's been needing desperately to confess to someone what she's done. "She's too young to understand. And I can't tell the police. If they thought I had anything to do with his death, she's going to wind up with some foster family I've never met. Which they're already threatening to do. I've only had her back for a few days, but there's supposed to be a visit soon, to see if I'm taking suitable care of her. Now how's that for irony?"

"I sincerely hope that doesn't happen." Though that's how this is likely to play out.

"Then what do you want?" Tasha asks.

"I just want to know who you gave the money to."

Tasha moves to the sofa, sitting next to her little girl. "I don't know. It all happened electronically."

I guess it would have been too easy for her to just say, *I gave Carmen the cash and the caffeine.*

"Where did you get the idea to have him killed?" Logan asks.

"Someone left me an anonymous note in my locker at work. They were offering their services." She holds up a hand before we can ask to see said note. "Obviously, I destroyed it. But I'd been complaining to a ton of people about Ryker. It could have been anybody."

"Were you supposed to get your money back out of the life insurance?" I ask.

"Life insurance?" Tasha puts a hand on her daughter's head. The girl looks up at her and laughs, offering her mother the game controller.

So someone else is profiting off Ryker's death.

"Did Carmen ever visit you at the hospital? Or ask you to get her any kind of pharmaceuticals?"

Tasha shakes her head. "You think Carmen might have something to do with this? She's been so kind, even though she doesn't know why I'm such a mess. I've been more depressed than I thought I'd be. I have so much guilt – and I've had to hide it, so that neither of my roommates suspect."

"I don't know if she's involved," I admit. "But Carmen's the one who found Ryker. She would have had an opportunity to remove anything incriminating from his body. I'm just trying to put things together."

"That's a bit of a stretch." Tasha looks disapproving for the first time since we came in. "If Carmen was charging that kind of money, do you think she'd have two roommates?"

"Sorry," I say. "I just had to ask." But Tasha brings up a good point. "I have wondered why she's still working for me, when she could make a lot more money in a hotel kitchen."

Tasha says, "Carmen won't apply anywhere because she's afraid people will realize she got fired from her first serious job – by a boss that was offended when she refused to let him kiss her in the walk-in. She's been through a lot in life, and most of it wasn't fair. I just hope you don't accuse her of something she didn't do."

"I won't accuse her of anything unless we find evidence to support it." I put a hand on Tasha's. "I promise."

Logan heads for the door, checking outside before gesturing me over. He's obviously decided we're not getting any more information, and is ready to go.

Tasha looks as terrified that we're leaving as she was when we arrived. "What happens now?"

"You should prepare yourself for the truth coming out," Logan says gently.

Once we're outside, I ask, "What's going to happen to that little girl?"

Logan glances back at the closed door. "Hopefully she'll wind up with someone who cares."

Tasha obviously cares. But there's little chance she's going to escape going to jail. I ask, "Do you think Tasha's going to take the girl and run? Should we do something to stop her?"

Logan shakes his head sadly. "No. I've seen enough people like that, back when I was a cop. There's no way she could live with what she's done. It's more likely she'll go to the police herself and confess before they come for her."

It's heartbreaking. I find myself just standing there, staring at the cracks in the pavement.

Logan's close behind me. "We should go before Carmen comes back."

I tell him, "She's got an afternoon worth of work if we're going to open tomorrow. She said something about complementary brownie bites." How could someone that responsible – and helpful – be a murderer?

Bruce comes up to me, pushing his head under my hand, forcing me to pet him.

Logan puts his hand out for Bruce to sniff. "Do you really think she poisoned her own dog?"

That's a big piece of what hasn't been adding up for me. But I have a sudden idea. "I know one way to find out. I have a friend at the hospital who can test Bruce and see if there are actual traces of theobromine in his system."

"You want to steal Carmen's dog?"

"Borrow," I tell him. And with all these emotions churning inside me, echoing my own loss and pain, I feel like we have to do it now. Right now. After our visit with Tasha, I need to do something useful. "We can have him back in an hour. Why don't you tell Tasha we're taking him? She'll take it better coming from you."

By which I mean, it will break my heart if I have to go back into that house. Because I can't help them. I need to focus on the problem I think I can solve, try to find whatever justice I can for Emma and Ryker and the rest of the victims – and that includes Ryker's daughter.

I text Sandra. Borrowing the dog is pointless if she's not at the hospital. She agrees to help us run tests on a dog, no questions asked. Those kinds of friends are priceless.

Now, I just have to figure out how to get Bruce into the back seat of Logan's car. The two seat halves are molded bucket-style, so he won't be able to just fit across it. The dog doesn't seem at all reluctant to be going with it us. Bruce keeps sniffing at me as I look for a way to level out these seats.

I wonder if Bruce knows something odd's been going on in his house. They say dogs can read emotion, can even spot physiological changes in their owners' blood pressure. The look on Tasha's face when she'd talked about her guilt of having paid for the murder of someone she'd once loved enough to have a child with. I can't imagine what that does to a person. I'd lost Kevin while still deeply in love with him. It's not a complicated emotion. But it had sounded like Tasha had realized too late that she might have still had feelings for Ryker.

Or maybe I'm just reading too much into it. Maybe it was just that she remembered he was a person and not a problem and a monster.

"Hold up," Logan says, walking quickly towards the car. He pops the trunk, and comes back with two folded beach towels. Which I guess he carries for ocean-related emergencies. He drops one onto each seat indentation.

"Aren't you going to spread one of those over the seat backs?" I ask. I'd be afraid the dog hair would be everywhere.

"Don't you think he'll be more comfortable this way?" Logan whistles, and Bruce jumps into the back seat. He fits. Barely.

I get into the front passenger side. "You have a dog back home?"

"Nah. I left the one I had with my sister when I left to go to Europe. I wasn't there when he died. Didn't seem right to get another one."

"Now that's just sad," I tell him. "If you want a dog, get a dog. There's plenty in the shelter who wish their owners had left them with someone they could trust."

Logan looks back at Bruce. "Yeah, maybe."

When we get to the hospital, I direct Logan around to the side entrance. Sandra's waiting by the door. I do a double-take. Sonya's usually the twin with the red hair. "Sandra?"

Sandra touches her hair. "You missed quite a party last night. By which I mean we all shared a bottle of wine and then Tiff and Sonya gave me a makeover."

"I'm sorry I missed it." I give her a huge hug. "Thanks for doing this."

She looks down nervously at Bruce. "He's not going to bite me, is he? I mean, it takes a good minute to take blood."

"I'll hold him and make sure he doesn't," Logan volunteers. He snaps a leash onto Bruce. He must have grabbed it when he went back into Carmen's house. Smart.

Sandra waggles her eyebrows at me. Seriously. Everyone keeps pushing me towards Logan.

I just roll my eyes and make a face at her.

As we enter the hallway, there's a group of people walking our way, several of them wearing scrubs. The only one I recognize is Dr. Ricci.

Sandra freezes. "That's not good. I can't afford to get in trouble again. Nobody's supposed to bring animals into the hospital."

Dr. Ricci walks over to us and pats Bruce on the head. Bruce noses at Dr. Ricci's pocket, like he's looking for a treat. It's like Knightley and his bunny love of parsley. He'll be best friends with anyone who feeds him. Only, Dr. Ricci doesn't have anything for Bruce, and after a couple of seconds, Bruce gives up.

Dr. Ricci grabs Bruce's leash and brings him back over to us. "It's okay. I told them he's an off-duty police dog."

"That's not something to joke about," Logan says, taking the leash.

"It is, if you want to keep him here at the hospital," Dr. Ricci ruffles Bruce's ears. "Personally, I love dogs. They make great therapy animals."

See? Everybody loves Bruce. Which makes it even more shocking that someone would try to hurt him.

I follow Sandra and Logan towards the elevator, and wind up sitting patiently on a little chair in her lab as she collects the sample and runs the test.

"Well?" I finally ask, when she's peering at the result. "Do we have a criminal mastermind on our hands, who dosed Bruce with something non-fatal just to trick us?"

Sandra's face looks doubly serious under the bottle-dye hair. "There are definite traces of theobromine in this dog's system."

Which means that Carmen's either not our killer – or she's a psychopath.

"This test doesn't clear Carmen. We need to bring what we know to the cops," Logan says. "Especially everything Tasha confessed."

I shake my head. "I promised Tasha I wouldn't accuse Carmen until I'm sure. Carmen's been a loyal employee. I owe her that much."

"Psychopaths often come across as loyal." Logan rubs Bruce's ears. "Don't be so charmed you lose your objectivity."

I should be excited that I've put enough of this together to convince Logan. But I still have questions.

"I just think there's more to this." I can't get that huge life insurance policy out of my mind. "Because seriously, where's the money?"

Chapter Twenty
Saturday

I still haven't come up with anything new by the next morning, when I have to meet with Emma's parents. I tried to talk them into meeting me somewhere other than where their daughter died, but they insisted on coming to the shop.

And now they're sitting across from me, holding paper cups from Starbucks. After having someone poisoned on the premises, I can't blame them for not trusting me to serve them coffee.

Carmen is in the back, making a list of supplies we need to replace, and I'm not sure I trust *her* to serve *me* food. What should I say if she offers me one of her brownies? Surely it wouldn't make sense to poison me. But what if Tasha told her we borrowed Bruce? Or that we suspect her of orchestrating Ryker's death?

Logan is at a table on the other side of the storefront, doing something on his cell phone. The dinner he made for me and Aunt Naomi last night was messy-looking and calorie-rich. And unexpectedly delicious. I have to admit, he's good in the kitchen. Outside, it's raining again. Bertha is on the move again, racing up the coast as a Category 3. The window for Logan flying me out of town has officially closed.

Emma's mom, Faye, looks exhausted. Beautiful, with perfectly coiffed blonde hair and flawlessly polished red nails, but under it, exhausted. "We just want to understand."

Emma's dad, Mitch, puts a hand on Faye's. He's a stocky guy, with a golfer's tan broken by the outline of sunglasses creating a pale mask around his eyes. "Did Emma have problems with anyone here? Because as far as I know, everyone loved her."

"I don't think so." Would it be more or less comforting if I told them I though Emma had been killed by mistake? It's just a theory, though. So I keep it to myself. And I'm certainly not going to tell them that Emma's killer could well be in this building. "I do have a question about one of her friends. Or, at least, someone whose number is in her phone. Have you ever heard of Monaco Ryan?"

Faye recoils as though I've slapped her. "You think Monaco had something to do with this? She and Emma have been friends since grade school."

"Monaco is a real person?" I blurt the question. I struggle to change tacks, to make it still sound like I know what I'm talking about. "I assumed it was another on-line persona. Like how Emma went by Emma Giselle."

Faye's mouth drops open, the fluorescent lights glinting on her bottom lip. "She what?"

Fay looks more upset about Emma's false name than about the idea she might have had enemies at the shop. I'm confused.

Mitch pats desperately at his wife's hand. But his expression when he looks back at me is somewhere between accusing and apologetic. "Giselle was Emma's sister's name. She died of meningitis her freshman year of college. Which is why we didn't force Emma to go to school. I know that sounds indulgent, but after losing one child . . ."

He trails off. My heart breaks for him. Here he is, losing a second one. It never should have happened. And if I hadn't bought those books, it might not have.

Might? Ha! Let's face it. I got Emma killed. On top of what I did to Arlo, I don't know how I'm supposed to cope with that. It's getting all mixed up in my brain, a solid layer of guilt and anxiety.

Much like Emma herself. Her sister's death must have done something to her that nobody understood. I'd instinctively felt that she needed help. But I hadn't guessed that that help should have included grief counseling. She hadn't even told me she had had a sister.

"Emma always liked to read," Faye says. "I always thought she would get herself together, maybe decide to teach."

Hoping it is the right thing to say, I tell her, "I think she decided to write. Emma signed a book deal, and she had a lifestyle blog. She had an amazing amount of motivation and drive."

I don't mention that that drive had turned Emma into a thief and a liar. But I can see how these people's expectations, coupled with the shadow form of a sister she could never replace, might have driven her to find success. Her family was well enough off, but not rich. Her parents self-absorbed, but not entirely.

"We should have made her come with us on the cruise," Faye says. "But she wanted to be here for your grand opening party."

That breaks my heart a little more. "I am so sorry."

I know. *I'm sorry* is the most pointless thing you can say to someone who's grieving. But even if they don't need to hear it, I need to say it. It's almost like there were two Emmas – and if the part of her that was still connected to her real life here in Galveston honestly cared about her job here and the success of my party. I should have handled things differently somehow. They're looking at me like they see how hollow my words are.

I ask, "Do you have contact information for Monaco?"

Faye shakes her head. "I lost track of that girl's parents years ago."

Dang. I really need to know why Monaco would have taken out a six-million-dollar life insurance policy on her boyfriend. Because if Monaco really did that, and there's not some massive insurance fraud scam here, then there's a lot less money to factor into the equation. All of the numbers on that ledger put together add up to roughly half a million. Which would be a lot easier to hide.

Faye asks, "Is there anything else you can tell us? Anything at all?"

There is one important thing. "Emma bought a Lexus shortly before she died. She let some friends of hers borrow it, but they're supposed to return it here on Monday. I'll make sure to drive it over to you."

Mitch gets up to leave, muttering, "What's wrong with the car she already had?"

After we usher Emma's parents out of the door, Logan flips my sign back over to *open* and joins me at my table. We will see them again in a couple of hours, at their daughter's funeral.

A few minutes later, I get a text from Miles. *Found out more about Emma. Her sister died when she was in high school.* He's a bit late on that one. I just found that out myself.

Another text: *She pulled away from her friends. Some of them described her as germophobic or heading for OCD. One of them said she had started applying hand sanitizer like ten times during class.*

And another: *There was a girl in both of the classes she was skipping who looked like her dead sister.*

And yet another: *Apparently, she was spending the time wandering around the beach, and around campus, taking landscape shots and selfies. Some of them are on old social media accounts that she closed at the end of that year.*

Miles's last text: *No idea how that might relate to who would have wanted to kill her. Sorry!*

Of course not. Because Emma had died over the contents of the ledger page I'd found.

I text Miles back: *It is starting to look like Emma wasn't the intended victim. Thanks for looking into it.*

After a minute Miles replies: *Not giving this up until we're sure.*

I can't promise him that. I don't know 100% that Emma died because of the ledger. But I have to say, Miles is nothing if not thorough. I should be equally so.

I pull up my snapshot of the ledger list, studying that first column of initials. If each pair of letters represents a person who has died, there should be information about them on-line. An obituary at least. But there aren't any dates. I don't even know where to start.

So I start on the estimated date of Ryker's death. I pull up the local newspaper's web site and start working my way backwards.

Okay, so it wasn't Miles's last text: *I'm going to go talk to her doctor. Maybe he'll tell me if she was taking antidepressants to treat OCD.*

I text back. *She never showed signs of OCD while working at the shop. Maybe the people you talked to were wrong? Or it was mild and she got treatment and got over it?*

Or maybe she channeled her anxiety into building a new persona. It seems mean to say that, though.

But seriously, it is like those tree sculptures. The one I'd photographed and Instagrammed outside of the café could have been made by anyone – not just the original artists who started sculpting them after Ike. The faked photos and the life Emma'd been pretending to lead could almost be termed performance art, whether she intended it as such, or if she had been trying to believe she could really transform herself into the character she had created. Horrible things had happened to her – and she was trying to take the ruined trunk of her life and sculpt something beautiful. It was never going to work. But in tragedy, the beauty is in the fall, and there was beauty in the vision she'd been trying to create.

Sudden tears bite at the back of my eyes.

Logan cuts a glance towards the kitchen. "I'm not comfortable with you being here right now. With her."

"You've said. Several times." I cup my face in my hands. "What am I supposed to do, Logan? I'm not a cop. All I know about investigating I picked up from books and TV."

"And considering that, I think you've been doing exceptionally well." He tugs at my arm, pulling my hand away from my face, making me look at him. "Following the money is logical. I've been over here looking into Tasha's financials. She made a transfer to an offshore account. The money goes nowhere. It's practically a Nigerian Prince scam. How did she even know whoever she hired would go through with it?"

Carmen comes through from the kitchen, her laptop in her hands. She's smiling. "What are you two talking about?"

"Nothing," I say quickly.

She looks from me to Logan, arching an eyebrow. "Um-hum. Well, I hate to leave you two lovebirds alone, but I've placed the order for the bulk stuff, and I'm going to the cake supply store." She looks out at the rain. "Though I'm glad they won't be sending us dry goods until after this storm passes. If we get flooding, who knows what might be ruined."

"I've been keeping track of the weather," Logan says. "They don't think we're in line for a direct hit."

Carmen nods. "Yeah, but there's still a possibility we will have to evacuate if the storm turns. The rain's already bad enough I've got Bruce shut in my room in the house. He usually has the run of the garage, but that's the first thing that floods."

She pulls an umbrella from her bag and heads out into the rain.

After the door shuts, I hold my hand out, emphasizing the direction Carmen's just gone. "Does that sound like a killer for hire to you?"

Logan holds up his phone, displaying the questionable financial data. "Certainly not a Nigerian Prince."

How? How is he about to laugh right now?

I tell him, "I'm just saying it feels a bit too obvious."

Logan looks even more like he's about to laugh. "You said you've picked up your investigative skills from books and stuff. Usually, they make it the last person you'd suspect. But as a former cop, I can tell you: it's usually the most obvious person who did it. No big puzzles, no curve balls, ninety-five percent of the time."

I take a deep breath, try to get this back on track. "Let's just agree that Tasha is trusting, to the point of vulnerability. The only other money to follow is the life insurance."

Logan slides his phone over to me. "This is the contact phone number listed for Monaco on the insurance policy."

I dial the number using my own phone. I get a message that starts, "You've dialed a number that is not currently available."

Seriously? What kind of person is set to inherit multiple millions, but can't currently pay a phone bill?

"What about the address?" I ask.

Logan puts it in his GPS. "It's an office building."

He grabs his keys.

"We can't just leave," I point out. "That would look super weird to Carmen."

While we wait for Carmen to come back and man the store, I get a trickling stream of customers. We aren't doing a bustling business, but considering the weather and the bad publicity, it's enough to keep me hopeful. In between customers, I keep scrolling through obits. There's a ST who died about a month ago, which matches the set of initials above Ryker's. Scott Thompson. The obit's pretty bland, and I can't find anything that implies his death was anything other than natural causes. But five minutes in the guy's social media shows he was a jerk.

Could that be the thing here? Carmen got harassed, and now she's trying to help people by killing the jerks in their lives? It almost makes sense. If it wasn't completely insane.

I use the edit tool to write Scott's death date out beside the column.

By the time Carmen gets back, I've possibly identified two other victims on the list. I can't look Carmen in the eye without feeling like I have to confront her and demand to know if she's the one who did this. So I scoop up Logan's keys and say, "We'll be back."

We take Logan's Mustang over to the address Monaco listed.

"I have to admit, I could get used to a car like this," I say. "It's certainly less awkward to park than a catering van."

"I have a work van too," Logan says. "For transporting people who use my charter service. But I don't want to have to drive it around all the time. It's like you told me, if you want a car, get a car. You can afford it."

I ask, "What about how I live tells you that?"

"Nothing. You're actually quite frugal."

We park in front of a square, cement building. The windows have been boarded over in case Bertha heads this way.

I point a finger at Logan. "Then you're just as trusting as Tasha. You're assuming that when you told me to pay you what you're worth, you and I are thinking on the same scale."

Logan opens the car door. "I am taking a chance on my ability to read people, that you're not going to stiff me when all this is over. But I'm not quite as naive as Tasha. I've had a look at your financials."

He gets out of the car before I can reply. Before I've gotten myself together enough to get my seatbelt off, he's already heading back to the car.

"What happened?" I ask.

He gestures to the building. "A sign on the door says 'Sorry! Come back later.' I assume whoever runs it preemptively evacuated."

Some people like to evacuate well ahead of a storm, so they won't get caught in the traffic trying to get out of town, which can, admittedly, take hours and hours of barely moving, even once the highways have been turned to all one way. The owners of this building must be that type of people.

Well, that's just great. If Monaco had put her home address on here instead of her work address -- like a normal person -- I could at least knot this thread in the puzzle we've been unraveling. Apologies to Sonya, that I've never actually made it into her yarn store, and probably mangled that metaphor.

But it's the biggest question: Did Monaco really take out the insurance policy on Ryker? And if so, why?

"There's really no home address for Monaco, anywhere?" I ask.

"It keeps showing up as unlisted," Logan says. "That's a girl who likes her privacy."

We're still in the parking lot when I get a phone call from Carmen.

She tells me, "Dr. Ricci came in to look at the books in the locked case. He said he had an appointment with you."

"Aww . . . I'm sorry." I can't believe I forgot. I've got a lot going on, but Dr. Ricci has to believe at this point that I'm blowing him off. "It's one of the travel volumes. Were you able to handle it?"

"I started to get the key out of your office, but he stopped me. He said he looked in the case, and the book he wanted wasn't there."

Logan is gesturing at me like he'd like to know what she's saying.

I hold up a hand, gesturing back that he should wait. "I'll contact him and figure out what title he needs."

Carmen says, "He didn't actually say it, but I'm guessing he was looking for the Jane Austen volumes. I know they weren't still in those boxes of books that got stolen. Please tell me you know where they are."

My chest goes cold, my fingers clammy in a way that has nothing to do with the weather. There's no way Ricci is interested in Austen. So why would Carmen be asking about those particular books, if she's not looking for that list? "I have them."

"Where?" Carmen asks. "I can get them back under lock and key for you."

I almost say *at home*, but fear stops me. Aunt Naomi is probably there right now, putting Elfa into that hall closet. "You know, that's okay. I'll take care of it after the funeral."

"I can find them in the office –"

"They're not there," I say quickly. "I've had an expert taking a look at their value."

"Autumn's library guy?" Carmen asks.

Now how could she know about that?

"Who?" I ask, feigning ignorance. I am a horrible liar.

"Autumn has called the store several times. She left messages that you need to get the info about the books to her library guy."

"No. It's not him." If Carmen is the killer for hire, Autumn's conservation librarian could be in trouble if she believes he's examining the books. I swallow hard. It's possible that right now, I could get an accidental confession. "Why do you care so much about *Sense and Sensibility*?"

"I don't," Carmen says. "I don't even like Austen. She's way too slow." Okay, so no confession, then. That would be too easy. And she's dogging one of my favorite authors. Carmen continues, "I'm just doing my best to take care of things here at the store. I – I don't guess you tried to check references at my last job. Or maybe you did, and you didn't care that I got fired. But either way, I didn't expect anyone to give me a second chance."

My emotions are in whiplash. I'm simultaneously more convinced that she's the killer – and less.

Chapter Twenty-One

After I say my goodbyes to Carmen, Logan drives me home. The whole way, he keeps asking me what Carmen said, but I'm still trying to process it myself. I just keep telling him, "I told her to close up the shop early, so she can get ready for the funeral."

He finally asks, "Did Carmen say anything that clears her?"

"No." I look down at my hands, wishing I had something to do with them, wishing I was back at my shop, making chocolate, where the worst thing I had to worry about was burning a batch of beans. "But maybe Emma was the killer's target after all. If she has Monaco in her phone, what if the two of them hatched this scheme together? Then it would make sense that Emma really was trying to take the books, that she was in my office, trying to see if I had the list."

"And you think Monaco killed her?" Logan pulls into my aunt's driveway.

I flip my hands over, looking at my palms. "Maybe. I think we need to know if she's taken out insurance policies on anybody else."

"I'll check on it," we both say at the same time.

Logan raises an eyebrow at me.

"What?" I raise *both* eyebrows back at him. "I have a friend of a friend in the insurance business. How do you think I found out who Monaco was in the first place?"

"You're saying the local gossip chain is a match for professional investigation?" He doesn't sound judgmental. More curious.

I shrug. "We all use the strengths that we have."

Logan leans back in his seat. "I don't think you would have said that two days ago. I think you're discovering strengths *you* never knew you had."

Heat suffuses through my face. I must be blushing red as a coffee cherry. "Fine. Your flattery gets you more work to do. You look into it, while I go get ready."

"Not until I've checked the alarm system first. Your aunt left the house for a significant amount of time."

I glance at him. His flight jacket looks a bit casual for a funeral. "Did you bring anything appropriate to wear later?"

"I try to plan for anything." He gets out of the car, then leans back in. "Don't worry. I clean up okay."

Okay. I roll my eyes. Logan has to know he's hot, even in the old Twins tee-shirt he'd worn last night with that pair of black pajama pants to sleep on the sofa. Which may have been part of why I couldn't sleep.

I follow him up the porch steps to the back door, trying to put his presence out of my mind and focus on the impending funeral. What do you wear to an event where half the people there probably think you're a murderer?

I step into the kitchen. It smells like Jambalaya, and there's a couple of lidded pots on the stove. Because, of course, you have to take food to a grieving family, and the funeral home is going to host the meal afterwards, instead of having everyone move over to Emma's parents' house. Aunt Naomi had cooked by herself. I should have thought to help.

Though she seems to have everything under control. Aunt Naomi is sitting at the island, already dressed in a sedate gray pants suit, accented with a short pearl necklace and matching bracelet. I didn't realize she owned anything that somber.

But nothing can repress the smile that takes up half her face. She cuts a glance towards the staircase, where my security guy has just disappeared. She asks quietly as she can stand, "How's it going with Logan? He's the guy, right? The one that lit up your smile after the disaster date I set you up on?"

Her smile is infectious, and I wish I could share her giddiness. "Logan doesn't date clients."

"Then fire him." Naomi fake-winces at the look I give her. "Kidding. Just wait until all of this is over."

My smile gives up entirely. "It would never work. I don't want a guy who has had bad guys chase him half way around the globe, and still carries a gun to feel safe. Yes, he's my type, physically. Like, sooo my type. But I can't get that invested in somebody who puts themselves in danger, because I can't lose another guy I love. And this one's broken, and comes with a ton of his own baggage. I need a fresh start, preferably on my own, and time to finish grieving. Not the exact opposite."

Her eyes go wide. "You've spent a lot of time thinking about this."

I nod. "I still miss Kevin. You can't imagine how much."

Naomi comes over and gives me a hug. "Greg's gone a lot. Sometimes I miss him fiercely, even though he's still alive. I can imagine . . . but I hope I never have to know."

There's a creak at the bottom of the stairs. Logan has to have heard everything we just said. My heart lurches, and I can feel my face going red again. I thought it would take him a few minutes to check the rooms upstairs.

"Light's out in the hall upstairs," Logan says, like nothing's fased him. Maybe it hasn't. He said he'd never fall for another client, so his feelings about me probably aren't nearly as complicated as my feelings about him. I've made an idiot of myself in front of him a couple of times in stupid, silly ways. But being honest makes me feel like the biggest moron of all. He gives me a smile that may be just the slightest bit tight, then turns to Naomi and asks, "Where do you keep the step ladder and the light bulbs?"

Naomi gets them for him, and when he's upstairs again, she looks horrified. She tries to get back some of her brightness, but her smile looks forced. "Well, at least he's not guessing how you feel."

"You think I just messed something up."

"Maybe." She purses her lips. "But if you're not ready, it's better that he knows." She comes back around and wraps me in a big hug. "I'm sorry I tried to push you too fast. But since you met Logan, you seem to be focusing less on what you've lost. It may not go anywhere, but you needed this."

I pull out of the hug. "I needed to be shot at and accused of murder?" It's a flippant comment, because she's struck something that makes me feel vulnerable.

"No. Of course not." But then Aunt Naomi taps her chin. "On second thought, yes. I think now you should stop getting shot at, and get your store back in order. And figure out what you do need to be happy."

"Uncle Greg says I'm using the shop to distract myself from my problems."

Aunt Naomi winces. "He told me he said that. He was afraid you'd gotten the wrong idea. I think you have a gift – we both do. Since you got into this chocolate thing, we've tasted a bit of single-origin chocolate, just to see what all the fuss is about. Yours is as good as people who have been in business a lot longer."

"You really think so?"

Aunt Naomi nods.

"You're biased, you know."

"Maybe a little." She grabs my hand and squeezes it. "But I'm also honest."

"You're clear," Logan says, coming back into the room. Then he heads for the living room, and I can see him digging in his duffle for different clothes.

I go upstairs and stare at the clothes in my closet. I change into a dark blue top and black skirt, and do my make-up. I don't spend a lot of time on my hair, given the miserable weather. I hope most of the proceedings will be inside.

I go back downstairs, and sit in the living room, in my favorite chair, off to the side.

Aunt Naomi is typing something on her tablet, and Logan must still be getting changed. I'm still mortified. I'd as much as admitted that I'm having to fight not to care about him.

I get another text from Miles: *Doctor's answering service contacted him and he called me back. He said he couldn't disclose anything about a patient. Also, he's not a very nice guy.*

I could have told him that he wasn't going to get any info with all the privacy statements patients sign these days. I text back: *Don't worry about it. You found out a lot. Will I see you at the funeral?*

He replies: *Probably not. I didn't really know Emma, so it might be weird.*

And yet, Emma's memory is driving Miles to find out more about who she was, what haunted her. It would probably be cathartic for him to attend the funeral. But I don't know how to put that into a text message.

I drop one hand down to the floor, and Knightley comes over to see if I have a treat for him. He delicately noses at my hand. I usually reserve kibble treats for training rewards, but I give him one out of the container on the side table. He cuddles up against my foot for a second, and then hops over my feet, comes back around and then starts racing across the rug. He stops before reaching the edge – Knightley hates to slide – and heads back the other way. In the middle, he binkies, leaping into the air out of sheer joy. It doesn't take much to make him happy. I lean forward and whip my head back and forth, letting my hair follow the motion in each direction, showing him that I too find joy in life. And maybe there is something to this fake it until you make it thing, because it makes me feel a little better.

If I was home alone, I might jump around with Knightley while he's binking. But there's no way I'm letting Logan see that. Heck, I won't even let Aunt Naomi see that. Knightley leaps a few more times, and then abruptly stops zooming and binking, sitting on the rug in front of me sedately, like it never happened.

Just because I'm in the mood to torture myself, I take out my phone and pull up Ash's *Gulf Coast Happenings*. Ash is prolific, I have to give him that. And one of his posts is a request for local freelancers to send him pictures, which he will pay for if he uses. Which explains how he keeps getting images of me.

Three entries from the top, there's a picture of me and Arlo. From high school. And then a picture of him walking next to me into the police station. From yesterday. And the headline *Local Chocolate Maker Sweet-Talks Her Way Out of Trouble.*

I'm getting just a little tired of hipster-guy Ash. The most maddening part is that he hasn't said anything untrue. I did date Arlo back in high school. I did get taken to the police station and questioned about Emma's murder. But the implication in that headline – that my relationship with Arlo is the only reason I haven't been arrested for murder – is insulting. And potentially bad for Arlo's career.

It's only a matter of time before I hear from Arlo. He's going to have to be a bit pushier about the case just so no one can cry favoritism. I won't be surprised if he does arrest me. I'm running out of time to do what he wants – find him the actual murderer.

"You okay?" Logan comes back into the room wearing a black button-down shirt and slacks, a steel-gray tie the only spot of lightness on him. He's holding a folded pair of jeans. His jaw is fresh shaven, and he smells of spice. Forgot okay. He cleans up amazing.

He has to know it, too.

The minute Aunt Naomi sees him, she's going to kick me for rejecting him. Even though he never actually offered me anything other than friendship. And it still feels like I have that. Unless he's really good at professional courtesy. Which is possible. I realize I have no idea where I stand with him at all.

I sigh, and try to focus on the blog problem. "Ash is dragging Arlo into this now."

"Let me see." Logan leans over me, taking the phone out of my hand. He reads over the article, then offers me back the phone. "It could be worse."

"I don't see how." I sound petulant, even to myself.

"You travel the world on your deceased husband's dime. If this guy starts doing his research, it's only a matter of time until he says something ugly about that."

My entire body goes cold. "There's no way I could have had anything to do with Kevin's accident. Why would anyone suggest otherwise? No blogger could be that cruel-"

Logan crosses his arms over his chest. "They might be. I just want you to prepare yourself for that possibility."

I blink up at him. "Wait. Did you think I might have something to do with it?"

Logan looks steadily at me for a long moment. And suddenly, even though his eyes are green, they're nothing like Kevin's. Of course they're not. Because Logan is a completely different kind of guy. "Not once I'd looked into the specifics. And for the record, I don't think you killed Emma either, now that I've gotten to know you."

"Thank you. I think." His steady gaze makes me suddenly uncomfortable. What might Logan himself have done, as a cop and in the intervening years? Would I even want to know?

"Come on. Let's get to that funeral. I want to be there before it gets crowded, so I can scope out the space and watch people coming in." He reaches out a hand to help me up.

As his fingers brush mine, I feel almost fluttery in my chest. I force myself to ignore the attraction. Like I told my aunt, it would never work.

Naomi comes into the room carrying a large casserole dish. There's a grocery-sized paper bag balanced precariously on top of it.

Logan takes the bag. He seems unprepared for the weight of it. "What's in here?"

"Boudin," I tell him, even though I haven't looked inside. Because what else are you going to want after a funeral?

It's definitely not crowded. There are about ten people, other than Emma's parents, in the funeral home. Most of them look around Emma's age, but there is an elderly woman sitting by herself, repeatedly dabbing her eyes with a lace-edged handkerchief.

I take a seat towards the middle of the room. Thunder is rumbling outside, echoing around the space. It's been raining harder and harder, practically since we left Naomi's house.

Aunt Naomi sits beside me, but Logan chooses to stand, brooding, over near the wall. He's studying each face. Does he imagine that the killer is here, that he can see the guilt in that person if he looks hard enough?

Logan stands even straighter, and his expression goes tight. I follow his gaze. Carmen has just come in. I guess she's still Logan's most likely suspect.

Carmen sits on my row, a few seats away from me. She's wearing a silver dress with black flowers printed all over it. It suits her better than solid black.

Logan moves over to us, climbing over Naomi and me to take a seat between me and Carmen. He really has decided she's a killer. His arm brushes mine, and he feels so stiff, I can practically feel waves of hypervigilance coming off of him.

Paul arrives and sits on the back row.

A few more people come in, but after a while, it is obvious that Carmen was right. Emma's funeral is not well attended.

A small man in a black suit with a green bow-tie comes to the front and announces that due to the weather, there will be no graveside service, and that we are waiting a few minutes to give people time to arrive. Which is heartbreaking.

How did Emma have so few real friends? Part of it has to be the double life she lived on-line. Many of her virtual friends are probably not even aware of her death. But Emma's lived in Galveston her whole life. Shouldn't she have impacted more people?

Maybe she did . . . just negatively. Kaylee's not here, for one.

At the last minute, the Mixed Plate family of bloggers come in, their three girls dressed in identical black satin dresses, Stewart Jr. in a miniature suit – also with a green bow-tie. They sit down a few rows in front of us. It must not have been difficult for them to figure out Emma's real name.

The kids are remarkably attentive during the short service, as people who knew Emma better than I did paint a picture of a kind girl, who was a good student, always curious, who loved clothes and design. I spend most of the time wondering how she got from that promising start to becoming the girl with almost no friends.

When it's over, Tam Binh comes up to me. She has her dark hair pulled away from her face and clipped back with a glittering barrette. "I wish I had known the real Emma."

"Me too," I tell her.

"We should talk." Tam Binh holds out her hand. "Give me your phone."

Logan is still hovering close. I move a little bit away from him to hand Tam Binh my phone. When she hands it back, she's added herself to my contacts, her name surrounded by pink hearts. A minute later, I get a text from her with a personalized Bitmoji waving and under it, *Tam Binh and Stewart Saveur*, and under that, a link to their blog.

I glance up to see Arlo standing at the door. He and Logan make eye contact, and something passes between them that makes me nervous.

Arlo walks over to Carmen and says something to her that turns her face crimson. She stalks out into the hall.

"Excuse me," I tell Tam Binh. I turn to follow Carmen.

Logan puts his hand on my arm. "Felicity, don't."

His tone puts me even more on edge. I pull away from him and rush out into the hallway.

Arlo has Carmen's hands cuffed behind her back, and is just finishing reading her her Miranda rights.

Carmen turns towards me, her eyes wide. "You know I didn't kill anybody."

"I'll call Miles's dad," I say weakly. Because what else can I do? If Arlo's arresting her, he must have evidence. She must really be a criminal mastermind, playing at being a care-free surfer.

Arlo gives me a kind look I don't expect. "When I suggested you find me a better suspect, I didn't expect for you to actually do it. I'm sorry I suspected you." He shakes his head. "Thanks for helping me. Imagine uncovering a conspiracy, right when you get back to town."

First off, I've been back for almost a year. And second, darn right, he should be sorry for suspecting me. But more importantly, "What do you mean I helped you?"

Arlo's smile fades a little. "Maybe you should talk to Logan. He turned over all of the information you uncovered, including the ledger and the information on Tasha's financials. Tasha's already been arrested for hiring the hit on her ex-husband."

Carmen already looks like she's freaking out, but her eyes go even wider. "Is that why you've been acting so weird around me? Because you decided I'm a murderer?"

"I thought it was a possibility," I admit. Embarrassed heat floods my face. "But I wasn't sure, and I certainly didn't turn over any information." I look belatedly at Arlo – who could still charge me with obstruction. "Yet."

Logan clears his throat. I hadn't realized he'd followed me into the hallway. But of course, what else is a bodyguard going to do? "Do you want me to take Bruce?"

Carmen's lips harden into a thin line. But then her shoulders slump. "Would you? Violet's never going to remember to feed him often enough to keep him alive."

My heart breaks for her, dumping defeat and grief into the mix of emotions I'm dealing with. More than anything, I'm frustrated that Naomi and I rode here with Logan. I can't exactly storm off, unless I want to try to find an Uber home in the pouring rain.

Carmen belatedly says, "Wait. Tasha hired someone to kill Ryker? Really?"

And there it is. That hint of doubt. Carmen sounds convincingly shocked.

But if she's the kind of psychopath capable of everything she's been accused of, she'd probably be able to handle that kind of acting just fine.

"Are you sure?" I ask Arlo, unable to completely articulate *what* I'm asking. I'm hoping he isn't rushing to arrest someone, just because of what the blogger had said about him and me, and how he was letting me get away with murder.

"We're sure," Arlo replies. "We followed up on the leads you gave us." He flicks his gaze over to Logan. "I guess you don't need a bodyguard anymore."

I look over at Logan. My chest goes tight. As much as I'm angry at him right now, I'm going to miss having him there.

After Arlo takes Carmen quietly out a side door, I go back into the room, looking for Aunt Naomi. I feel distant and numb, but I still can't help but notice Paul has disappeared.

Chapter Twenty-Two

Logan is driving us home. I'm in the passenger seat, and Aunt Naomi is sitting behind Logan, looking quietly out the window. She can't be seeing much past the rain.

Naomi says, "They did a good job on her makeup, didn't they? It's so important – that's the last memory her parents have."

I shudder. I hate funerals, especially the part where you walk past the coffin. I'd have given anything not to have had to see Kevin's face with a layer of makeup that couldn't even begin to mimic life. I hadn't looked that closely at Emma. "She was a beautiful girl," I murmur.

"I wish they had covered the bruise on the side of her thumb." Aunt Naomi's still not looking at us. "It was so small. It would have been easy."

Desperate to change the subject I ask Logan, "Do you need anything for Bruce?"

Logan doesn't take his eyes off the road. He just shakes his head. "If I think of anything, the PayPal transfer you sent will more than cover it."

Because I'd just been his client, and now that I'd paid him, what else is there? We ride in silence, broken only by the sound of the rain outside.

Finally, Logan says, "They found money in an account Carmen hadn't touched since college. It was at her parents' credit union."

"How much money?" I ask. We'd been trying to track the money. I should be relieved that all of this is over, but somehow it feels anticlimactic that Arlo's the one who found the last pieces of the puzzle.

"Two hundred thousand dollars." Logan glances at me, then returns his eyes to the road. "And there's nothing in her background that explains it."

"You still shouldn't have talked to Arlo behind my back." I had to say it.

I can practically feel the heat of his glower. "What you uncovered are facts, Felicity. You don't own them, didn't create them. This has more to do with justice than anything I owed you as an employee."

Ouch. He could banter and smile at me, and still keep me that distant in his mind. He wasn't kidding about not falling for a client. I'm not even sure he wants to be friends.

When we get back to Naomi's house, Logan comes in to get his duffle, but he doesn't make me let him go first, and he doesn't check the house for danger. Why would he? The intruder had turned out to be Carmen. She'd been the one taking those shots at me in the dark. It's still hard to imagine a gun in her smooth, small hands, but my brain is starting to get used to the idea. Logan was right. It is usually the most obvious suspect.

So why am I so disappointed? Maybe part of it was Logan making me acknowledge all the self-confidence I've gained from trying to solve this. And now he's leaving.

Logan stops, still holding that ridiculous duffle with its giant baseball. "You going to be okay?"

His expression says that maybe he does care, on some level, after all.

"I'll open the shop tomorrow, and hope customers show up, even though Carmen poisoned someone." I'm not looking forward to it, though. One of my assistants is dead, and the other is in jail. It is going to be very quiet, with the reminders of both of them everywhere. Plus, I will either have to find new employees, or else break down and bake.

"Keep an eye on the weather," Logan says. "Bertha is still moving in the Gulf. She might be headed this way. It would be a shame to have protected you, only to have something happen to you in the storm."

He touches my arm, and it feels like the end of something. Which I know is stupid. We're both still living on the same island. We're bound to run into each other again sooner or later. But it won't be the same.

"You be safe too," I tell him.

And then he gets in his car and leaves.

I can't stand just being here, in someone else's house, realizing that I have nothing left to move towards. No mystery to solve – either of Emma's death or of Logan's personality. "I'm going to the shop."

Naomi looks up from her phone. "Keep your ringer on. They're talking possible evacuations again. I'll be going by your grandmother's."

It's probably too late to ask Miles to board up my shop windows. When I called him to ask if his Dad had time to go look into representing Carmen, he'd said they were leaving ahead of the storm, but that his Dad would make some phone calls from the car. "I'll bring my go bag to the shop, just in case and either way, I'll bring some chocolate by Mawmaw's later."

Aunt Naomi's eyebrows go up. But she probably doesn't dare comment, in case it makes me change my mind. "I'll tell her you're coming. And that, when she starts making coffee, you're going to need decaf."

"Don't remind me." I grab the backpack I use as my go-bag, quickly checking the expiration on everything, especially my back-up medication. I'm not sure if granola bars really go bad, so I hesitate to toss the ones I've got, even though they are a few months over. You never know how long you could be stuck in traffic trying to get out of town via the bridge, which is the only way off the island now. The ferries don't run in this bad of weather.

I take my catering truck over to the shop. If we do wind up having to evacuate, I can bring a goodly portion of my stock with me. I have bins stacked in the back, and a system planned out that will let me get it all packed in an hour. When you grow up with the temperamental Gulf in your back yard, you learn to be prepared for anything.

Mandatory evacuation still seems unlikely. We get threatened with it several times a year, but it rarely actually happens. Still, I cast a worried glance at my plate glass windows. Maybe I should have boarded up.

I hate to pack everything for nothing. So I just grab a couple of gift boxes of chocolate bars and head over to my grandmother's condo. It had been easy to tell Aunt Naomi that I was ready to do this. But the longer I'd stayed away, the harder it was going to be to face Mawmaw's innocent smile, harder to explain how I could live on the same island as someone who I know cares about me and not find time to stop in.

When I get to her building, I bring both boxes of chocolate bars into the lobby with me and leave one at the desk downstairs, before I take the elevator up to the fifth floor. It's a nice building, and everything here is relatively new. It had been rebuilt after Hugo put a hole straight through the center of it.

There was a time when I would have let myself right into to my grandmother's house. Even after she got moved into the condo. But after this long, that feels weird. So I knock.

Mawmaw comes to the door. She's short and a little plump, with hair dyed raven black, and reading glasses perched on her nose. She pushes the glasses up on top of her head, and without saying anything, she opens her arms for a hug. I fall into them, leaning down awkwardly. She pats my back, then rubs at it soothingly.

"I'm sorry," I tell her. "I should have come sooner."

"It's okay, Kit." Mawmaw pats my back some more. "It's been a hard year."

I finally pull away, rubbing my hand across my nose and trying to stop suddenly impending tears. Maybe . . . maybe she's doing better.

"I know," I whisper.

"Stay strong, Kit."

Kit is a family nick-name for me. I've always had a soft spot for animals, and I am told my first word was an abbreviated form of the word kitten, when I had been reaching for the neighbor's grey-and-white fluffball. That cat had always run away from me. Probably with good reason.

I look deeper into the condo's living room, over to where Naomi is sitting on the sofa. The room is warm and overstuffed with knick-knacks and floral upholstery. I remember most of these things from when I was young, from Mawmaw's house. The hope in my heart must be shining in my eyes. Mawmaw could be doing better. Naomi shakes her head, and my hope comes crashing down, even as Mawmaw asks, "How's Kevin?"

Just like she does every single time I see her. Her neurologist has diagnosed her with mild cognitive impairment, said there's a chance it won't get much worse, but there are some things she just can't manage to hold onto. Especially things that are uncomfortable to remember.

Heat at the back of my eyes and stinging deep in my nose, I tell her softly, "Kevin's gone, Mawmaw. You know that."

I can see her putting it together, digging into her brain, finding the memory, and the shock of it, and the pain of the loss washing over her anew. Washing over me, as I watch.

I suppose it could be worse. She could just not remember him at all.

My grandmother and my late husband had had some kind of special connection. Part of it had probably been Kevin insisting on learning her style of cooking, and dragging me into the kitchen with them, even though I'd resisted learning to cook as a child.

Mawmaw makes me a cup of decaf Community coffee – a pointless product if ever there was one – and I go sit next to Aunt Naomi on the sofa. Her memory problems haven't affected her cooking abilities, but there's sensors on her stove and oven that shut them off after certain amounts of time, just in case she forgets.

I give her the box of chocolate bars. "I made these, Mawmaw. I hope you like them."

"Your mother always tells me you have such talent. She's coming to see me next week, if the hurricane warning passes." See. Mawmaw can remember most of the present. She opens one of the chocolate bars, takes a taste. "Kevin used to bring me chocolate every time you two came to see me. Good stuff, too. Not as good as this." Does she remember now that he's dead? Can she hold onto that much? She looks up at me and smiles. "When are you two going to have kids?"

The tears are stinging at my eyes, strong and insistent. I put my cup down on the coffee table. "Excuse me."

I make it to the bathroom before I give into the tears, and they turn into wracking sobs that shake my body, and leave me feeling cleansed. Afterwards, I look in the mirror at the absolute mess I've made out of my makeup. I wipe most of it off.

I'm back at square one, feeling like I'm back at *day* one, trying to figure out how to deal with being a widow. Uncle Greg was right. Work is not enough to fill the holes in my life. And I have no idea what else to fill them with.

I have to go back out there and face this microcosm of my family, and I'm terrified of the pitying look I'll see in Naomi's eyes. She'd wanted me to come here. She'd wanted me to face this. My mom hadn't even pushed me to come see Mawmaw.

There's a knock at the bathroom door. I open it. Naomi is standing there. "You okay?"

I nod. "Yeah."

"She wants to play Scrabble." Aunt Naomi gestures with her chin back into the living room, where my cup has been moved to one side and Mawmaw is indeed setting up the Scrabble board on the coffee table. She may have trouble holding onto isolated memories, but she can still beat the socks off of us at word games. "And she says she has something to tell you."

I wash off my face, and go sit back on the sofa. After we play for a little while, it starts to feel like I'm a kid again, drinking coffee milk on board game nights when my cousins were all in town, getting to feel like one of the grown-ups. Mawmaw's dark eyes are still sharp, and her strategizing to monopolize the triple word scores completely on point.

There's a bruise on the inside of her elbow, visible beneath the cuff of her short-sleeve cotton blouse.

I point at it. "Did you hurt yourself?"

She looks down. "No. That new guy they have coming to draw blood took three tries to hit a vein."

I study the bruise. Even on someone fragile like my Mawmaw, the discoloration should be a lot smaller than that. "I may have to talk to someone downstairs."

"Don't do that," Mawmaw insists. "He's sweet, and he doesn't treat me like I'm old. Seeing him's one of the things that brightens up my day."

I can't help but laugh. "Okay then. I wouldn't want to take that away. You call me next time they're scheduling you for tests, and I'll come show him how to do it properly."

"I may just call you anyway. I miss seeing you. I know you've had a hard year." Her eyes are uncertain, like she's held onto that fact, but can't for the life of her remember why.

"I've missed you too." There's heat at the back of my eyes, but also embarrassed heat creeping into my cheeks. No matter what, my grandmother is family. She was there for me when I was little and I needed it. And I haven't been here for her. "What was it you wanted to tell me?"

"I made you something." Mawmaw hands me a thick rectangular book. "For your grand opening. I think I'm a few days late, but I wasn't feeling up to going out. I'm sorry. I wish I could have been there."

My heart aches. I hadn't even considered that she might want to go. My mom had just sent a congratulatory e-mail. I look down at the book in my hands. It's a scrapbook. I open it, and the title page says *Kit's Chocolate*. "You didn't have to go through this much trouble."

The first page is a collage of mine and Kevin's wedding photos. Mawmaw taps one of them, which she's captioned *Caught Red Handed.* The centerpieces on the table are white and gold, the gold from foil-wrapped chocolate hearts we'd used to fill the vases underneath white roses. She tells me, "Kevin caught me eating all of the chocolates out of the centerpiece on my table. That's when he started bringing me chocolates, every time you two came to visit. And it was never the same kind, like he always wanted me to have a little surprise."

"I had no idea he was doing that," I tell her. I refuse to cry again.

She flips through pages of me, as a child, my face smeared with chocolate, in school, selling generically-packaged chocolate bars for some kind of fundraiser, me with my family eating chocolate cake and just living life, and at the end there's a double spread of me holding up a double-handful of beans I'd roasted myself. Mawmaw flips the page. It's blank. "There's a lot more pages here. You send me the pictures, and I'll add them. My doctor says this kind of thing is good for my memory. Or take the book with you, and you can do it yourself."

I wipe at my cheeks, traitor tears refusing to stay put. "Maybe we can do it together. Only, I feel like I've hit a dead stop, after losing both Emma and Carmen." I explain to her what's been going on since the grand opening, including how Ash the blogger had re-named my shop Sympathy and Condolences, and how I'd gotten an offer to do an order of 100% dark using that title.

"What did the club owner say when you called him back?" Mawmaw asks. "Is he still letting you do it?"

"You don't think it's tacky?" I ask.

Both Mawmaw and Aunt Naomi shake their heads no. The family resemblance is heightened by the incredulous look in both their eyes.

"I'm not letting you leave until you call and secure the contract." Mawmaw grabs a pencil out of the cup on her desk and starts sketching boxes onto the first blank page of the scrapbook. I see her pencil in the caption *100% Success*.

She's right. I need to put this mystery behind me and get back to my normal life.

If I can figure out how to do that.

Chapter Twenty-Three

If I'm going to get my rhythm back, it'll be at the shop. So I head back there, leaving my dripping umbrella at the back door. I've got my phone ringer on, so if there's another weather alert, or if Aunt Naomi calls me, I won't miss anything.

I haven't been in the shop for more than five minutes before my phone rings. It's Autumn. "How could you not call me?"

I bring a hand to my forehead. I never did remember to call her back. "Aw, man. I forgot to tell you about the books. Those wonky endpapers had been altered-"

"To hide a secret hit list. I know. The gossip train has already made it back from the police station. What I don't get is why you've been dodging my calls. Seriously, girl, you uncover that one of our friends is a killer for hire, and you don't even think to tell me?"

I hadn't realized Autumn thought of Carmen as a friend. And, wow, gossip travels at the speed of light on this island. "I got overwhelmed by everything that was happening. So how did you find out?"

"My library guy called me. He wanted to know if your books are the same ones he heard about. I sounded like an idiot, okay? You're supposed to be my best friend, and I have no idea what's been going on."

"I'm sorry." I sigh. "How can I make it up to you?"

"Chocolates. Obviously."

I smile. "That's easy. Come by here later."

"Can't. I'm meeting my librarian for dinner, assuming we haven't all washed away." A lot of people would be cancelling dates in the face of a potential hurricane. But Autumn's lived on this island most of her life. Her philosophy has always been that if you cancel everything every time there's a weather issue, you'll miss out on a lot for no reason. And yeah, there were a lot of times we evacuated when I was a kid and then nothing happened. That's just the way the Gulf is. "But tomorrow, lunch?"

"Of course." My smile gets wider. "But I thought you said you sounded like an idiot to Library Guy."

"Maybe he likes idiots." She laughs. But then her tone gets more serious. "You know how hard it is to meet someone. I work from home, so that makes it even harder. I don't want to mess this up."

"You won't," I assure her.

I take out a bain-marie, and get water simmering in it on the stovetop. When I'd first thought about becoming a chocolate maker, I'd wanted to be a purist. No inclusions and no flavorings. Cacao and sugar, and that's it. It's like being a wine maker, able to focus in on natural flavors to make specific effects.

But I'd soon realized how much that limits my market potential. So I'd made the concession to do truffles – despite the confusion that creates, and the potential for people calling me a chocolatier instead of a chocolate maker, not understanding where my real passion lies. But I've had to think of the truffles as a gateway drug, a way to show people what can happen when you combine familiar flavors with stunning chocolate.

I don't want to focus on a process where I already know the end profile, like finishing processing the batch of chocolate I'd started yesterday. I just want to noodle around with flavors, try and re-capture the spark of excitement I used to feel in this shop.

I pour cream into a saucepan, to make a ganache. I grab some of the nibs I made yesterday from the deep bin in front of the winnower, so that I can sprinkle them on top of the finished truffles. I still wear a painter's mask when winnowing, but the treatments have helped so much with my asthma symptoms that I haven't had problems lately.

Now all I need is a flavor. While looking for some fresh herbs to infuse into the mixture, I find a couple of lemons Carmen left in the fridge. I drop the herbs – thyme and basil and tarragon -- into the cream, bring it just to a simmer, and then turn it off, letting the herbs steep. I zest the lemons, and after I strain the cream, discarding the herb solids, I toss in the zest and a spoonful of white pepper. I smell it, then add a few drops of lemon oil and a splash of bergamot. On impulse, I add a few drops of rose oil too.

I put some pieces from the test batches of Columbia chocolate into the bain-marie, to melt to make an outside coating for the truffles. I chop more of the Columbia into small chunks and put them in a glass bowl for the ganache. I heat the cream back up, then pour it into the bowl, allowing it to soften the chocolate before I start whisking it smooth.

Someone comes into the front of the shop. "Hello! Is anyone here?"

I still have the glass bowl and the whisk in my hands when I move from the kitchen into the shop.

There's a tall woman, with thick long brunette hair and even features standing there in a black miniskirt and sleeveless purple blouse.

"Hi!" I move towards her. "Thanks for coming in despite the weather. Can I offer you some samples?"

She tilts her head. "Are you making candy in this humidity?"

I nod. "We have a serious dehumidification system. But today, I'm just experimenting." I grab a sample spoon out of the container on the counter and spoon up a bit of the ganache. "Want to try?"

She takes the spoon and brings it up to her mouth. She hesitates. "Why does this smell like Arlo's cologne?"

After she says it, I realize it does, a bit. Somewhere in my subconscious, I'd stored that almost-moment yesterday, and it had come out as this delicate chocolate concoction. Maybe I haven't found as much closure there as I'd thought. Heat's coming into my face. "You know Arlo?"

"Yes. Very well." She puts the spoon in her mouth, making a happy little noise as she swallows the ganache. "I'm Patsy."

I don't know why, but I'd pictured Patsy blonde, with frizzy hair and maybe a penchant for country music and denim. But she's tall and brunette. Like me. Though, she's a bit more polished, and I think prettier.

First impression: I like her. But I doubt she's here to make friends.

I find myself stammering. "Whatever that blogger said. You know he was wrong. I would never. Not someone who's taken. I mean-"

"Okay." She rescues me, taking another spoon from the container on the counter and piling it high with ganache. "Can you blame me for wanting to see for myself? You are his ex, after all."

I smile, cautiously. "You like the ganache? Want me to make you some truffles? On the house?"

She smiles back. "Can I help? Maybe see what I've got to live up to now that I'm trying to get the guy to take things serious."

I gesture her towards the kitchen. "I dated Arlo back in high school. I wasn't the world's best cook back then. My late husband and I spent a lot of time learning together in the kitchen. We were pretty broke when we were both in college."

Before she comes around the counter, she moves over to the shelves and picks up one of my variety boxes that comes with four bars. "What all is in here?"

As she moves the box, something slides out from between it and the wall, falling to the floor with a plastic *crack*.

I put the bowl on the counter. "What's that?"

She peers down at it. "I think it's a microphone. Like somebody's been spying on you."

I gasp. I knew this couldn't be over. I struggle to remember what I've actually said to people in this room. We've hardly been open. But I talked the cops here . . . and to Emma's parents. And Logan and I had a couple of private conversations, including our theories on the murder. Oh, no. What might I have said? And who was listening?

I bring a finger to my lips and gesture Patsy into the kitchen. She follows, bringing the bowl of ganache.

I pull out my phone, and my first thought is to call Arlo. But I'm not about to do that with Patsy right here. We've made a fragile sort of peace, and she might still get the wrong idea.

Plus, the microphone might be related to the security system Logan put in here. And I'd feel stupid getting the cops out here for nothing.

I'm still not over Logan handing information to Arlo, cutting me out of the equation.

I call Logan anyway.

When Logan answers, he sounds sleepy, like he was napping. I wonder how much sleep he actually got over the past few days, down on that couch. I feel guilty for not considering that.

"Have you been listening to me?" I ask.

"I didn't realize that was part of the job." He's half asleep and still able to banter. "Don't you need a therapist for that? Or a boyfriend?"

I make an exasperated noise. "Not like that. I found a listening device, in my shop."

"Are you kidding me?" He doesn't sound sleepy now. "Are you there alone?"

"No, but I feel safe. I'm here with Arlo's girlfriend, and we're making truffles."

"That sounds surreal." Logan's holding back a laugh, I swear. "Lock the doors. I'll be right there."

I waggle my eyebrows at Patsy. "Just wait until you meet my hot bodyguard."

She thinks I'm joking. Until Logan shows up. He comes to the back door, and we let him into the kitchen. Patsy hands him a truffle, the chocolate coating still damp, but the nibs sprinkled attractively on top, like I showed her.

Logan breaks it in half and tries it. "I told you I like lemon, but Felicity, this tastes like Arlo's cologne smells."

Okay. Maybe my subconscious is storing more confused ideas than I thought. Was I inspired by one of these guys? Both of them? Random co-incidence because Carmen left lemons in the fridge? I look at Logan. "So you don't like it?"

"I'm not saying that." He pops the other half of the truffle in his mouth. "But I'd prefer it made with the chocolate you gave me last time."

"I can see that. But take a look at this." I quietly lead Logan into the front of the shop and point him towards the microphone. Patsy follows us, not about to miss a thing.

Logan crouches down and examines the device, then goes over to the counter, picks up a glass cloche dome and places it over the microphone. He speaks softly. "Do you think whoever planted this knows you discovered it? I mean, did you talk about finding it or being spied on?"

I nod. "Unfortunately, yes."

"Damn." He lets out a long, slow breath. "Okay. We can still hope that they've stopped monitoring this, now that Carmen's been arrested. Honestly, Carmen's probably the one who put this here. If she's been operating on the level required to have pulled off that many hits without getting caught, I wouldn't be surprised if she has an extensive surveillance network."

"Where's all the gear? Wouldn't the police have searched her house?" I cross my arms and face Logan. "I think this proves Arlo arrested the wrong girl."

"But what about the money in her account?"

Déjà vu hits me as he says that. I feel sick to my stomach. "Logan, you and I sat right in this room, talking about how we suspected Carmen, and about the list, and how we needed to follow the money. We might as well have given the real killer a checklist for setting her up."

His mouth drops open, revealing his white, perfect teeth. "That could be a distinct possibility."

Patsy says, "Arlo doesn't usually make mistakes."

Logan looks amused. I don't know if it's because Patsy's body posture looks like a bear defending her cubs, or because he knows why she's here in the first place and he thinks it's funny that she's getting defensive with him instead of me.

Or maybe Logan's just relieved that he's not the only one who makes mistakes.

I can't help but remind him, "You're the one who gave Arlo the information he followed."

The humor fades from Logan's smile. "I still don't regret doing it. And no matter what, a part of me will always be a cop. And cops follow the evidence. There's still a chance that Arlo's already got the right person in jail. If so, confirming that doesn't hurt. But if not . . . we just didn't look at the evidence right."

I guess he does have a point. And I have to get over it, or we won't be able to work together and get Carmen out of jail.

I look over at Patsy. "I don't suppose you could hold off on telling Arlo that we're still investigating the case."

I assume that protective-bear is going to say no.

But she tilts her head again. "That depends. Just how many truffles are involved."

I grin back. "You want to try some of my single-origin bars?"

After Patsy leaves, Logan asks me, "You are aware you just gave her like three hundred dollars' worth of chocolate?"

"Oh, I know how much my products are worth." And here I am with Logan, right back where I'd started. "So what do we do now? I don't know how else to follow the money. Do you think we could get the ME's report? We just have Arlo's word for it that the poison was in the coffee. Maybe there's something we missed."

Logan takes out his phone. "Finally something law enforcement can do that your gossip chain can't."

"Fair enough. I never said I had access to everything."

He finished typing in some information. "I should get that report relatively soon – and I called in a few favors to get it, so you owe me one. In the meantime, I say we find Monaco." Logan takes a mini chocolate-chunk beso off the plate that had been under the glass cloche. "If Carmen's innocent, then Monaco's our main suspect. Unless you think it was Paul."

"I'm not sure it was either of them. Neither one ever showed any interest in the books, and Monaco wasn't even here the day Emma died." I shrug. "I mean, theoretically, Paul could have gotten to the cups, but I don't see him being organized enough to have created that ledger."

"These pastries are amazing." Logan says. "What about that guy who kept asking you about rare books?"

"Dr. Ricci?" I hadn't even considered him as a suspect. I think back to the day in question. "No, he never went near the coffee. He's my GP, and he says if he can give up caffeine, so can I. And he never got close to Emma. He wanted to help her after she collapsed, but I didn't let him."

I pick up one of the besos too and bite into it. Besos are a traditional Mexican sweet bread, made from a raised dough baked as two half spheres. Carmen had added chunks of my fruity Sierra Nevada chocolate to the mix, and joined the pieces with home-made strawberry jam and rolled the whole thing in fine coconut that had been infused with lavender. Traditional, yet elevated.

If we can prove Carmen innocent, I hope that makes up for getting her arrested in the first place. I really want her to work for me again.

"What about your writer friend? She'd have the organizational skills and the creativity to plan multiple murders, and handle the bookkeeping. You said you still don't know what she does all day. And she left several messages asking specifically about the endpapers."

I gasp, sucking in crumbs, both into my lungs and up my nose. I cough them back out. "Autumn?"

But when I think back, I remember her jokingly saying she wasn't a suspect. Her leading me directly to Carmen as a suspect. Even our last conversation – where she'd already found out what that list was for before any of this had even hit the news. Hesitantly, I say, "It's possible. Logistically." Then I shake my head. "Autumn's too sweet of a person. You don't know how many people she rescued and defended back in high school. Nobody wound up eating in the cafeteria alone if she was there."

"I know she's your friend," Logan says. "But think about it. Ryker was a scumbag, using that little girl as a pawn with his ex. If Autumn's about defending people . . ."

He trails off, gives me time to absorb his words with growing horror. Autumn had been right there, closer to me than anyone, from the moment Emma had collapsed. If Autumn was our killer, Emma wasn't murdered by mistake. If Autumn had intended to kill me, she would have had ample opportunity to finish the job, and I would be dead.

Emma had alienated Carmen and Kaylee – and who knows who else in her desperation to build a new life. Theoretically, Emma could have upset someone badly enough for them to make a case to Autumn about why she deserved to be killed.

Autumn had made that joke about doctors missing things. Could she have been trying to figure out if I'd realized how Emma had been killed? Would I have been in danger if I hadn't laughed it off? My breathing comes heavy. I force myself to slow it down.

Because, seriously. This is Autumn. Who fosters kittens on a fairly regular basis. But who also took quite an interest in me investigating Emma's death. What if she was only pretending to help, because she wanted to control what information I was getting? Volunteering to go with me to question Carmen. Feeding me information on Tasha. A chill shivers down my spine as all those questions she'd asked about the Austen novels – especially the endpapers – take on sinister meaning.

Heat bites at the back of my eyes. How could I have not seen it all as it was happening? Because I love Autumn, that's how. Because she was there for me after Kevin died, texting me every day when I was in Seattle. Someone who does that couldn't be hurting people, could they?

We all trust our friends, especially if the face they've always shown us is kind and good. But how many times are there television reports about people who have done horrible things, and their friends and neighbors are being interviewed, saying how friendly they are, how much a part of the community?

I don't want to believe it. Especially because she would have had to have poisoned Bruce, which, given her love of animals, is almost harder to believe than her hurting a person. But everything lines up. I try to slow my breathing again.

I look up at Logan, moisture dancing in my eyes, threatening to become tears. "I can see the logic here. But promise me, this time, we will make sure before we accuse anybody. Autumn is very dear to me."

"Promise." His eyes are hard as emeralds. I feel like I can trust that promise.

My phone starts going nuts with a weather alert. I move over to silence it. I read the text and groan. "That's the notice for recommended evacuation. They're pretty sure Bertha's going to sideswipe the Island as a Category 2." Mainly because it had lost strength over Freeport. "If everybody leaves, there's no way we're going to figure this out."

Logan moves closer to me. "You know half the people here won't leave. There's too much traffic on the roads already."

Logan may say he's from Minnesota, but he's lived on the Island long enough to reason like a Texan.

But I always follow evacuation orders. Always. When it's mandatory, it's technically against the law not to.

As if to emphasize Logan's point, my phone buzzes with a text. It's from Tam Binh.

Just been invited to a Hurricane Party at the Bergamot Hotel. Meet us here tonight? I'd love to interview the hero for my blog!!!

My first thought is – shouldn't she be evacuating, since she's got kids? My second thought: I sooooo want to walk into the Bergamot, having been vindicated, after they ditched me because they were afraid I'd caused a scandal.

But the third thought seals it: Autumn loves the Bergamot. We've done their afternoon tea together there more than once. And I'd like to figure out for sure whether or not my best friend is a criminal.

Even if it means staying put.

I feel all queasy, and I'm itching for my go bag. I should run, with everyone else, and let the storm pass me by.

But if I go, I'll always consider myself a coward.

So I discuss my plan with Logan, and then I call Paul. I need to know how much he's willing to risk to clear Carmen. I'm not going to put him in danger without his consent. If Autumn really has been bumping off the awful people in her client's lives, I need a name to dangle as bait. And from the outside, before you get to know him and his ambitions to improve his life for the sake of his son, Paul seems like a total jerk.

I tell him, "It isn't likely that the killer-" I'm not even telling him I think it is Autumn, "would take action without me giving her the money. But just in case she decides she's doing me a favor, there's a slight chance you could be her next target."

I cringe, waiting for Paul's outraged reply.

Paul laughs into the phone. "It wouldn't be the first time someone's tried to kill me. And it's not like I can do anything else for Carmen. It's been so frustrating, knowing she didn't do it – isn't capable of something so cold -- but not being able to say a thing."

I'm blown away by the conviction in his voice. "You really care about Carmen. You should tell her that. Even if it's complicated."

"I will. As soon as she gets released. I'm allergic to police stations."

Which means he's counting on me to get things right. If I screw this up, I could wind up getting myself – or him – killed.

An incoming call from Naomi beeps into my conversation with Paul. I let him go to talk to her.

Naomi says, "I've got your Mawmaw downstairs at her complex and we're ready to evacuate. How soon can you be here?"

How can I tell her I'm not going? Our family always follows the rules. I want to take the stock from my shop, and my collection of maps and get in the van. But whatever evidence there is that Autumn did these horrible things might get washed away in the storm. I need her confession, and I need to get a recording of it to the cops.

"I'm staying here," I tell Aunt Naomi. "I think-" It sounds stupid, when I say it out loud. "I don't think Carmen killed anybody. And I think I have a way to prove it."

Naomi doesn't try to talk me out of it. "I have your maps, in the fireproof box with the important documents from Greg's office."

Aunt Naomi really does care about me. I find myself smiling, despite everything. "Will you take Knightley?"

"He's already here, in his carrier. Your grandma's trying to calm him down. But not even sprigs of parsley will get him out of the back corner."

Rabbits don't like to travel. They tend to freeze up. "Put the carrier on the floor until you leave. The closer Knightley is to the ground, the happier he'll be."

"What about your chocolate and the shop? If you need us to, we could come by and take your stock in your catering truck."

I can't imagine Mawmaw having to spend who knows how many hours on the road in the catering truck's less than comfortable passenger seat. "No, I'll figure something out. You go."

I start moving stock from lower shelves into plastic bins, stacking them on top of the counter. Logan takes the cue and starts putting books from the half-empty bottom shelves higher up on the bookcase.

I text Autumn, spreading the word about the party, and asking her to come after her dinner – and bring her date. Because if Library Guy is real, I need to talk to him. And if he's not – then Autumn isn't the person I thought she was.   I make the concession that Logan can tell Arlo we have a lead, and that we may have information for him tonight, if he wants to send someone to the area near the Strand. Assuming he can spare anyone, since he'd likely have officers evacuating Carmen, and anyone else unfortunate enough to have been in the local jail.

Arlo sends me a text. *Lis, you need to step back in this one. YOU ARE NOT A DETECTIVE. Confronting a murderer could get you hurt. Just tell me who and why, and I'll take care of it.*

Ordinarily, I would agree with him. But I respond, *I'm in a position to get information you might not be able to. I'll be careful.*

Autumn texts back. *That sounds Ah-Mazing! But I don't know if my guy will be able to make it. He says he needs to get over to his mamma's. He might even cancel dinner.*

Oh, Autumn. I don't even want to believe you're capable of doing what's outlined on that ledger. How am I supposed to get you to confess?

Chapter Twenty-Four

Despite growing up in Galveston, I've never been to a hurricane party before. The concept of getting a group of friends together, when everyone else is leaving town, in order to drink booze and tempt nature, is completely alien to me. Which makes this both frightening and exciting.

I wish I could enjoy the party, but I keep spacing out and missing what people are saying to me, because I'm worried about what will happen when Autumn shows up.

"I'm sorry," I tell the girl with the purple ombre hair. She was at Emma's funeral, but I hadn't stayed long enough after to talk to her. I hadn't wanted to face Emma's parents, because at that point I had believed that Emma had been killed by mistake, that it should have been my funeral. "What did you say you do again?"

"I'm a reputation manager. I could boost your personal brand." The girl hands me a card. She glances behind me, and her expression lights up. "Oooooh. Jacque broke out the champagne. I'll be back in a bit."

I move into a corner, and try to regroup. There's about sixty people here in the hotel ballroom. Somebody has cued up techno music, which has Logan half dancing, even as he follows me around the room. I feel like I'm at a networking event for young professionals. I'm 32. I still qualify, right?

Once I'm sure no one can see my phone screen, I pull up the image of that ledger page. Of all the initials on the list, I've figured out possible identities for a grand total of five. Earlier I had added Marshall Klein to the bottom of the list. I'd found tons of information about him, so I know he was declared dead ten days ago at exactly 2:03 AM.

It's not much to work with. I need to catch Autumn in a lie, so I try to commit the details to memory.

I shift my hand, and the business card flutters to the floor, shiny purple paper on thick lush carpet. With the gold wallpaper and elaborate crystal chandeliers, this room looks fit for a fairy tale. I start to bend awkwardly in the only dress I own trendy enough for a party here.

"Let me." Logan reaches down and picks up the business card. He holds it instead of giving it back. "Felicity, did you even read this?"

I take the card from him. Monaco Ryan. It has an e-mail address on it, and a Skype handle, but no phone number.

I'd been desperate to find her, but hadn't even realized it when I had.

Monaco is on the other side of the room, a heavy bottle in her hand.

The lights flicker, and then go out. An audible groan carries across the room, and then eerie lighting sprouts as just about everyone in the ballroom turns on the flashlights on their phones.

I turn on the light on mine and start to head towards Monaco.

Logan's hand comes down on my shoulder, pulling me to a halt. "Not on your life. This room, in the dark, is a tactical nightmare."

I hadn't been sure whether Logan was still thinking of himself as my bodyguard. I find it comforting that he is. I gesture towards Monaco, who has started pouring champagne into plastic cups. "What's she going to do?"

"She could hit you with that champagne bottle. It looks heavy." He says it deadpan, but I think he's joking. "You don't know whether she's involved with insurance fraud. Her name came up as beneficiary on two other insurance policies. I got the information after Carmen was arrested, so I didn't think to forward it to you."

I turn towards Logan in the dim light. "Are the guys on those policies dead too?"

"Not as far as I could find out."

It's frustrating, standing here in the dark, so close to the source of information I need, unable to do anything about it. I'm close to Logan too, the dark making me hyperaware of him as he moves, and I find my treacherous heart beating a little faster, my breath trying to catch. I'm glad Logan can't clearly see my face flushing with conflicted emotions.

When this is over, I'm going to have to let Logan go, get back to my life. And that will be hard. But I have no claim on him. I've made that clear.

I turn away before Logan can see the pain in my face.

I make my way over to Monaco, forcing Logan to follow me. She's standing alone now, by the table with the booze.

Monaco smiles and hands me a cup. "I see you couldn't resist the good stuff."

Good stuff indeed. She's just emptied the last of a bottle of Veuve Clicquot into my cup.

Logan clears his throat, signaling me not to drink it. I'm tempted to ignore him. If you have to die, poisoned by Veuve has to be the way to go.

Logan tells Monaco, "I'm sorry about Ryker."

Monaco blinks. "I'm sorry about him too. What's he done this time?"

My mouth drops open, and I take a drink of the champagne without thinking. "Have you not been checking your messages?"

She shakes her head. "It felt like a good time to do a social media detox." She looks down at her own cup of bubbly. "Emma was my first client. She stuck with me while I was learning, and I got her everything she wanted. But it was for nothing."

"Ryker's dead," Logan says.

Monaco's eyes go wide with shock. "Has anybody told his girlfriend?"

Now it's my turn to be shocked. "I thought you were his girlfriend. You're the beneficiary of his insurance policy."

Monaco laughs, but it's a brittle, horrified sound. "I'm not his girlfriend. I'm his employer. I work in a solo office as a regional part of a larger company. I hired Ryker to set up situations that can be newsworthy. I used the same terms as my parent company – which includes outrageous life insurance policies on all the employees. The premiums make for a handy tax deduction. Faust Images has one on me."

"But for six million dollars," I blurt out. I take another sip of the Veuve. This time, Logan doesn't even try to stop me.

Monaco's mouth bows into an 'o.' I think it's just dawning on her how big of a windfall she's in for.

I'm re-evaluating what I thought I knew about Ryker. Maybe he was starting to get his life together, right when his ex had him killed.

Autumn comes into the room. She's holding a dripping umbrella, and her plum-colored dress is speckled with dark spots from the rain. She waves at me from the doorway, her eyes wide and her mouth pressed into a plum-lipsticked purse of excitement. She's excited I invited her here. Which makes me feel awful.

Is it possible for her to be both a murderer and my oldest friend? Could the part of her that I know be a real and valid side of her personality – even as it coexists with a callous dark side? She never would tell me why she stopped writing. I've known for a long time that Autumn has her secrets.

I need to know for sure if the logic chain – following the Evidence, as Logan called it – is right. And if Autumn is a killer for hire, I need to know why she's doing it. Because if we're friends, I need to know what that says about me.

Nervousness dances in my stomach. This is what had been missing when Arlo had arrested Carmen: the confirmation that I'd found the right solution to the puzzle. Unfortunately, that means confronting the killer. Which, like Arlo said, is inherently dangerous. I almost wish I'd told him exactly where I was going to be.

I play with the screen on my phone, making sure the voice memo recorder can be accessed with a single touch. I wave Autumn over and introduce her to Monaco.

Neither of them seems to have a reaction to the other's name.

Monaco introduces us to some of her other friends – including one face I recognize.

With his square glasses and skinny tie and smug smile, there's no mistaking Ash. One corner of his mouth tugs up as I offer my hand for him to shake. "Felicity Koerber. As I live and breathe. So nice to finally meet you in the flesh."

I do the polite thing and shake hands. But I can't keep the sarcasm completely out of my voice. "I'm sure it is."

"Whoa." He takes his hand back. "Nothing personal, you know?"

I tilt my head. "You called my business a death zone, practically accused me of murder, and said I was trying to break up a friend's relationship. That sounds personal to me."

"I never *actually* said any of that." Ash shrugs. I stare at him, until he adds, "I just never imagined I'd be wrong."

It takes every ounce of self-restraint I have not to slap him. I'd made my own assumptions about Emma's murder, and, despite my best intentions, Carmen had wound up in jail, and right now is probably undergoing the most terrifying hurricane evacuation of her life. I owe her. Big time. And here's Ash, acting like there's nothing he owes me. "At the very least, you could say something nice about my shop. My aunt is one of your readers, and I think that would make her feel better about the whole thing."

The other side of Ash's mouth quirks up. He's probably flattered to know how far his readership goes. "Sure. You can count on it."

But I doubt that he'll actually do another article. Or if he does, if it will turn out to be all that positive.

"I'll be looking forward to it." Tam Binh walks up to us. "I might even link to it off my article. Since Felicity's a friend of mine."

The smugness falls from Ash's face. "Okay," he stammers. I can't tell if he's embarrassed, flattered, or what, but I think my relationship to Ash has just changed completely.

I get the feeling that Tam Binh's Mixed Plate is a much bigger deal in the blogger world than I had realized.

"Let's talk," Tam Binh says.

I look over at Autumn, who is chatting with Monaco. I hate to leave the two of them alone, but honestly, Monaco doesn't know anything Autumn should find threatening. And it's not like Autumn's planning to murder anybody at this party. That I know of.

So I go with Tam Binh. She blinks when Logan starts to follow us.

"Private security," I quickly explain.

"Really?" Both of Tam Binh's eyebrows delicately arch. "He comes across as your boyfriend."

Logan blushes, but says nothing, just follows us into a side room where Tam Binh interviews me, asking about the places I've been and the people I've met and how that's changed my perspective on the world. I talk about how, for the most part, people are welcoming wherever you go, if you are showing an interest in them and the things they are passionate about, if you show respect for their language and etiquette. And how it helps to share a common interest. In my case, chocolate. There are farmers who love their trees, would spend time in their little bit of rainforest, even if the crop wasn't lucrative. There are fellow bean-to-bar makers, who share your bliss when you try their chocolate. There are chocolatiers in Paris and London and Tokyo, hungry to try out new takes on single-origin chocolate. Chocolate opens doors. Chocolate makes connections. There's a reason for that joke meme: chocolate understands.

In the course of the interview, the lights go out again. And they stay out.

Even after Tam Binh finishes the interview and excuses herself, saying she needs to go check in on Stewart and the kids.

"That was impressive," Logan says. "I wish there was something in my life that I felt that passionate about."

"Keep looking," I tell him. "You'll find it."

I hear him moving closer in the dark. "The only thing I care about right now is keeping you safe. I still don't like your plan. It requires me to leave you alone and vulnerable. And that feels like another mistake."

My anxiety, already high, kicks up a gear. "You agreed to it earlier."

"I know. But I was ignoring my gut. And that's the same thing that got Mari killed. I'm not making the same mistake, for a third time. I'm not letting you do this alone."

"But Autumn won't talk to me if someone else is here," I protest. "She's certainly not going to offer to kill someone for me."

"Felicity?" Autumn's voice comes from the hallway.

Logan switches off his phone and takes a step backwards, into the shadows. I can still sense his presence in the room, but that's probably because I know he's there. It's about as good of a compromise as I'm going to get.

"What?" I reply, like I'm distracted. I pretend to be absorbed in my phone. If I look too eager to talk, that might put Autumn's guard up.

"Someone said you went this way. You have to try this cocktail. It would make a great white chocolate truffle." She comes into the room, her phone held awkwardly against the stem of a cocktail glass. She has a matching glass in her other hand.

She sits down at the table and puts one cocktail in front of me. I peer down at it, dismay growing in my gut. I'd kind of forgotten how the intruder at my aunt's house had shot at me in dead earnest. Might still want me dead, if she thinks I know her true identity.

I don't need Logan to tell me not to drink this drink. I pretend to take a sip. She's going to want flavor notes. I can smell the alcohol coming off of it. "It's a bit strong, don't you think?"

"Strong?" She looks startled. "The way it's blended, you can hardly taste the alcohol at all. I'm talking about the way the pineapple rum blends with the raspberry."

"I can see that," I lie. "And yeah, that could work with white chocolate." I hesitate a beat, trying to think of a way to change the subject. "How'd your date go?"

"It was fun. Way too short, because just when it started getting interesting, he started getting texts from his mama that her kitchen was flooding, and he headed over there with some more sandbags." She takes a deep sip of her cocktail, emptying half of it. "I told him to be careful. The roads might not even be passable. He said if they weren't, he'd head over here."

That gives me pause. Is it possible that Library Guy is real? Worried now that I might be making a mistake, I still have to launch into my plan, turning on the voice memo function on my phone to catch her confession. "Sounds like a good guy. I wish more of them were." I grimace, like I'm thinking of someone in particular.

"I didn't think you were seeing anyone. Who are you having a problem with?" Autumn sounds sympathetic.

"Do you remember Emma's ex-boyfriend Paul? He keeps hitting on me. Says he's dying to get with an older woman." I manage to keep from giggling, as I imagine Paul's face if he ever finds out he supposedly said such a thing. "And now, he's threatening to blackmail me if I don't go out with him."

"Blackmail? Felicity, you're the one person I know who always follows the rules. What could someone possibly have on you?"

I look down at the table, hiding the fact that I'm not the best liar, while hoping it makes me look guilty of something. "I'd rather not say."

Autumn nods. "Fair enough."

She has her secrets. She's prepared to let me keep mine.

"I wish Carmen wasn't in jail," I tell her. "I wish I could still hire her to get rid of Paul."

Autumn recoils, spilling her drink across the tablecloth. "Felicity! You don't mean that."

She grabs my drink and takes another deep sip. I guess the cocktail wasn't poisoned after all.

This isn't the reaction I was expecting. At all. I try to recover. "What I'm trying to say is – I'm pretty sure Carmen isn't creative or organized enough to have pulled off all those murders. I'm still hoping to hire the person who actually did it."

Even by the light of the phones, I can see emotion flitting across Autumn's face, settling on shocked. "And you think it was me?"

If I can't lure her into a confession, maybe I can push her into one. "Isn't it? I mean, everything adds up. You kept asking about the books where we found the killer's ledger. And you were at the grand opening when Emma died. You even teased me about how I wasn't considering you a suspect. And you used to write murder mysteries, so you've got all these 'handy' facts. Including how Carmen's roommate had access to ampules of caffeine."

"You're accusing me because I'm a mystery author?" She looks incredulous, even in this dim light.

I followed the evidence. She's the most likely suspect. "Can you prove to me that it's not you? I mean, I hope it's not. But as much as I love our friendship, Carmen's in jail and people are dying."

"How am I supposed to prove that? That's why the justice system says innocent until proven guilty."

"Where were you two weeks ago Monday?" I ask. "That's the day Ryker Brody disappeared."

"I'm usually at home on Mondays. I was probably researching the provenance on the vintage jewelry I bought over the weekend. That's how I can buy a piece sometimes for fifty cents and sell it for fifty dollars, okay. But I tend to clear my browser history, because it bothers me when things get that cluttered." She gasps and stares at me, her eyes wide and luminous in the glare from her phone. "You're right. It sounds like I did it." She looks down at her phone. "There's no way I can account for my time on a lot of days."

I want to believe her. "If you didn't do it-" I pause, and she shakes her head emphatically no, "the only other time of death I've figured out for sure is at two in the morning on June third."

"Girl, do you know where I was that night?" Autumn slaps a hand on top of mine. The lights flick back on, and Autumn looks up at Logan, who is standing a few feet behind us, his gun in his hand, just in case. She blinks, but seems to take this in stride. She focuses back on her phone, looking through the video files. "You know my brother owns a restaurant down in Padre. He's been hosting after-hours events to get the revenue up. I was MC-ing a karaoke contest that night until about three in the morning." She pulls up a video of her and her brother, singing *Life is a Highway* as a duet. The date at the top of the screen matches, with a timestamp that says 1:12 AM. It's a four-and-a-half-hour drive from Padre back to Galveston. It is still possible she could have done something to Marshall Klein that would have had a delayed effect . . . "I got there two days before, so we could practice. Want to see me playing hide and seek with his kids?"

It's seeming less and less probable that Autumn's our killer. Logan's put away his gun. I turn my voice memo recording off. My stomach is sinking like a lead weight, even though I'm relieved. I may have just ruined my longest friendship, and gained nothing. Not justice. Not even a clue to the mystery. "I'm sorry." I swallow, trying to think of a graceful way past this huge faux pas. "I hope we're still friends."

Autumn puts her hand on mine again. "You owe me a lot of chocolate. I mean a lot."

"You're not mad?" Logan asks.

"A little. More hurt." Autumn looks at me when she answers. "I thought Carmen was the killer, and I was wrong. Felicity was just doing the same thing I did, putting the clues together to solve the puzzle. Though I *thought* we knew each other better than that."

"There's a lot about you I don't know," I say before I can stop myself.

"Like what?"

I hesitate. But there's one thing she's withheld that I keep wondering about. "Like why you quit writing."

Autumn looks like I slapped her, more upset by this question than when I'd accused her of murder. But Logan and I are both looking at her, and her face goes from panicked and trapped to resigned. "Something I wrote happened."

I blink, not sure what to say to that.

"What do you mean?" Logan asks her.

Autumn takes a deep breath. "You know I'm not superstitious. But did you ever see that movie *Stranger Than Fiction*? I wrote a scene about a hit-and-run, and then next day it actually happened. To another writer I knew. And it was almost the same as what happened in my manuscript. I know – *I know* -- it was coincidence, but I kept thinking about that movie, and every time I sat down to write, it was like I was just paralyzed. I know it's stupid, but I couldn't write another murder."

"Oh, honey." I've moved and put an arm around Autumn's shoulders before I even realize I sounded just like my aunt. I agree – it was just an unfortunate coincidence. But I don't want to focus on trying to convince her of that. Writing has always been what brought her joy. Whatever her reasons, I don't want to try and talk her into doing something painful with it. "You could write something else. Romance, maybe?"

Autumn looks up at me, a you've-got-to-be-kidding expression on her face. "I can't even figure out real-life love."

There's a long moment of silence, which stretches into awkwardness.

Finally Logan clears his throat. "About this karaoke. Will you be doing it again? Because I would drive out for something like that."

Bless him for trying to lighten the mood.

Autumn scrunches up her nose. "He wants to do Clue night next. With his sister the mystery author as a draw. Even though I haven't done a book in years."

"It's nice that he thinks highly of you," Logan points out. Maybe he's imagining what his sister thinks of him, after all his mistakes.

Autumn smiles. "There is that."

"We could do karaoke night here, at my shop. I could use a way to bring in the community." They both look at me sharply, so I add, "After we solve Emma's murder, obviously. If we can. We're back to square one again."

"We have the files," Logan says. "Both from the scene and from the ME's office."

He slides his phone over to me. I start scrolling through the information. I get to a list of everything Emma had on her when the police took her body. In her purse, she had a men's Breitling Avenger dive watch. That's a five-thousand-dollar watch. I should know, because I had bought Kevin one as a gift for our second anniversary. I keep it in the locked drawer of my desk. At least, that drawer should have been locked. I remember playing with that drawer when Arlo had questioned me in my office, too distracted to realize it wasn't normal that it wasn't locked.

Emma didn't dive, and I doubt she would have worn a men's watch. She wore a smooth bracelet-watch that paired with her phone. She was more likely getting text messages when it looked like she was checking the time. I check the list. The bracelet-watch was on her when she died.

It probably doesn't mean anything, even if she did steal Kevin's watch. But it's the only thing I've got to go on that just doesn't add up.

"I need to get back to the shop," I tell Logan.

Autumn says, "In this weather?"

Chapter Twenty-Five

The wind is getting high, and pieces of paper and leaves and bits of dirt and plant matter are blowing down the alleyway between the shops. I'm having to hold hard onto my umbrella, as the wind threatens to snatch it away. I should have evacuated. I didn't have the answers after all. But it is too late for that now.

Logan goes into the shop ahead of me, and the door blows shut behind me, pushing me inside.

Logan leaves me at the back door of my own shop, insisting on going in to clear the building first. I close my umbrella, as Logan disappears through the doorway into the processing room.

I can't blame Autumn for not wanting to come with us, since I don't even know what I'm hoping to find. And the party was getting into full swing.

We all get a group text from Tiff. She's been on the road all day, and has finally made it to Dallas. Even her text message sounds tired. It ends with: *Don't forget, you guys, get on Facebook as soon as everything's clear. The hurricane's listed as an event, and you can check in as safe.*

Which is actually a cool way to use social media.

Sandra and Sonya evacuated, too, but they are still on the road. Sonya sends pics of bumper-to-bumper traffic in the pouring rain. And of Sandra, driving.

I heart their pictures. Then I wait for Logan to come back. For a good long while. I stand there, just looking around the kitchen, wondering how long it will take for me to feel comfortable working alone in this space again, knowing how easily someone broke in, how easily they'd managed to kill someone here. It feels cold and clinical, like a hospital in a horror movie. And with my wet clothes, and the pounding rain outside, and the feeling that I should have evacuated . . .

Suddenly, I can't stand to be alone.

"Logan?" I call.

He's not in the processing area, or past that in the bean room, or out in the shop. The hall light is off, but the light to the men's bathroom is on.

"Logan?" I call again, hesitating near the door.

It's hard to hear through the door, but I think he says, "Give me a minute."

Geesh. He could have told me he'd cleared the place before ducking into the bathroom.

I head down the hall, towards my office. I turn on the light, and stand there, studying the cluttered room, pretending to be Emma on the last day of her life. She knew she'd been caught stealing, might not have a job much longer if she didn't straighten up. Looking at the desk, there was only one drawer I ever bothered to lock. There are wear marks on the edges of that drawer, showing I'd used it a lot more than the other ones.

So if I'm Emma, and I'm looking for valuables, that's the drawer I open. There's only one key. She must have copied it, at some point when I wasn't paying attention. Either that, or she'd picked the lock. I examine the mechanism. There's something sticky below the lock. Careful to touch nothing but the ring-shaped drawer pull, I slide the drawer out. There's more adhesive on the bottom of the drawer, and a tiny piece of plastic that looks like a chip broken off of something bigger.

I think about the bruise on Emma's thumb. So tiny. So insignificant, the ME had barely noted it. But it could mark an injection site.

If Emma had been sitting down, with her wrist at just the right angle, it's possible her thumb could have lined up with the bottom of the drawer. A prick of a needle, and she could have been poisoned. But wouldn't she have felt that, realized she needed help before it suffused through her system?

Hadn't someone mentioned a pain-free injection system? Sid, of all people, had been saying something important, and I hadn't really been listening. I think back to that disastrous date. He'd said it was someone local.

If it was painless, maybe Emma wouldn't have noticed, not if her focus was on listening for me potentially coming back for my phone.

There's a noise from outside my office, like a chair falling over or something. It's probably something outside the building. The weather must really be getting bad. I should go check, make sure my windows are still intact.

I do a quick Google search, which gives me the piece of information I need for everything to fall into place. Dr. Ricci had invented the pain-free delivery system. Dr. Ricci, who sometimes had business at the hospital, where he could have encountered Tasha – and could have faked a reason to access concentrated caffeine, or any number of other drugs. Dr. Ricci, who had wanted so badly to talk to me about the books – and had never actually said he wanted a travel book. The same guy who had been there at the café the day my coffee got switched, with something ominous in his hand.

A chill goes down my spine. Had he planned to inject me with something that, after all that coffee mixing with my meds, could have been chalked up to natural causes? I feel a cold certainty that Logan really did save my life that day.

Every interaction I've had with Ricci since I bought those books takes on a new, ominous meaning. Even seeing him getting into that black Acura at the coffee shop. Aunt Naomi might easily have mistaken an Acura for a Lexus, from across the street in the rain. It had been just a coincidence that Emma had actually owned one.

Dr. Ricci must have thought I knew what was in the books I'd bought when he'd grudgingly agreed to come to my grand opening. Had he thought I was blackmailing him?

I head back into the hall, towards the bathrooms. "Logan! Hurry up! I know who the killer is."

"I was afraid you were going to say that," Dr. Ricci says, coming into the hallway. Which puts him between me and the exit. He's holding Logan's gun. And he's wearing gloves.

"Where's Logan?" I ask. Though I'm certain I don't want to know the answer to that.

Ricci gestures towards the bathroom with his free hand. "He noticed the ceiling tile I'd removed to get back in here from next door. Since they don't have any pesky cameras – or fancy alarm systems."

"So it was you who broke in after the police were here. A fuzzy figure on the camera breaking in, but no sign of you leaving." I'm trembling, but I manage to keep my voice steady. The night of the party, Ricci must have gone into the men's bathroom and waited for me to leave my office to go do my makeup, then slipped into the office without anyone noticing. Emma hadn't been lying about the door being open. And that boot print on the counter -- Ricci'd obviously come back to remove whatever had been taped to the bottom of the desk. I'd just assumed that intruder had gotten up on the counter because he been looking for something. I'd been looking at all of this wrong.

"Of course I'm the one who broke in. And I made it easy to come back. Even then, I was sure I would eventually have to kill you. And if it couldn't be natural causes, I might need it to look like suicide." He nods and takes a step towards me, gesturing me back into the office. My chest goes tight and cold with fear. Logan's probably lying dead on the bathroom floor. No one else is coming to help me. And Ricci, who's already taken down Logan, just announced he's planning my imminent death. I can't count on help from the police – in the middle of a mandatory evacuation, there's no guarantee they're even still in the Island

My only goal is to stay alive long enough to plot an avenue of escape. My heart is beating loud in my ears as I back into the office.

Ricci sounds proud of his plan. And he's probably not been able to tell anyone how clever he's been. He strikes me as a guy who likes looking clever.

"How are you going to explain what happened to Logan?" I ask. My phone is on the desk, too far away to reach. I'm sure he'd see me activating the voice memo anyway. So likely, no one will even know I'm hearing his confession.

Ricci snorts. "That's the best part. Your bodyguard will wind up claiming you knocked him out. He called your name right before I dosed him, thinking you'd followed him into the bathroom. So when he finds your lifeless body, and sees your confession, especially the heartbreaking part about your aching guilt over having accidentally killed Emma, who was an innocent in all of this, he's going to confirm the story I'm building."

"Logan's not dead?" I say with relief.

Ricci makes a face. He snags my phone off the desk and puts it in his pocket. "I don't kill people if I don't have to. Not people who aren't cancers on their families and friends, who need to be excised from society. I don't want to kill you, honestly. But you just wouldn't leave it alone. Not after I warned you to. Not even after I got someone else arrested."

"I knew someone planted that money in Carmen's account." But there's still something bugging me. "But if the poison that killed Emma was in an injection system, why were there traces of it in some random coffee cup?"

Ricci smiles sheepishly. "I load the injection system with little gelatin balloons. I intended to flush the extra one, but when the police arrived, I couldn't get back into the bathroom, so I dissolved it into a cup of abandoned coffee and threw the coffee in your ficus tree."

I hadn't even considered the cup might be the way to dispose of the evidence. I shake my head, trying not to show how terrified I am. "But your real objective was whatever you did to the desk."

Ricci nods. "It was delicate work. The mechanism had to be positioned so that wouldn't be noticed once the drawer was closed and the needle retracted. And that wouldn't strike again if someone else opened the drawer."

I fake a smile that I hope comes across as admiration. "My husband was an engineer. I know how hard it is to get a design just right."

He smiles back. But it doesn't affect the aim of the gun. "And not only were you not the one who opened that drawer, you'll get credit for all the good work I've been doing."

Good work. As in killing people. I shudder. "Your first mistake was when you missed the estate sale. How did you even let books that important slip through your fingers?"

Ricci sighs. "Because I didn't get the threatening letter from Marshall until days after I had killed him. He was always so vague, so fond of his puzzles, by the time I figured out he hadn't been able to resist telling me what he'd done with the ledger page, more days had passed, and it was too late. It usually takes longer to plan an estate sale." He seems wistful, regretful.

"How did Marshall even know you killed all those people?" I ask. "Were you working together?"

Ricci splutters out a laugh. "Goodness, no. He just stumbled across me excising someone in the hospital. He put it together with other things that had happened at the hospital and then he broke into my house to find evidence."

"Murdering them," I correct. "You can't excise a human being."

Ricci shrugs. "That's a matter of semantics." He gestures towards my chair. "Sit at the desk, and sign the confession. I want to do this as humanely as possible."

He says it in the same tone as if he was asking me to hop up on the exam table at his office.

"No." His plan hinges on my death looking like a suicide. I'm not going to just sit down and let him do it.

"What do you mean no?" He looks shocked, like it never occurred to him that I might resist. I guess, with his methods that look like natural causes, none of his other victims had ever seen it coming.

"My death would be pointless, Doctor," I point out. "Even if they believe I killed Emma, there's no way the cops are going to believe I killed all those other people."

Dr. Ricci smiles sadly. "Lieutenant Romero already believes you murdered Emma. I heard that with the listening equipment I left in this shop. Why else would he think you would have killed her, if not over the stolen list? By logic, he must believe you killed all the others."

"But I handed that ledger over to the cops myself," I insist.

"And then immediately framed your friend." Ricci shakes his head. "And it will be easier to believe when they find your final victim."

I feel my eyes go wide. "You said you wouldn't hurt Logan."

"Not Logan. Just someone else who's been digging into my secrets. Who actually showed up here to try and rescue you. I caught him just before I came to find you. Don't worry. You don't actually have to kill him. I'll just make it look like you did."

My heart lurches. Who is he talking about? Arlo? Paul? I don't quite dare ask.

We're at a stalemate. He can't shoot me from where he is and have my death explain away all his crimes. And I can't get close enough to try to take the gun, or get past him out of this closet-sized room, without him shooting me anyway first.

If I want any power in this situation, I need to be the one to break the impasse. "At least let me die surrounded by my chocolate. That'd be more believable than in here anyway."

"Fine." Ricci backs into the hall. "But you try anything, and I will have to go back and put a bullet in Logan's head, so this all makes sense later."

He's not bluffing.

"I do have one question," I say as boldly as I can. "Why did you steal all of my Guayas River bars?"

Ricci smiles as I pass him. "Because that's the most delicate chocolate I've ever tasted. And good thing I took them, too. They're about to be limited edition."

At the end of the hallway, I can go into the shop or into the bean room. And I have about five steps to decide. The shop has the front door, but I'm not likely to get very far, running on foot into the heavy rain. And this guy will kill Logan before he comes after me.

There's a muffled noise from the front of the shop. I glance towards it. There, tied to one of the chairs, a bright white gag forced into his mouth, is Miles. My heart freezes. I'd thought he had evacuated with his family. Miles is such a good kid, with such a bright future.

Dr. Ricci has made it clear: If I die, Miles dies. And that would be my fault too: I should have told him all the way back at the restaurant not to investigate this.

Miles looks at me, his eyes wide and terrified. Pleading for my help. It hurts me inside, but I pretend I don't notice him at all.

With such an innocent life on the line, I can't let Dr. Ricci win. I turn towards the bean room. I'm going to have to use what's there to defend myself.

Ricci considers the space, all the machinery, the heavy bags of beans. "Where do you want to stand?"

I walk over to the winnower, with the deep bin of cacao nibs in front of it. I bury my hands in the nibs, bring a double handful up to my face, inhaling deeply. Earthy and aromatic, redolent of all the adventures in wild places I'd planned to take, the scent of fresh-roasted chocolate fills my lungs. My plan. Me. Not in memory of someone else. Not to fill in the voids. I find, here when it's hopeless and I'm about to die, I'm hungry to breathe it all in.

And the heady fragrance leaves me completely bereft. For this one brief moment, it doesn't even matter that both Logan and

Miles's lives are in danger too. I grieve for myself. That photo album my grandmother gave me may have been highlights of the life I'd shared with Kevin, but the Instagram feed I'd started when I launched the business shows highlights of my new life. I'd tried to make it sound exciting for my potential customers. Me, arm in arm with a family of cacao farmers in Ecuador. The simple meal we'd shared afterwards had been some of the best food I've ever eaten. Shots of me standing next to a fully-grown cacao tree, holding a shallow box filled with potted cacao seedlings, marveling at the way the wrinkled beans crack open and split to reveal the tiny leaves inside, the first signs of new life. Me, hiking in the mountains in Colombia, the sky behind me looking like it was painted in, my knee a little scratched from climbing up to the impossibly high rock where the shot was taken. I would have been too afraid to make that climb before, had been terrified while doing it.

And you know what? Forget trying to convince the readers. My life *is* exciting. It does have the potential to make me happy, for me to be the "together" person my social media says I am. And I'm supposed to just give that up? And let Ricci take at least one other life in the process?

I know the odds are against me. But I'm not going out without a fight.

I run the nibs through my fingers, digging deeper into the bin, looking for larger pieces, sharper edges. Ricci doesn't try to stop me. I've got one shot at distracting him, maybe taking the gun. I hold my hands out towards the doctor, piled high with nibs. He's still a good four steps away. "Have you ever smelled anything so amazing?"

He shakes his head, takes a step closer. "Probably not. You know what? Hold them if it makes you feel better. I'll forge your signature and put the gun in your hand after. And then I'll get your prints on the syringe with the overdose for Miles."

He takes one more step, close enough now to make his scenario look real, not close enough for me to make my move. I have to try anyway. With all my might, I fling my hands up, showering him with cacao nibs. It's not as effective as if I'd been able to hit him straight in the face, but he does bring a hand up, shielding his eyes.

I bump into him, trying to take the gun, but he doesn't yield and I wind up sprawled on the floor. Ricci growls and levels his gun. My phone starts ringing in his pocket, which startles him enough to make him hesitate. I'm between him and the door back into the hall, but there's no way I'm getting up and out of the way before he fires. "Please, just don't kill Logan!" My heart's hammering as my hands scramble for purchase on the smooth floor. I sob out a breath I didn't think I'd get to take.

Ricci puts a hand in his pocket to silence the phone, almost says something, decides not to. Because what I should have said is don't kill Miles.

And then I see Logan, who has snuck into the room, launch himself at Ricci, tackling the doctor from the side. Together they crash into the tray by the roaster, knocking it over on top of them as they struggle for the gun. I can't see what's happening. The gun goes off, and my heart goes cold.

If Logan's just died for me – I don't think I could cope with the loss.

There's still movement under the tray, which flips over, away from the fight, scattering cacao beans everywhere. But which one of the guys threw it?

Logan gets up, and relief floods through me, melting me back onto the floor. He reholsters his gun. He looks down at Dr Ricci, scowling. "That garbage you injected me with made me throw up. And then there's the splitting headache."

Ricci groans. He brings a hand to his leg, where blood is seeping from a hole in his slacks. "You should have been out for at least another hour."

"I've always had a high tolerance." Logan moves over to me, helping me up off the floor.

Ricci looks from Logan to me, obviously realizing he's not going to get anywhere with Logan. "I don't suppose the ambulances are still running in the middle of a hurricane."

"Probably not," Logan says. "But the police should be here soon. I called them as soon as I woke up."

It takes a second for the implications of that to really hit Dr. Ricci, but after a moment his face crumples into defeat. He looks down at his leg and sighs. As wounds go, it's not terrible. "And there's zero chance of me bleeding out peacefully before they get here."

I go to release Miles from the chair.

I tell him, as I untie the gag, "I thought you'd evacuated."

Miles says, "We were on our way out of town, and I thought I saw a car like Mrs. Thibodeau described seeing across the street from y'all's house parked out front of Sandwich Town. I mean, an Acura looks a lot like a Lexus. The employees were giving out food to people getting on the highway to evacuate, so they were packed. I hung out to find out who got in it, and it turned out to be the doctor I'd just been talking to. He had nine pictures of himself on his web site, so that wasn't hard to figure out. I followed him around for a couple of hours, until he came here and broke into the shop next door. I couldn't believe that was really happening."

I get him untied, and we head for the back.

Miles adds, "I knew you were here – or at least your phone was. I was afraid the Doctor was going to hurt you, so I snuck in the back, trying to be a hero. I'm sorry I just made it worse."

"He got the drop on me too," Logan says. "You're still a hero in my book."

"Mine too," I say.

"Oh please," Dr. Ricci says.

Logan is still picking cocoa bits out of his jacket cuffs when Arlo and Officer Beckman show up, just a minute or two later, banging on the shop's locked door.

Meryl must be one of the only cops able to make it through the storm, if Arlo's bringing a beat officer into this situation. I wonder if this means there might be a promotion in her future.

She shouts "Police!" in a way that has me sure they're about to shoot out the glass.

I hurry to the front of the shop to let them in. "We have Dr. Ricci in the back. He's not going anywhere."

Arlo looks me up and down. "Not a scratch on you."

Something about the admiration in his gaze sends a blush across my cheeks. Officer Beckman catches the exchange, and gives me a sour look. Oh boy. I hope she's not friends with Patsy. Otherwise I'm never going to hear the end of it. I get that Arlo's taken. Really, I do. But the reason Arlo and I have a history is because I was attracted to him all those years ago. And he isn't any less attractive now. I won't act on it. But I can't help the blush.

Arlo says, "I'm going to need another statement."

I smile. "Gladly. This time I have solid information. Ricci explained a lot, because he was planning to kill me."

"Then I'm glad you're still around to testify." His tone is dead serious, but he's teasing. Right?

Officer Beckman asks, "Did he mention why he decided to become a killer for hire?"

I point towards the back room. "He seems to think he was helping heal society. Still wanting to be a doctor, I guess."

"That's crazy," Arlo says.

"Tell me about it." I try to act like the whole ordeal was nothing, but I'm still trembling, still seeing that gun barrel in Dr. Ricci's hand sighting down at me when I'd been on the floor. "I'm not sure why he felt the money was important, though."

"Don't worry. We'll get him to tell us. You did a good job on this one." Arlo smiles. "I guess I do have a 'one more thing' after all."

"And what's that?" I ask.

"Don't do anything like this again. Regular people aren't supposed to be facing off with murderers, because they usually wind up getting killed. Patsy is addicted to your truffles now. If anything happens to you, I'm the one who will be in trouble."

Arlo moves into the back room and pulls Logan aside, obviously asking for his side of what happened during the fight with Dr. Ricci. I think he's just forgiven me for the past. I feel light in a way I hadn't expected.

Officer Beckman tells Dr. Ricci, "The ambulances aren't running. They've downgraded the storm, but there's still a lot of rain flooding the roads. Lieutenant Romero and I will get you to the hospital in Houston, one way or another."

Ricci says, "Lovely."

Then she reads him his rights.

I survey the mess. There's another batch of beans ruined, this time before they even got conched into chocolate. And with the blood spatter from Ricci's wound, I'm going to have to sanitize this entire room before I feel comfortable making chocolate in here again. I wonder if my insurance covers that?

Logan sticks around after the cops take Ricci away and Miles home. I don't know where Logan and I stand, because now that the killer has been caught, I don't need a bodyguard anymore.

"You want to grab a cup of coffee?" Logan says. "Decaf, of course."

"As soon as I find a new doctor, I'm going to find out how soon I can get off these meds. I'm getting sick of decaf. Ricci said one more month. But Ricci said a lot of things." Then I realize what he'd actually meant. I don't think he's proposing a date, rather that we grab coffee as friends. And as attractive as he is, I'm okay with that. I just discovered in that moment when Logan saved my life that I'm okay forging a connection with someone Kevin wouldn't have approved of, who's lived a life I might not completely understand. Whatever that connection eventually turns out to be.

And really, right now, I want to figure out how to live without the shadows of the past haunting me. To have those adventures in the chocolate-heavy rainforest in a way that honors my love and my memories – but that are also just for me. I think that's what my Uncle Greg meant. But I'm not sure yet how to balance that.

The rain outside the window is already less intense. And even though I hadn't managed to get anything boarded up, my shop is safe despite the threat of the storm. The hurricane had fizzled after making landfall. Tension is going out of my shoulders, and suddenly I am very tired.

"I'd love a cup of coffee," I tell Logan. "But where are we going to find a place that's open?"

"Dang. I didn't think of that." Logan looks a bit abashed. "I'm just so relieved I didn't make a third mistake."

His way of saying he's happy I'm alive.

"Don't worry. I can make us some coffee here." I gesture toward the kitchen. "I'm not completely helpless without Carmen. Have you ever had a dirty horchata?"

"No." Logan arches an eyebrow at me, and I just want to drown in his intense green eyes. He really is hot when he looks intrigued.

Epilogue
Two Weeks Later

I'm finally getting to have a proper grand opening. It's somber without Emma, but everyone in town seems curious about Greetings and Felicitations and meeting the hero who stopped a killer. As in me. A hero. Who knew?

I'm launching the Sympathy and Condolences line at the party, a week before my Houston clients feature it at their club bash. There are three bars – an 80% with a peppery profile, a 90% that tastes of earth and rain, and the 100% with the notes of pecan and cherry. We put Bruce's picture on all three – with a clear note that chocolate should never be given to dogs – and did the wrappers in deep gray and silver. Despite the name of the line, we've left the message space blank, so people can gift them for any occasion they want. We're only printing Sympathy and Condolences across the bars intended for the club. The rest of them just say S&C. I've dedicated the 100% bar to Emma, and the sales from that one will go to Emma's parents. It's not much closure to offer them, when their vibrant, spunky daughter died for no real reason.

Carmen keeps giving me dirty looks in between making rounds of coffee and pulling tiny chocolate-filled empanadas out of the oven. I don't know what to say. I feel embarrassed for having suspected Carmen of murder – especially after she agreed to come back to work. I've managed to keep from telling her it was Autumn who put that idea in my head. If Carmen ever does become a closer friend, it wouldn't do to have two of my besties hating each other.

I go over to where Carmen is pulling espresso shots for the custom drink orders, for people who don't want plain coffee out of the carafes. "I just want to say I'm sorry again."

Carmen sighs. "I know. It's just – do you know how rare it is to have the kind of waves that were going on the whole time I was in jail? And Bruce. He hasn't been the same since Logan had him. I think Logan was feeding him people food. And letting him sleep in the house. And now he's totally spoiled."

I can't help but laugh. "What can I do to make it up to you?"

"Find me a new roommate?" Carmen pours two shots of espresso into a paper cup and pulls out milk to steam for froth. "With Tasha in jail, Violet and I can barely afford rent, let alone luxuries like toothpaste and breakfast."

"How about a bonus? For prepping a second grand opening party basically by yourself." I'd been too busy working on the new chocolate.

"I'll take it." Her face brightens instantly. "Wait. How much?"

I send her PayPal account a couple thousand dollars. Which I hope will make up the missing rent long enough for Carmen to make other plans. And the sour looks get replaced by happy little smiles.

I wish everything was that easy. Especially because Kaylee is the next person who comes into the store. I brace myself.

The bookstore owner tuts disapprovingly at my tiny book section, and makes a face at the display case holding the now infamous Austen Assassin volumes – which had been the center of the positive blog post Ash had made, and a draw on their own, to get people with morbid curiosity to step into my shop.

Autumn is sitting over in the corner with her librarian – a tall black man with elegant taste in clothes – after convincing him to come into the shop just to look at those books. My grandmother is sitting with them, playing Scrabble. She'd insisted on bringing the board game so that I wouldn't feel she was underfoot or had to be entertained. Last I'd checked in on the table, she'd been winning. Against a writer and a librarian.

But Kaylee's not about to go join the table of literary types. I'd sent her some chocolates as a peace offering -- and an apology for accusing her of being a thief. I'm half afraid she's come to throw them back in my face. I relax my shoulders, trying not to display defensive body language.

Kaylee comes up to the counter. "Do you have any more of the truffles with the pecans on top and the Belizean chocolate?"

That's the one inspired by whiskey sauced bread pudding. It's the booziest thing I make. I crack a grin. "Of course. They're one of my favorites."

I don't tell her they're all my favorites. She buys an entire box, and I throw in two extras on the house. Which actually gets me a smile, before she turns and heads straight out the door. I don't think I've made friends – more gained a grudging respect from a rival. But I'll take it.

Paul comes in. He hasn't spoken to Carmen since she got released from jail. And he made me promise not to tell her that we'd used him as bait to try to get her out, when I'd given his name to Autumn as a potential murder victim. Which I can't tell her anyway, because that would mean I would have to explain everything that happened with Autumn, including how she thought Carmen had to have been the killer.

"Carmen," I say loudly. "Paul wants a custom coffee." Even though he had said no such thing. I whisper to him, "Tell her how you feel."

"I dunno, Mrs. Koerber," he mumbles as he walks towards her. And orders a coffee, the two of them totally awkward with each other.

I'm not going to push any harder to get the two of them together. Whatever happens there happens.

As I turn to go check on the chocolate in the melanger, a new batch ready for the long-awaited bar-making demo, I hear Carmen ask Paul, "How's your son?"

The chocolate looks perfect – smooth and dark and glossy. I look at the line of molds, and the row of brightly colored sugar sprinkles, the same brand as the ones Emma had ordered. The moment is so bittersweet.

Suddenly, I catch a whiff of chicory coffee in the air and my heart jolts, because for a split second, I imagine I might be burning chocolate again. But I'm not roasting today. Puzzled, I turn back to the kitchen and see Naomi showing Carmen – and Miles, who Naomi talked into helping out during the party – how to make dark Cajun-style coffee. That scent will always remind me of family. My parents were here an hour ago, but I told them they didn't have to stay for the party, since it's a perfect day for the beach. I look over to where my grandmother is sitting, and she gives me a little wave. I'm sure in a minute, she's going to ask where Kevin is. But somehow, I don't think it will hurt quite so much.

The door opens again. It's Logan. He's got a bag in his hand, from the café where I took him once for lunch. He walks over to me and holds it up. "I brought you a burger. Your chocolate's great and all, but I wanted to make sure you got some real food."

"Thanks," I say. "This is perfect."

As for whether I'm talking about the event or the food, or the fact that he's decided to stay in my life, I'll let him decide.

I pull my phone out of my pocket and gather all my favorite people for a group pic.

"Airdrop this to me," Aunt Naomi says after she's verified that everyone's eyes are open and no one looks like a goofball.

"Oh don't worry," I tell her, even as I Airdrop to half the people in the room. "This one's going on Instagram."

ACKNOWLEDGEMENTS

Special thanks to Jael Rattigan of French Broad Chocolates in South Carolina, who consulted on this manuscript. And to Sander Wolf of DallasChocolate.org, who put me in touch with so many experts in the chocolate field. I also want to thank the Llanderal Familia of Chocosolutions in Monterrey Mexico for their generosity in giving us a private tour of their facility, and sharing so much knowledge. I would also like to thank Cindy Pedraza of CocoAndré Chocolatier and Horchatería, who inspired me to make Felicity's chocolate shop also serve dirty horchata at the coffee bar. And Yeli of Yelibelly chocolates for sharing her chocolate enthusiasm. There have been so many others, who have showed us behind the scenes at their shops, or simply taken the time to talk about how they do things and why they're passionate about chocolate. Thank you all.

I'd also like to thank Dr. Robin Murphy of Texas A&M for sharing her knowledge of hurricane patterns and movements, and Rhonda Eudaly, who shared information on emergency preparedness.

I'd also like to thank Leah Hinton for sharing her expertise on planes and how to fly them.

I have to thank Jake, as usual, for reading the manuscript umpteen times, being my biggest fan and cheerleader, and doing all the formatting things to make this thing happen. He always keeps me going, even when things are stressful.

And thanks to my agent, Jennie, for her input on this manuscript, which took my thoughts on social media in this manuscript from muddled to powerful.

And on this book especially, I'd like to thank both my family and Jake's (especially my mom and dad, who evacuated up here during the last hurricane, and reminisced about storms and food from when I was a kid). Before she passed away, Jake's grandmother passed down recipes for gumbo and jambalaya, which he still makes. And my own Mawmaw taught me about the Cajun waltz and how to can pickles and fig jam. Though I've gone a lot of directions since then culinarily, her house is where I put down roots, drinking a splash or two of Community Coffee in warm milk, so that I could feel like the adults around her dining room table.

Thanks to James and Rachel Knowles for sharing their knowledge of bunny behavior (as well as videos of their ADORABLE bunny).

I'd also like to thank Cassie, Monica and Tessa, who are my support network in general. I don't know how I would have gotten through this year of social isolation without you three.

Thank you all, dear readers, for spending time in Felicity's world. I hope you enjoyed getting to know her. Her second adventure will be available for you soon.

Did Felicity's story make you hungry?

Visit the Bean to Bar Mysteries Bonus Recipes page on Amber's website to find out how to make some of the food mentioned in the book.

AMBER ROYER writes the CHOCOVERSE comic telenovela-style foodie-inspired space opera series (available from Angry Robot Books and Golden Tip Press). She is also co-author of the cookbook There are Herbs in My Chocolate, which combines culinary herbs and chocolate in over 60 sweet and savory recipes, and had a long-running column for Dave's Garden, where she covered gardening and crafting. She blogs about creative writing technique and all things chocolate related over at www.amberroyer.com. She also teaches creative writing in person in North Texas for both UT Arlington Continuing Education and Writing Workshops Dallas. If you are very nice to her, she might make you cupcakes.

www.amberroyer.com   Instagram: amberroyerauthor

CPSIA information can be obtained
at www.ICGtesting.com
Printed in the USA
LVHW031512090221
678834LV00002B/280

9 781952 854088